I0667752

THE MIDNIGHT VISITOR

The Midnight Visitor

Gordon Lawrie

Dean Park Press

First published 2022 by Dean Park Press
An imprint of Comely Bank Publishing

ISBN: 978-1-912365-23-4

Copyright © 2022 Gordon Lawrie

The right of Gordon Lawrie to be identified as author of
this work has been identified by him in accordance with the
Copyright, Patents and Designs Act 1988.

All rights reserved. No part of this publication may be
reproduced, stored in or introduced into a retrieval system,
or transmitted, in any form, or by any means (electronic,
mechanical, photocopying, recording or otherwise) without
the prior written permission of the publisher. Any person who
does any unauthorised act in relation to this publication may be
liable to criminal prosecution and civil claims for damages.

Cover art by Comely Bank Design

Text printed in Adobe Garamond Pro

A CIP catalogue record for this book is available from
the British Library.

This book is sold subject to the condition that it shall not,
by way of trade or otherwise, be lent, re-sold, hired out, or
otherwise circulated without the publisher's prior consent
in any form or binding or cover other than that in which it
is published and without a similar condition including this
condition being imposed on the subsequent purchaser.

For Nicola, who cares for many,
and who brings much joy into our lives.

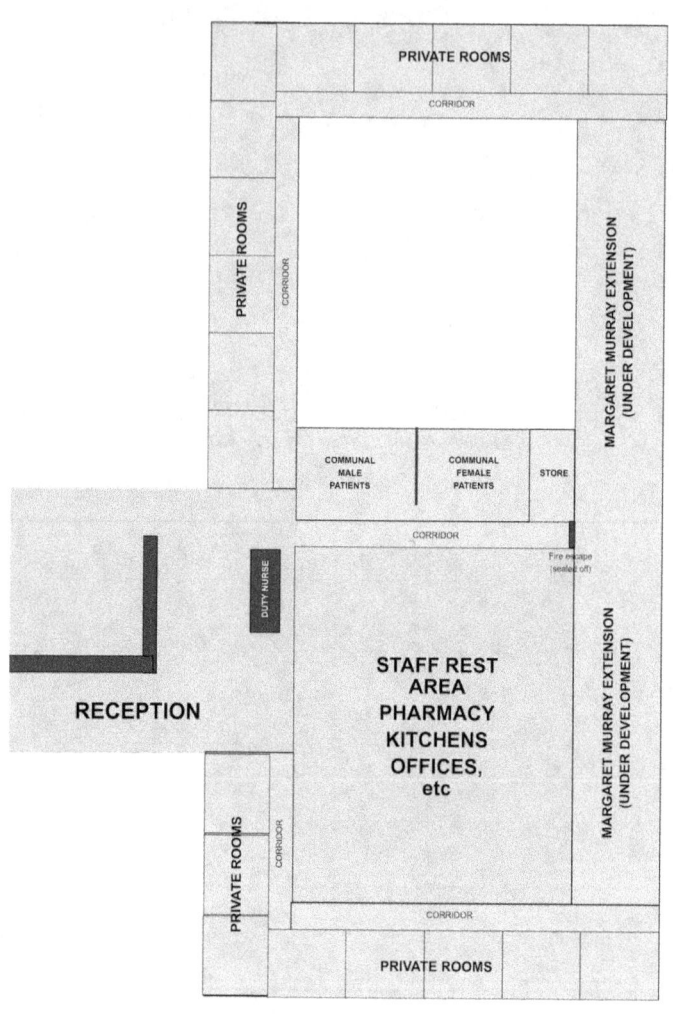

Plan of St Ninian's Haven

ONE

THE WOMAN LEANT OVER THE MAN, listening to whatever faint, whispering words he could manage in these, his final days. She knew his needs: peace, reassurance, comfort and, above all, company. It was a role she played at around midnight each evening. As for the man, he was barely aware of anything at all, doped up as he was each night with morphine; but had he been able to take her in, he'd have enjoyed the experience. She believed in making every possible effort for those *in extremis*. Today's effort involved a glorious deep red dress, perfectly-fitted to show off every detail of the figure of a woman who, despite being closer to sixty than fifty years old, was fortunate enough to retain the tall, slim shape of one fully ten years younger. To top off the show, she wore a liberal quantity of Chanel No.5.

She said a brief prayer, wondered if she would see the man again 24 hours later, then moved on to the next bed. Its occupant recognised her well enough, reached out towards her, and had his hand firmly placed back on the bed. The woman was there to provide company, not to fondle. When he tried again a moment later, his wrist was abruptly slapped, followed by a sharp warning that no matter how ill he was, some things remained firmly out of bounds. The woman had long noticed that an individual's true character always emerges at the approach of death. Her first thought was that this one would be no loss, but then she reminded herself that she shouldn't condemn the man: he would soon be judged by an authority higher than herself. Pointedly though, she spent less time with this particular man, who was stronger than the first. She listened to him briefly, said another prayer over him, but then decided he'd had enough attention.

Moving across, she noted that one of the beds was empty. On Monday, the patient had been quite full of life, albeit without the slightest idea of who or where he was. She knew much more of this man and his past. He wasn't pleasant, not pleasant at all, and her momentary feeling of relief not to have to minister to him now caused her some slight pangs of guilt. But of course death at the nursing home could strike at any moment, indeed as often as not it was ushered in like a welcome visitor by the staff. Keeping patients alive needlessly wasn't the highest priority at St Ninian's.

The final bed in the 'male' area contained a relative newcomer. The woman greeted this patient with a smile and asked how he was. It was a stupid question to ask a dying man, but what else can you say to anyone if you want to maintain normal conversation? The man croaked a polite answer – clearly his demise would involve his throat or his lungs – but patted the bed, and so the woman decided to offer him a little more of herself. Sitting beside him, she leant over to whisper a few quiet words in his ear, bringing the two close enough that they could actually feel each other breathe. The newcomer clearly enjoyed her proximity, but kept his hands to himself. The woman said a prayer over him, and promised to return the following night at the same time. She made a mental note that this patient was deserving of all of her intimate attention.

Run by a charitable foundation, St Ninian's Haven had once been a sanatorium but these days was part nursing home, part hospice. For a hefty weekly payment, it offered single private single rooms to allow wealthy patients – either terminally ill or needing full-time nursing care – the chance to die in peace. Care homes don't normally have doctors available on call, but St Ninian's patients – or at least the patients' relatives – were prepared to pay whatever it took to retain a full medical team in the building at all times.

There were those, though, who couldn't afford the payments, whose funds had run out, or whose children were unwilling to spend money on them. They had to make do with this communal area, comprising the unimaginatively-named Blue Room and Pink Room, each of which had four beds. But it was free, which was where the 'charity' came in.

In any event, there wasn't enough space in St Ninian's for twenty single-roomed residents all at the same time. Edinburgh had an ageing, dying population and the demand for end-of-life care was soaring with each passing year. Currently, the shortage of single rooms at St Ninian's was compounded by a roof leak that had taken two of these private rooms out of commission, and there was the little matter of the ongoing building extension. The new 'Margaret Murray Memorial Wing' currently being constructed at the end of the corridor would eventually contain a further twelve single rooms, but in the meantime two existing ones had been lost to make way for toilets and emergency exits.

The woman in the red dress invariably began her rounds in the private rooms, and this turn into the two four-bed rooms was the final part of her journey; for although she was a remarkable woman, she was also a creature of habit. She was assured that these occupants had apparently chosen to spend their last days in the company of each other anyway, although she wasn't certain which of them had the slightest idea what was going on. Wherever possible, St Ninian's tried to get each of the patients out of bed each day, resting them at night with the assistance of medication. It aimed to relieve its patients of both boredom and pain. Some patients were extremely lucid, others less so.

Her work with the men complete, the woman moved through to the female Pink Room area. This time the four beds were clearly occupied, although one of them had its curtains drawn. The visitor knew not to disturb that patient: perhaps a dressing was being changed or a bedpan was in place. Perhaps the palliative care doctor was attending, although for the moment the visitor could hear no sound. Most likely the patient was simply asleep.

The three women who were visible had been there for over three weeks already, and the visitor wondered if they'd each been admitted too early. But that was none of her business. Her visits to the female patients were naturally different: if they were lucid, they'd discuss clothing, perfume, and of course men. Although the visitor naturally made less obvious use of her feminine charms with these inmates, she maintained the rest of her routine of quiet chat followed by prayer.

The visitor leant over the one lucid woman in the room. The patient complimented her on her red dress, the quality of its material and most of all its tailored fit, for that was indeed the most striking feature of the visitor's clothing. The visitor let the woman reminisce about her past, some long-ago travels with her husband to distant lands, but after a minute or so it was clear that she was rambling. The visitor said nothing other than the occasional word of encouragement, before the patient dried up quite suddenly and there was silence. Once again the visitor said a short prayer, then crossed over to repeat the same words over the comatose figure across the room. Let her rest in peace, the visitor thought, hopefully for ever.

The curtained-off bay had remained silent throughout, but now there was a grunt from behind. The female visitor wondered if she should leave it, but something in the tone of the noise told her that there was a problem. Unwilling to intrude at first, she crossed over to the other side and listened from outside the curtain: nothing. She considered peering in to reassure herself that the figure was asleep, but she knew that several machines would silently be recording the last dregs of the patient's life anyway.

Then there was another grunt from behind the curtain, then a louder grunt. Perhaps the patient was in distress after all? The visitor pulled the curtain back slightly just in case.

The woman in the bed was breathing with some difficulty; she lay on her back, unaware of anything around her, perhaps in a drug-induced sleep. The visitor glanced at the clipboard at the foot of the bed: Eileen Lamb. But Eileen Lamb's breathing difficulties weren't really down in any way to illness; they were down to circumstance. Eileen wasn't the only occupant of the bed. On top of her, face down, lay a bald man, semi-dressed in pyjamas insofar as the jacket was pushed halfway up his back, while his pyjama bottoms were lowered to his knees. Like the woman, the bald man lay motionless, but in his case the visitor could detect no sound of breathing from him at all. She shook her head: a frequent visitor to geriatric hospitals and psychiatric wards, she'd seen the sight of elderly men and women in a state of undress before. Loss of dignity and self-control was sometimes one of the saddest aspects of the end of human life. Meantime, there was little doubt that the man in pyjamas was dead.

The woman in the red dress said a quick prayer over each of the occupants of the bed, the comatose woman and the deceased man. She was glad of her Chanel No.5, although she wasn't aware of much smell, suggesting that the man had only recently passed on.

At first glance there was little reason to doubt the cause of the man's demise: the handle of a decent-sized kitchen knife protruded from his lower back. The handle bore the engraved initials 'LP'. There was blood, but it was oozing rather than gushing from the wound, and there was no chance that the lady visitor was going to risk changing that state of affairs by touching it herself. Instead, she drew herself up to her full height, silently counted to five, then fetched help.

Then the fun began properly.

***

'I've called the police, Mary,' the overnight receptionist said. 'They said they'll be here shortly. At least that's what the 999 woman said. I hope they take less time than they did last year when our house was burgled,' she added.

The woman in the red dress nodded her thanks. She didn't feel like hearing about Lisa's burglary at that point, so she said nothing. Instead she drew up one of the chairs from the corridor, placed it with its back against the communal ward door, and sat down.

'It was funny calling for an ambulance to come here,' Lisa continued. 'You know, us being a hospital.'

Mary just gave a tired smile and closed her eyes.

'Would you like a cup of tea, Mary?' Lisa asked. 'Coffee, perhaps? Or maybe just a glass of water?'

Mary weighed up these options carefully, giving herself something other than dead and dying bodies to think about for a moment. Lisa made her own tea a deep brown colour, which she then flooded with instant milk powder, a concoction to which she then added artificial sweeteners because she was 'making an effort to get the weight down'. St Ninian's tap water never seemed either cold or fresh, no matter how long it ran. But Mary needed another few moments of silence to herself.

'Coffee would be nice, thanks, Lisa. Black, no sugar.'

'Don't you think a little sugar would help the shock?'

Mary looked up at her from the seat. 'How would sugar in *my* coffee help *your* shock, Lisa?'

'I'm only trying to be helpful.'

Mary sat back, sighed, and closed her eyes. 'Yes, I know, I'm sorry. But I'm trying to compose my thoughts here before the police arrive, and to be honest before Dr Davis and the other St Ninian's bigwigs start to swarm around here.' She added with a smile, 'I'm fine thanks, Lisa, but that coffee would be nice.'

Since she'd discovered the body to a nearby auxiliary on the Communal Ward Team, Mary had been approached by Lisa, a nurse called Magda, the on-duty doctor called Helen, and another auxiliary called John who lived in the next street, as well as wee Hamish the handyman who lived just across the road and had come over to see. Each in turn had said the following, and in the same order: first, 'How awful'; second, 'What a shock for you'; third, 'Are the police coming?'; fourth, 'Are you all right?'; and finally, 'Can I get you anything?'

In fact, the one thing Mary craved most was a little peace.

Of the various passers-by, Mary had prevented all but Dr Helen Wolstencroft and Magda the nurse from going inside. Wolstencroft wanted to check that the other patients were fine – which they were, it seemed, because the woman under the dead body was still out for the count, while Mary had been so discreet that none of the others were aware of anything at all. Wolstencroft insisted that at the very least she and Magda rescue the comatose patient from under the dead body and lay her on the one empty bed in the room.

She'd actually wanted to clear the other patients from the room, but Mary had suggested that, as far as possible, the crime scene should remain untouched. Wolstencroft assured her that, yes, there would boxes of disposable gloves inside that the nurse and she could use too; Mary had no need to worry. Roughly two minutes later the doctor had emerged to say that she could get no pulse from face-down man, which together with the knife in the back, just to the right of the lower spine suggested... he was dead. When Mary asked for a little time to herself to think, the doctor kindly took the hint and said she had paperwork to complete in her office while they were all waiting for the police to arrive. Meanwhile, taking the red silk handkerchief bunched up in Mary's right hand to be a sign of tears, Wolstencroft invited her to use the staff toilet to wash her face.

When Mary returned, Lisa had appeared with a plastic cup filled with instant coffee: too weak, instant milk, two sugars. Out of politeness Mary took a sip, then another, then set it on the floor with the excuse that it was still a bit hot to drink. Mercifully, she now heard sirens in the distance, which meant that the coffee could stay undrunk without offending Lisa, who after all was simply trying to be kind. She heard talking at the St Ninian's entrance, presumably Helen Wolstencroft briefing the investigating officers quickly, then the voices started to get louder.

There were two uniformed police constables, a man and a woman. Each of them looked as though they were well practised in the role of counsellor to the grieving. Directly in front of them was a young woman who wore her longish dark hair tied back, black shoes, a short black jacket, white shirt, and black jeans. In other circumstances Mary might have disapproved of the jeans, but her attention was fully occupied by the young man leading – in all senses – the arriving group.

In his early thirties, he had matured considerably in the years since they'd last been in touch. No longer in uniform, he was nevertheless smartly dressed and his suit seemed to fit him perfectly. Mary wondered for a moment if he had lost a little weight until she remembered that uniformed police constables often wear slightly protective waistcoats that make them appear bulkier. She might have been in her mid-fifties but she felt a pang of regret as memories of the past flooded through her mind.

'John,' she said, standing. 'You've come. Thank God it's you.'

'Hello, Mary.'

They each left 'it's been a long time' unspoken.

'You discovered the dead body?' the policeman asked.

'Yes. I didn't need a doctor to tell me. Face down, not breathing, and with a Sabatier knife in the back isn't usually consistent with life.'

John gave a wry smile. Mary's sense of humour was still there, he was relieved to hear, even although he knew that shock might be playing a part, too.

'A Sabatier knife? Are you an expert?' Then the detective suddenly panicked. 'You didn't touch anything, did you?'

Mary smiled sadly. 'John, how could you think such a thing? Of course I didn't touch anything. But I know a Sabatier 18cm filleting knife, made by Lion in Thiers, when I see one. The sort that fishmongers would treasure. Expensive. Rather a waste, really. Lesser knives would have done the job just as well.'

'And you know it's a Sabatier because…?'

'The blade isn't all the way in. The maker's mark is quite clearly visible. As are the initials on the handle, 'LP'.' Then she said, 'Don't you and your colleagues want to take a look?'

The detective smiled. 'But of course. Thank you, Mary. I'm sorry this happened to you. Dreadful.'

'Worse for the victim,' Mary pointed out. 'Don't worry about me, I'm fine.'

'I presume it's one of the patients?' John said as he turned to go inside.

'Oh yes. I knew him well. I only wish I didn't, in fact.'

The detective stopped again. 'Sorry?'

'It's Uncle Lenny.'

TWO

JOHN KNOX, RELATIVELY RECENTLY PROMOTED by Police Scotland to the rank of Inspector, had understandably little experience of murders. He'd dealt with a domestic dispute that had turned fatal, and a drug-related knife killing; in each case the guilty party had confessed in less than thirty minutes. Superintendent Jack O'Malley never tired of saying that most murders were 'accidents gone wrong', and although Knox wasn't quite sure if that made any sense, he'd picked up the general idea that most killers didn't really mean to kill. In fact they generally didn't really know what they meant to do and were totally confused by their own actions.

To a casual observer, O'Malley's 'accident-gone-wrong' theory might have looked promising this time, too. After all, the nursing home was full of patients whose grasp of right and wrong was dulled or distorted by pain or pain-killing drugs, and Knox doubted if anyone in this area especially had the ability to think straight enough to kill a man already close to the end of life. On the other hand there was the small matter of a Sabatier filleting knife, and a new one at that, which was unlikely to be casually lying about in any sort of old folks' home.

Knox now found himself in charge of an investigation slightly more challenging than anything he'd previously dealt with, and he could already see obvious problems. It was going to be difficult to take statements from comatose witnesses. The crime scene had been tampered with: Dr Wolstencroft had taken the unilateral decision to remove all of the other patients, including Eileen Lamb on top of whom the victim had been discovered. Of course Knox knew that as far as possible nothing should ever be touched until the Scene of Crime people and police photographer had all done their thing, but the doctor was concerned for the safety of the remaining patients.

His compromise was to ask Lucy to coordinate the crime scene outside the little ward, while he himself stood just inside the doorway and made a note to touch nothing. It took a seemingly interminable period before the SOCOs people made it – how could the general public stand it, Knox wondered? – and he was treated to a scowl from team leader Jodie Wilson when they eventually appeared.

'OK, who's messed up the crime scene this time?' she said.

'Only the medics on duty, Dr Wolstencroft and the nurse called Magda have been in there.' Knox explained that he could hardly prevent the other patients from being moved out. 'Nice to see you, too, Jodie.'

'Haven't you been in there yourself?'

'Well, yes, but I was wearing gloves and those shoe cover things.'

'But you *breathed*,' Wilson said. 'That means the DNA samples will be all messed up.'

'Really?' Knox asked.

'You know, if it weren't for policemen, we might actually find one or two bits of useful information for you,' she said. 'But no, you guys have to contaminate the scene.'

'Excuse me for existing,' Knox said, chuckling. He knew Wilson wasn't being serious. Not entirely serious, at any rate.

Wilson laughed. 'No, of course not.' Knox guessed he was being teased, but didn't mind; Jodie Wilson was good at her job and he liked her as a person. 'One thing about hospitals,' she added, 'they're supposed to be clean. Except that they're usually anything but.'

Knox let that pass by without comment. 'There were eight patients in the two rooms altogether, including the deceased. The doctor on duty and one of the nurses have moved all of the other patients out. So that's a total of ten people who were in there. Plus the lady who found him, of course.'

'Of course. Plus all the staff who might have gone in that day, plus all the ones who weren't around but whose shift it might have been earlier. Plus all the visitors. Plus Santa Claus if they haven't cleaned the chimneys since Christmas.'

Once Jodie was on one of her cynical rants it was best to let her get it out of her system.

'I gather you're not impressed with the hygiene standards in the typical hospital, Jodie,' said Knox eventually, when he felt it was safe to say something.

'For the most part it's not the hospital's fault, they've got lots of germs being brought in. Some of them very nasty indeed. By why they have to have the heating so high, I don't know. It just helps everything multiply.'

Knox smiled in acknowledgement. He'd discovered early in his career that the less he said, the fewer people he offended. And it helped keep him out of trouble with superiors. Accordingly, he had few enemies in the force, even although it was widely acknowledged that he was destined for high office. And without anyone to wind her up into a frenzy, Jodie and her SOCO team had nothing better to do than get on with their work.

Lucy Grant was still in the corridor, sitting with Mary.

'I've been talking to this lady, sir,' she said. Knox encouraged Lucy to use his first name in private, but when the public was present he insisted on the formalities. 'I get the impression that you know each other.'

'Indeed, Sergeant. She used to be my piano teacher,' he said, before adding, 'amongst other things.'

Lucy decided that it was best to ignore that. 'She says her name is Mary Maxwell-Hume, she's 57 years old, and… she's also a nun?'

The lady in question drew herself up on her chair.

'Excuse me, young lady, I can speak for myself, you know,' she said firmly. 'And the Inspector and I do indeed know each other.'

'I'm sorry, madam. I wasn't sure if you might be suffering a little from shock. We have to look after the welfare of witnesses. And… you appear to have discovered the body, so you're quite an important witness.'

'I'd imagine that I *am* an important witness. I can understand you want to make sure I'm well looked after. But I'm not an invalid. I can speak for myself.'

Knox wanted to laugh. Mary Maxwell-Hume could be a hard woman to deal with at times, as Lucy was finding out first hand. But the seriousness of the situation meant that he had to try and keep a straight face.

'Sergeant Grant wouldn't have meant to offend you, Mary, I can assure you of that,' he said, trying to calm things a little. 'How are you, anyway? Busy?'

Mary looked away. 'I'm still teaching piano…' she hesitated – 'do I call you 'Inspector'?' She glanced towards Lucy Grant as if to add, 'while she's present'.

'Call me 'John'. DS Grant here is a grown-up.'

Mary Maxwell-Hume had a fine line in knowing smiles.

'Do you call each other 'Inspector' and 'Sergeant' in private, tell me?'

It was the detective sergeant who answered this time. 'My name's Lucy, Ms Maxwell-Hume. Would you feel more comfortable if you called me that?'

Mary thought for a moment. 'More comfortable? Hmm… now that we've got that far, I suppose it makes sense, doesn't it?' She turned back to Knox. 'I'd heard that they'd made you an Inspector. That was quick. Were you ever a sergeant at all?' she asked, mischievously. She was testing Knox in front of the sergeant.

'For a couple of years, yes. Everyone has to go through the hoops, Mary, even if we fast-trackers hopefully pass through them more quickly. I've only recently reached these giddy heights.' Anxious to ensure his detective sergeant remained a part of the conversation, Knox added, 'My colleague Lucy here is just a couple of years behind me, that's all, but she's on the same programme.'

Mary arched her eyebrows. 'Another one destined for high office, then?'

Knox smiled. 'I'd say so. Certainly, if it were left to me.' Lucy Grant looked a little embarrassed, and shuffled awkwardly in her chair.

Mary turned to the detective sergeant. 'So you're on the graduate entry programme, are you? What did you study at university? I know that John here has a background in History.'

'My degree's in Applied Mathematics, actually.'

'Really? How does a Mathematics graduate end up in the police force? I'd have thought all sorts of doors would open to a woman of your education.'

'A lot of doors did open, Ms Maxwell-Hume, but they were all in the defence industry. Making weapons, that sort of thing. I decided I'd rather devote my life to protecting lives, not ending them.'

Mary smiled towards John. 'You're right, John, she *is* destined for high office. I'm impressed.' She changed tack slightly. 'And what about that odious little man who was your superior officer? At least you won't be answerable to him now, will you?'

This had the potential to be enormously embarrassing, at least with Grant present as well. She knew that Maximilian Plews was the officer Mary was referring to, and shared Mary's contempt.

'It doesn't work like that, it seems,' Knox began to explain.

Mary stiffened in surprise. 'No?'

'Inspector Plews was himself promoted to Chief Inspector on exactly the same day that I started in this job.'

'My, there's a coincidence,' Mary said. 'Couldn't stand not being able to give you orders, perhaps?'

'Perhaps. I wouldn't like to speculate.'

'In which case I'm surprised he's not here.'

'Perhaps he's on his way. He gives me orders, Mary, not the other way around.'

'More's the pity,' Mary said. 'And what about Superintendent O'Malley?'

'Still there,' Knox said. 'That hasn't changed.'

'Has his command of English improved?'

Knox heard Lucy Grant snigger to his right; Knox himself briefly lowered his head and closed his eyes to avoid doing the same thing himself. He made another attempt to retake control of the conversation.

'So you still teach piano?'

'None of my present pupils are as good as you were, John.'

'Oh dear, that sounds awful,' Knox chuckled.

'It is. Believe me it is. And you? I do so hope that you still play the piano, John.'

'I don't get so much time as before, but I still try to play.'

'Does Alice like when you play the piano, John?' It was the first mention of Knox's partner. They'd met almost three years ago, and Knox had felt that it would be better if he distanced himself a little from Mary from then on. He was pretty sure Mary had been hurt, even although she was almost twice his age. He wanted to steer the conversation away again from these dangerous waters.

'How about the Sisters? How are they all?' Knox could see Lucy looking bemused. 'Ms Maxwell-Hume is also a nun,' he reminded her.

'We are well, thank you, John.' Mary turned towards Lucy. 'I told you that I was a nun, but not that my order is the Order of the Sisters of Mary of the Sacred Cross. Have you heard of us?'

'Can't say I have, Mary. You don't look like a nun, though.' Lucy began to look at the woman's red dress with a keener eye. It was incredibly well fitted, so much so that anything worn underneath would show through, except that…

Knox read Lucy's thoughts.

'Mary's no ordinary nun, Lucy. But then I suppose you've worked that out already.'

'Our order believes that the purpose of clothing is to preserve modesty,' Mary said, 'and we should wear only whatever is necessary and no more. Christ died naked on the cross for us.'

Grant was left speechless for a moment, which allowed Knox yet another chance to ask a few questions.

'How long are your visits normally, Mary?'

'Oh, it depends. Twenty minutes, perhaps thirty if there are appreciative patients. Tonight, one was too appreciative and I was keen to get away. Do you understand?'

Knox gave a wry smile to indicate that he understood only too well.

'So, today you'd been here for only twenty minutes or so?'

'About that.'

'And you saw nothing untoward?'

'Nothing. But then I don't really watch out for potential knife killers when I do my nightly rounds, John.'

Knox soaked up the little jibe quietly. Even in the handful of years that he'd spent in the force, he'd already learned that it paid to be patient, and to listen to witnesses, rather than interrogate them forcefully. He liked to analyse how the witness prioritised information they were giving, as well as analysing the information itself. If something was missing, or wasn't clear, he could always fill the gaps later. It was certainly always worth listening carefully to Mary Maxwell-Hume.

Puncturing the silence, Lucy Grant ventured a question.

'You referred to the victim as 'Lenny', Miss Maxwell-Hume.'

'Ms.'

'Sorry. Ms Maxwell-Hume. You called him 'Lenny'. Did you know all of the patients by their first names? It must be quite hard to remember them all.'

'Of course. If you look, you'll see that the patients' names are on the outside of every door – it's not so hard, really. You've only got to remember the name from the doorway as far as the patient's bed. And, yes, dying patients often like to feel that they're doing so in the company of friends.'

Knox said nothing. He knew there would be more to come.

Eventually Mary felt compelled to go on. 'But you're quite correct, I knew the deceased. Does that make me a suspect?'

'You're a witness rather than a suspect, Mary,' Knox said. 'Technically, we don't even know there's been a crime committed yet.'

Mary straightened up again in theatrical amazement. 'No crime committed? Really? I'd have thought a Sabatier fish knife in the lower back suggests a crime has been committed, don't you?' Then she added, with a waspish smile, 'Inspector?'

Knox caught a glimpse of Lucy Grant's grin and smiled. 'One should never jump to conclusions in this job, Mary.' He'd forgotten how much he'd enjoyed these exchanges with Mary, even now in these extreme circumstances. And she wasn't finished.

'I demand that you do your duty and arrest me,' she said with a commendably straight face, holding out two slim wrists for handcuffs.

Now it was Knox's turn to grin. 'Are you planning on making a dash for it, Mary?' Lucy, meantime, was both amused and bemused by the conversation, so yet again Knox tried to regain control of things. 'Look, Mary, it's nice to see you again and we can catch up on old times later if you want, but in the meantime a man's dead in that room there and Lucy Grant and I need to find out what happened. Please.'

Mary's shoulders slumped. 'So no handcuffs, no strip search?'

'No handcuffs. Definitely no strip search. Just tell us what you know, please, and let's get on with it.'

Mary smiled again. 'Masterful, John. I always said you'd make a good policeman.' But then, remarkably, she switched into 'reliable witness' mode and in less than five minutes she'd managed a detailed account of everything she'd seen, done, even said from the moment she'd entered the building right up until the moment she'd handed over to Dr Wolstencroft. Grant, who was taking the notes, went so far as to compliment her on her clarity; while Mary finally apologised for her earlier behaviour, which she acknowledged 'had not been helpful'.

'I'd imagine that it was all a bit of a shock finding the body,' Lucy said.

'Perhaps,' Mary conceded. 'Thank you for allowing that possibility. It's not every day I stumble across a murder. But I still need to apologise.'

'We don't think you need to apologise, Mary,' Knox said, 'but if it makes you feel better then thank you, and that's the end of it.'

'Am I likely to have to speak to Plews at any point?'

Knox shrugged his shoulders. 'I'll try to prevent it, but I can't promise anything. To be honest, I'm really surprised he's not here yet, getting in the way.' Grant raised her eyebrows again.

'So what now?' Mary asked.

'We'll need fingerprints, DNA samples, that sort of thing. Probably easier to ask you to do that back at the station, though. Would you be able to manage tonight?'

'Why not? My social diary for this evening doesn't have any entries.'

'That's good. I'll arrange a lift – '

With a loud crash, a fire door down the corridor swung open and banged against the wall. Making a remarkable racket stood a short, slightly stocky man wearing a three-piece suit and a contemptuous snarl.

'Where is he?' said Chief Inspector Plews.

Knox nodded in the direction of the room where the dead patient lay along with the other seven, and the unpleasant man dived inside. Suddenly there was a wail: 'Daddy!', taking the growing crowd gathering in the corridor by surprise.

A few moments later the little round man re-emerged, looked at Knox and said, 'So he's dead. Murdered, obviously.'

'Looks like it, sir.'

'Who found the body? Whoever found it is the prime suspect, of course. Basic.'

'You think so, sir?' Knox asked. He rarely found it worth questioning his boss directly, even although most of the time the man talked nonsense.

'I know so. In the meantime, how are you getting on with the Jaguar thefts? Have you found my brother's stolen car yet? I understand six have been taken now.'

Knox was understandably thrown by this sudden change of subject, all the more remarkable from a man who had just found out that his father had been murdered. There had been a spate of high-value Jaguar car thefts. One if the victims had been Theodore Plews, brother of the Chief Inspector and director of a local auction house.

'Not yet, sir. I was prioritising this case.'

'The man's dead, Sergeant.' Knox suspected that the temporary reference to his previous grade was deliberate. 'On the other hand, the cars keep getting stolen. I gave you no permission to prioritise any particular case.'

'I understand, sir.'

'Regarding this murder, have you arrested the culprit yet?'

'This lady discovered the body, sir. Sister Mary Maxwell-Hume, during her nightly rounds. Do you remember her?'

Plews looked down at the woman in the red dress.

'You?' he sneered. 'What are you doing here? You're like a bad penny, you keep turning up.' He turned to Knox. 'Arrest her. A night in the cells will teach her a lesson.'

'But sir – ' Knox and Grant both began to speak at once.

'Don't argue!'

Mary stood up. 'Inspector Knox, Sergeant Grant, just let's do it. Put the handcuffs on. Take me to the station, do the fingerprints and DNA swabs, everything.'

As she was being led away, Mary turned back to Plews and said, 'Perhaps you'd like to perform the strip search yourself, Chief Inspector. Shall we ask them to wait?'

'Get out.'

'By the way, I'm sorry for your loss,' she added. 'I mean that.'

'He was no loss to anyone,' Plews muttered.

'I know that, too,' Mary said, and left with two uniformed police officers.

THREE

KNOX ALLOWED LUCY GRANT to take witness statements from all those able to make them. She was good, he knew that, and he liked working with Lucy, whose similar fast-tracked career path allowed him the chance to talk about his job without the sniping that his immediate superiors came up with. But Knox also wanted some time to wander around St Ninian's by himself.

He began with the area immediately around the twin rooms where the murder – for that's what it surely was – had taken place. St Ninian's 'private area' consisted of around twenty single rooms, accessed by corridors which turned at right angles at each end of the building. These rooms had views to the outside world. By contrast, the two rooms for charity patients sat directly opposite the administration area, and what little view they had was of an internal quadrangle. Anyone could see that St Ninian's needed more space, not just for the patients but even more for the staff. One of the auxiliaries had confided to Lucy that the only place where staff could lay their heads was on one of the two sofas in the 'Rest Room'. There was a solitary staff shower, but male and female staff had to share it, which had led to several embarrassing incidents.

St Ninian's wasn't poor, though. Huge donations by the grateful families of recently-deceased patients continued to ensure that there were more than enough funds to allow St Ninian's to build a staff wing and to extend the entire building which would eventually allow all patients a room to themselves. It was a work in progress, though, and in the meantime space was tight.

As he wandered around the building, Knox once again bumped into Helen Wolstencroft.

'Can I help you, Inspector?'

'I suppose I'm just getting a feel of the building. You don't mind, do you?'

'Of course not, you've a job to do. It's a dreadful business.'

Knox pointed up at the ceiling. 'Am I right – is that a CCTV camera?'

'Yes. Officially it's for the patients' safety, although to be honest the staff are more in danger in most hospitals than the patients are.' Then she added, 'Or so I'd thought.'

'Have you had problems?'

'Not many, to be honest. NHS Accident and Emergency Departments get the biggest share of drunks and difficult people, and clearly we don't have an A&E. But we've had the odd difficult relative. People often act differently when someone close to them is dying.'

'I dare say. Will we be able to see what the CCTV cameras recorded? Half the time these things don't work, you know.'

'These ones do, Inspector. Yet another advantage of having a little more money to spend than the average NHS hospital – we can afford to maintain our buildings. I'll make sure you get what you need. It's the usual thing, there are several cameras covering every area from the car park and the front desk to the corridors.'

'Thanks.'

'Exactly who's in charge of this investigation? Is that you?'

'So I'd imagined. But my superior officer, Chief Inspector Plews, is here because he's the son of the deceased man.'

'We seem to have another senior officer here as well, a Superintendent O'Malley.'

Knox took a deep breath. 'Ah. The Superintendent is here as well. Sorry if it all seems too much at the moment. He's probably right, though – Chief Inspector Plews really can't make any useful contribution to this case, given his close connection to it. It's likely that Superintendent O'Malley is here to make sure of that.'

'Naturally. And to offer a little emotional support to your bereaved colleague, I'd hope.'

Knox allowed that to pass for the moment. He'd couldn't find much to sympathise with in Plews, and moreover he didn't think O'Malley would be any more skilled. Anyway, Knox knew a little of the history of Leonard Plews.

'I've left Sergeant Grant with the job of taking statements, doctor. Will that be all right?'

'As you wish, Inspector.'

'Were you on your rounds yourself?'

'I was in my office catching up on some paperwork. I usually try to stay out of Sister Mary's way when she comes. She appreciates a little privacy, I think.'

'I can imagine.'

'There's always the emergency call system if they need me. Will that be all? I should really take a look at each of the patients inside – when can we have access again?'

'Soon, I suppose. Just one question, Dr Wolstencroft – are these patients able to do anything? Are they in comas, or asleep, or what?'

'Oh, none of them are in comas apart from Eileen Lamb, Inspector. That's the one who was found… under Mr Plews. All the rest could be awake. They can almost all make it to the toilet across the room, even. But for most of them that's about all they can manage in the entire day, and we do sedate them at night a little. And there's the little matter of pain management. That tends to knock them out.'

'Of course,' Knox said. 'Sorry, I should have thought of that.'

'I don't know, Inspector. You're supposed to know about your job, I'm supposed to know about mine. I think that's all.'

'You've seen the body. Before the police doctor arrives, do you have any thoughts, observations to make? Anything at all?'

'Not really. Nothing beyond what Sister Mary said to me as she came out having found Leonard Plews.'

'That she'd found him, you mean?'

'No, no, about having that knife in his back.' The doctor allowed her mind to wander for a moment. 'You know, we have an identical one at home ourselves. I'll never be able to look it in the same light again.'

Knox smiled. 'Who fillets the fish in your household? You or your husband?'

'My partner does. She's very good at it, actually.'

Knox blushed at his own crassness, and it took a moment or so to recover his composure. 'Sorry to be so insensitive, doctor.'

Now it was Wolstencroft's turn to offer an easy smile. 'Don't worry, We're both used to it. Anyway, that's not what Sister Mary said about the knife. It was the fact that there was so little blood.'

Knox used his own silence to encourage her to continue.

'Mr Plews was already dead before the knife was inserted into his back.'

'You're saying that the whole scene with the knife was for effect?'

'You're the detective, Inspector.'

'And Sister Mary pointed it out.'

'Yes. I think she's right, too. Now, can I ask a question?'

'Please feel free.'

'Are the photographs we took likely to be of any use to you?'

'Photographs?'

'Before Magda and I moved the other patients, we took as many photographs of the scene as possible. We thought it would give you a better idea of what it was like, wouldn't it?'

For the first time, Knox smiled. 'That was very thoughtful. I'm not sure they're admissible in evidence, but I'm certain they'll help us put together a picture of the crime scene, yes. Thank you very much, Doctor.'

'I wish I could say it was a pleasure, Inspector. But it wasn't, I'm afraid.'

With seven patients in various states of consciousness now in corridors and spare corners, Knox explained to the doctor that Lucy Grant would need to take a more formal statement. Then he completed his reconnaissance of the building, before heading back to find Superintendent O'Malley. As it transpired, the Superintendent and Plews were standing in the corridor, so Knox knew he really couldn't put off speaking to Plews any longer.

'First of all, sir, I'm sorry for your loss.'

'As I said, Knox, he was no loss. In fact, the world's a better place now that he's dead,' he said. 'Now get on with your work,' he added, swivelling on his heels and marching out of the building without another word.

O'Malley disliked Plews as much as everyone else, but circumstances compelled him to be sympathetic to a man who had just lost his father.

'Son,' – that was his standard way of addressing Knox – 'I've just been explainin' tae the Chief Inspector there that he cannae hae nowt tae dae wi' the investigation, he's far tae closely linked, ken?'

'Yes, sir.'

'That leaves youz wi' the job, yez understand? Dinnae mak a pig's ear o' it, mind.'

'I'll obviously do my best, sir. While you're here, sir, about Ms Maxwell-Hume…'

O'Malley muttered. 'Aye, son, ah ken whit yer thinkin' an' yer right. He'd nae business arrestin' that wumman. He's no' oan the case, he shouldnae be arrestin' nae wan.' Then he added conspiratorially, 'Although between you an' me, son, I wouldnae mind haein' her in handcuffs masel'.'

Knox had several strengths as a policeman, and the ability to stay silent at the right times was his most useful – such as when utterly revolted as he was now by O'Malley's suggestion this time. He even managed a small smile.

'Anyway, I let the wumman go,' O'Malley said. 'I'm not a pathologist, but I reckon Plews's faither had been deid fur a wee while. Nae blood frae the knife wound, ken?' He looked at Knox. 'Did they teach yez that at university, son?'

Again, Knox decided that this was not the moment to display what little knowledge he did have. 'I'm very much a beginner. Learning all the time – perhaps you'd explain?'

O'Malley chuckled. 'Good answer, son, good answer. Ah knew ye'd go far. Yez ken far mair than yez are lettin' oan'. Still, there's nae harm in sharing intelligence, like. So tell me whit yez think.'

Knox took a deep breath. 'Well, sir, you like to say that most murders are accidents gone wrong. Although I'm not ruling out an accident in the case, the presence of a knife in his back, and with his pyjamas pulled away to expose him, suggests malice aforethought.'

'I think I might agree wi' that, son. 'Malice aforethought."

'Then there was the knife. That's an unusual choice of murder weapon – if indeed it was the murder weapon.' Knox scratched his head. 'How does a brand-new upmarket knife designed for filleting fish get in amongst a roomful of terminally ill patients?'

'Havenae a clue.'

'What's more, the knife had the victim's initials on it, which is unusual.'

'Naw, ah cannae help yez wi' that wan either. We'll need tae find out the answer, though. *You'll* need tae find out.'

Knox let that go, and changed the subject. 'I wonder how long it'll take to get a time of death?'

'As long as it takes the furrensic pathuligist tae get here.' Looking round, he pointed to the entrance. 'Which ah'm glad tae see is around about now. Have yez met Dr MacIntosh yet?'

Whatever Knox was expecting from a forensic pathologist, this wasn't it. The woman who appeared was tall, blonde, in her early thirties; she wore green scrubs and a cycling helmet. She carried a large rucksack and from it she took out a bagful of medical equipment. She popped the cycling helmet into the space left in the rucksack and suddenly she was ready to go.

'Sally MacIntosh, nice to see you. It's often quicker by bike,' she explained, glancing towards Knox adding, 'I'm not sure we've met.'

Knox chuckled. 'I'm sure I'd have remembered. John Knox. Nice to meet you, too, maybe get a chance to talk later. The body's through there, along with one of the other living patients.'

'She's still there with the deceased?'

Knox pointed her in the direction of the body. 'Take a look.'

No sooner had she gone than O'Malley laughed rather dirtily. 'Well, John, ye didnae expect that, did yez? A fabulous-looking doctor tae gaze at.'

'There have been a few surprises tonight, sir. I'm beginning to expect the unexpected.' Knox hadn't failed to note that, for the first time ever, he'd called Knox by his first name.

O'Malley could read his mind, it seemed. 'And when no one else is listening, yez can call me Jack. But only when we're alone, mind, and definitely not when the Chief Inspector's anywhere around.'

'Understood, sir. I mean... understood. About Dr MacIntosh – do pathologists normally visit the scene of a sudden death?'

'No' really. But Dr Sally's an exercise freak and likes cycling around the city. Are yez complainin'?'

Knox shook his head. 'Hardly.'

'Anyway,' O'Malley said, 'I'm off to make sure that Chief Inspector Plews remembers that he's the son of a recently-murdered man, not the examining officer here. I'll try and keep him out of your hair, but you know what he's like.'

'Thanks....' Knox managed to cut himself off as O'Malley turned and left the building.

As he waited for Sally MacIntosh to emerge, Knox noted that it seemed unusually busy for just after one in the morning. Perhaps staff were genuinely busy because of the number of patients that had to be re-settled. Perhaps they were just rubber-necking. This time, though, it was Magda Czeslawska – the nurse to whom Mary had reported the murder – who appeared down the corridor.

'Poor Mr Plews.' She spoke English well, but with an Eastern European accent. 'He just seemed his normal self when we were playing cards in the dayroom today.'

'He did? In the dayroom? He was playing cards?'

'Oh yes, we play games in the dayroom every day. It's one of our activities, it passes the time,' she said, and continued down the corridor, leaving Knox looking baffled. He called after her, 'We'll need to take a formal statement from you in due course, Ms Czeslawska,' to which the nurse simply shrugged her shoulders and said 'OK', without looking back.

A moment later he was knocking at Helen Wolstencroft's open office door. She was at her desk, filling out a variety of forms, and when she saw Knox standing she held out a piece of paper in his direction.

'I've made out a certificate of death, Inspector. After all, I was the first medic to pronounce Mr Plews dead. This is a new situation for me, though, and I'm not sure if I'm allowed to do it.'

'It's a new situation for me, too, doctor,' Knox said. 'Thanks – I'm sure it's all we need. If not, it can't exactly do any harm.' He took the certificate, then carried on, 'But that wasn't what I wanted to ask you about.'

Wolstencroft motioned him to sit down.

'So, how can I be of help?'

Knox waited to gather his thoughts; he needed the doctor to sort this out for him. 'Exactly what does this care home

31

do? I thought these patients would be at death's door and quite incapable of doing anything.'

'You're half right, Inspector. Those eight patients are all terminally ill. But care homes like ours provide palliative care, which means we aim to make the end of their lives as high-quality as possible. Above all that means pain control, even if we trade a few days off their lives to achieve that.

'But it doesn't mean that they're comatose vegetables. On the contrary, we try to create 'days' and 'nights' for our patients. Where possible we do things in the daytime, and at night they're sedated to help them recover for the next day.'

'If there is a next day, I suppose,' Knox said.

'There's always that. But what we try to do is to give a shape to their days, make even their last few days – or weeks, or months, however long it takes – something worth waking up for. We have programmes of activities, we show movies, and we even play games.'

Knox allowed himself time to absorb that, then asked, 'Where do the visitors fit in? Mind you, I haven't seen many visitors, come to think of it.'

Wolstencroft looked surprised. 'You really don't know very much about us, do you, Inspector? The Blue and Pink rooms at St Ninian's cater for those without support from family or friends. It happens for all sorts of reasons. Perhaps they never had any children. Perhaps they moved to the city with a partner who died. Or they have dementia and visitors have long since stopped seeing any point in coming. Perhaps they simply didn't know anyone. It happens more often than you'd imagine.'

Knox thought of the Plews family. 'Perhaps they were unpleasant people who drove all their friends away.'

Wolstencroft sighed. 'That, too, is fairly common, I'm afraid.'

'Mr Plews might have fallen into that category?'

'I think he might, Inspector. Mind you, I didn't care for either of his two sons when I met them. I gather one of them's a policeman?'

'He's my immediate superior, Doctor.'

Wolstencroft laughed, covering her mouth with her hand instinctively to hide her embarrassment. 'Oh dear. That must be awkward. Could you perhaps keep my thoughts on him to yourself?'

'Naturally.' Changing the subject yet again, Knox asked, 'So, is it possible that any of the other patients in that room could have got out of bed to kill Mr Plews?'

'Some of them, certainly. But once they're sedated, even slightly, they should have been more or less out for the count. Some of them might have been faintly awake, perhaps, at that point – sometimes sedatives take a little longer to work. We use a mixture of drugs taken orally, plus of course there's the morphine drip.'

'Regarding Mr Plews... would he have been capable of...?' Knox was a little embarrassed to ask the question.

Wolstencroft chuckled. 'Sexual intercourse? I don't think so, Inspector. Whatever his desire – who knows what goes through a man's mind? – the act of physical love would surely have been beyond him. But in any case the knife wound surely wasn't what killed him, was it?'

Knox felt that everyone to whom he spoke seemed to understand the significance of the lack of blood. Oh, for conversation with someone with very little scientific knowledge.

'No.'

'I don't know what killed him, Inspector, but to me it looked like some form of oxygen starvation. Mr Plews had a few bluish tinges in some areas of his skin. The knife seemed a later… addition.'

Knox was about to reply when he became aware of someone behind him.

'I'd agree with that, Inspector.' It was Sally MacIntosh, wearing her cycling helmet and equipment once again in her rucksack. 'Here's a certificate of death, although perhaps Dr…' she looked at the nameplate on the door '… Wolstencroft has already written one out for you?'

'One can never have too many death certificates,' Knox said. 'Any idea of a time of death?'

'It's complicated by the heat in here. However I'm pretty sure that the gentleman died somewhere between an hour and two hours ago.'

'Well that lets Sister Mary off the hook at least,' Wolstencroft said. 'Not that I thought for a moment that she was involved, she does good work here. She comes in each night and visits each of the patients in turn as they drop off to sleep. I like to think that if someone doesn't make it through to the following morning, their last vision will be of Sister Mary Maxwell-Hume.'

'It's a nice thought,' Knox admitted.

'A latter-day Florence Nightingale?' said Sally MacIntosh. 'Anyway, you can move the body as far as I'm concerned. Now I need to go and write up some reports. It'll be a long night – I had to deal with that road traffic accident this afternoon, too. Bit messy, I'm afraid.' A four-car pile up on the Edinburgh City By-Pass had been the talk of the police station since around 4.30 p.m.

Knox watched as the scrubs-clad figure disappeared out of the door, then he turned back to Wolstencroft.

'We'll need the corridor CCTV footage as soon as possible, doctor. Can you manage that?'

'We'll do our best, Inspector. We have quite a small staff at night, so it should be possible to narrow it down quickly to the culprit.'

'Let's hope so,' Knox said. 'My life will be hell until the Chief Inspector's father's killer is caught.'

FOUR

I T WAS PAST FOUR IN THE MORNING by the time Knox made it home; Alice was still in bed, but despite his best efforts his entrance was enough to waken her from a drowsy half-sleep.

'Sorry if I woke you,' he said.

'I was worried,' she said. 'You might have texted me, let me know somehow.'

'Sorry,' he said, 'the reception wasn't good in the hospital. You know what it's like in these places.' In truth, he'd been distracted and simply forgotten.

'Hospital?'

Alice always wanted to know about John's cases, and even at this hour of the night she wanted some detail. Knox sensed she might have desired something else as well but he himself felt somewhat soiled by what he'd seen and was in no mood for romance. Instead, he found himself sharing more detail of the crime scene, more of the investigative procedure as well, simply to deflect any passion. She listened carefully, though, aware that this was only her lover's third murder case, and his first serious one, since his promotion to inspector.

Eventually, Knox dropped his bombshell.

'Guess who discovered the body?' he said quietly, before going on to explain Mary Maxwell-Hume's good deeds in and around St Ninian's Haven.

'She was there?' Alice had never met Mary, but had always suspected that she and John had been lovers at some stage. Alice was wrong, but John could never quite convince her, and in any case there had been a couple of close shaves. Neither John nor Mary could truly say, hand on heart, that there wasn't a physical bond between them. Despite being almost twice his age, Knox found Mary an attractive woman, and she'd made it clear that – nun or no nun – she too could have been willing to share her bed with him. But then Mary Maxwell-Hume was no ordinary nun.

Understandably, then, he felt Alice stiffen slightly at the mention of Sister Mary's name.

'Does that mean they'll have to give the case to someone else?' she asked.

Knox was genuinely confused for a moment. 'I don't understand.'

'I mean, because you and Mary Maxwell-Hume used to know each other.'

'We still do, I suppose. But not any way that might compromise the case,' he said, although he knew that wasn't really true. He was afraid of losing the case, and so he had no intention of confessing to his seniors his real connection with her: that Mary had secretly helped him resolve several crimes in the past. Knox might have been on the fast track programme, but he owed a significant part of his rapid promotion to Mary's subtle assistance. He suspected that Superintendent O'Malley had guessed as much, but Mary seemed to have some hold over O'Malley as well – it didn't take much imagination to work out what that might have involved – and the Superintendent seemed content to let stones remain unturned.

'Will you see her again?' Alice asked.

'I'd imagine so. She's the key witness.'

'Not a suspect?'

'I think we'll find that the time of death will be too early. It'll be before she arrived for the evening. She's in the clear, I'd imagine.'

Knox began to wonder if sex might not be a bad idea after all, as it would at least change the subject. Neither of them usually wore anything in bed, and he pulled back the duvet a little to expose her breasts. He gently kissed each one in turn, then stood up and removed his clothes as she watched him.

'You're not really very turned on, are you?' she said.

'Appearances can be deceptive.'

'But perhaps not this time,' she said. 'Anyway, hang up that suit before it gets completely crushed.' He did as commanded, but then she turned over onto her front and added, 'I'm not sure that after tonight I don't deserve a little tender loving care all to myself. Get that bottle of body oil you gave me for my birthday. It's on top of the chest of drawers. Make me feel like the woman you love.'

Knox pulled back the duvet fully and began; the crisis was past. He took his time, slowly working the lotion into every square inch of her arms, back, shoulders, and then continued further on down, right to her feet, before finishing in the most intimate areas once more. Then, whispering in her ear, he invited Alice to turn over; but now she really had fallen asleep, so he carried on for a while, massaging gently as she lay. But just before he pulled the duvet back over her, the thought suddenly crossed his mind that, despite their differences, in some ways Alice and Mary weren't so different seen from behind. Perhaps he was just imagining it. Either way, he found it a little disturbing.

***

First thing the following day, O'Malley phoned Knox to ask if he could sit in on the case meeting due to be held that morning. Not that it was really a request, and in any case he knew that the Superintendent would want to be kept informed of all developments in such a sensitive case. As well as Lucy Grant, Knox had been assigned two detective constables, Isobel Bryce and Dave Lander. Each had experienced life a little.

In her forties, Bryce had joined the force after leaving school, then married and left shortly afterwards to raise a family: police shifts and parenting don't mix terribly well. That had all changed when she discovered her husband had a betting problem and had gambled their house away. Fortunately, her two children were on the point of leaving school by now, but Izzy needed a decent source of income quickly and rejoining the police was the obvious choice. Knox liked her businesslike energy, but he also liked her no-nonsense style. She'd scored a major hit with the staff after an incident with O'Malley, of all people. Fed up with the Superintendent's too liberal use of his hands, Izzy had finally taken action one day in a crowded canteen. O'Malley had just followed a quiet word of praise with yet another couple of pats on Izzy's bottom. Izzy had turned round, thanked him grinning broadly, and informed the Superintendent that he was welcome to pat her down the *inside* of her knickers instead in future if he preferred. O'Malley knew he'd been caught, was embarrassed and might even have flown into a rage, but then Izzy defused the entire situation by reaching up and giving him a hug and a quick kiss on the cheek. From then on, O'Malley and Izzy Bryce got on like a house on fire. But he kept his hands off her – and every other woman as well.

Lander was an ex-Army man who had served in Afghanistan. He'd been caught by a roadside bomb, and although outwardly he appeared fully recovered, he had his dark moments. However, the police force wanted to be seen to be keen to engage a man who had seen live combat with the armed forces, and he'd been welcomed with open arms. Lander could drive but preferred to let Izzy do any serious pursuit chases. He was an amiable enough man on the surface, but difficult to get to know, and rarely spoke seriously about anything other than his work. His real strength was a steely determination to do his job well and respected Knox's leadership qualities, even although he was almost ten years older.

Knox knew he was lucky that these close colleagues were so reliable. Lucy Grant was reliable and loyal too, but there was no way Lucy would be around him for very long. As Mary had observed, she was destined for high office. Lucy was on the same graduate fast-track programme that he'd recently emerged from himself, but she had two clear advantages over him. First of all, she was very, very good at her job – better at the same stage than he was himself, for sure. Secondly, she was a woman, but more importantly she was mixed-race woman. Her mother – now a respected academic – had become pregnant as the result of a one-night stand at a party celebrating the end of her undergraduate final exams. Lucy's mum had worked hard to raise her only daughter without compromising the demands of her own career; Lucy was keen to show that she had either inherited or learned the same drive. Police Scotland was keen to give her every chance. Indeed, one very senior officer had quietly confided that he hoped that Lucy would one day become the 'public face' of the Scottish police service.

So Knox knew that, sooner or later, he'd lose Lucy as she advanced her own career. He'd long ago recognised that one day – perhaps not so very far in the future – Lucy would be his commanding officer, not the other way around.

Some technical and auxiliary staff had come along, too. One of them started the morning off.

'Two provisional reports are on your desk, sir. One's from the Scene of Crime people, the other one's Dr MacIntosh's provisional report.' Marc Logan was a Records Bureau Assistant, which effectively meant he was a glorified filing clerk, albeit with enhanced IT skills.

Knox looked a little bemused. 'Well, what do they say?'

'Was I allowed to look, sir?'

'I should hope so. The job's a little easier if we share our information, Marc.'

'It's just that Inspector Plews – I mean Chief Inspector Plews – likes to see all reports first.'

Knox looked in dismay across the room towards a chuckling O'Malley, who was hiding in a corner.

'Aye, yez cannae be tae careful these days, son. Dinnae blame yez masel.'

Knox was about to take a look at the report when Logan suddenly continued.

'The SOC report is a bit disappointing. There are so many fingerprints and traces of DNA that it's impossible to eliminate anyone. Everyone has been everywhere.'

'What about fingerprints on the knife?' Knox asked.

'Just one set. Eileen Lamb, the woman on whose body Mr Plews was discovered.'

It caught Knox by surprise.

'Just hers? They're saying the knife was wiped clean before it was put in her hand? There must be traces of something.'

'They're saying that there were never any fingerprints on the knife at all before she touched it. Ever, they think, in its entire life.'

'Wow. That takes some doing. And I think we can rule out the comatose Mrs Lamb.'

'Apart from her, the knife only ever appears to have been held by people wearing gloves. Actually, Jodie Wilson offers you the alternative possibility that the knife might have a life of its own.' Marc Logan was growing in confidence, so he added, 'I don't think that suggestion will appear in her final version for the Procurator Fiscal's Office, though, sir.'

Knox laughed. 'I wouldn't be so sure, Marc. Jodie is intimidated by no one. She particularly dislikes men who attended posh schools and routinely wear bow ties to work.' Ranald Thompson-Moir, the local Depute Procurator Fiscal, was rather too fond of parading his Fettes education, especially the Latin and Greek he'd learned there.

'Let's move on to Dr MacIntosh's findings.'

'It says the deceased died of asphyxiation,' Marc continued. 'Pillow over his head, almost certainly, judging by the fibres Dr Sally found there. Time of death around 10.00 pm.'

'Quite early,' said Knox, amused that Logan had read this report as well, and at the reference to 'Dr Sally'. 'There was nobody around?'

'Dr Wolstencroft explained that terminally ill patients get tired early,' Lucy said. 'It makes them easier to manage, too, if they're tired.'

'I'll bet. The sooner they can sedate the patients, the less the staff have to do.'

'I think she really felt it was for the best, sir. And she did point out that these patients are pretty lonely, too. There's not much to stay alive for.'

'It makes you wonder why anyone would bother to murder someone who was going to die anyway.'

'Mercy killing? Oh, sorry.' It was O'Malley from the corner; he'd promised that would just be an observer, but couldn't help himself.

'A mercy killing would be possible, sir,' said Marc. 'But although Dr Sally said the Chief Inspector's father was suffocated, the knife was used on him first.'

'He survived the knife in the back?'

'That wasn't where the knife was first used, sir.'

'Go on.'

Marc hesitated. 'Well…'

Dave Lander intervened to help him out. 'There are little cuts here and there around the genitals, sir. Nothing too obvious, and they look as if they might have been done from behind. And the knife had been inserted slightly into his anus. There was slight internal bleeding there. Dr Sally suggested that the knife might have been held against the victim to encourage him to keep still.'

'While the pillow was placed over his head?' Knox asked. 'That must have placed Mr Plews in a difficult position.'

'That's the idea, sir. But whatever the reason for holding the knife down there it was definitely only after Mr Plews was dead that the knife was jammed into his back.'

'Ouch. Somebody didn't like the victim,' said Izzy.

'The Chief Inspector himsel' wisnae tae fond o' his ain faither,' O'Malley chipped in. 'Ah think he n' his brither got a fair few hammerins when they were laddies.'

'Any signs of resistance?' Knox asked, before adding, 'I know, I could read the report myself but I'm being lazy this morning.' He might have added that he was also making sure that everyone else was familiar with the report.

'Not really,' Izzy said. She wanted to make it clear that she, at least, had done her homework. 'There's a little bruising on the arms and so on, but nothing suggesting any significant struggle. It's almost like he was a willing victim. Mind you, with a knife there cutting him apart every time he wriggled...'

'On the other hand, he wasn't a well man. It wouldn't have taken much of an effort to pin him down. What was his problem, incidentally? What was he dying of?'

'He had Alzheimer's, but he also had quite bad COPD.' Lander said. 'That's – '

Knox cut in. 'Chronic obstructive pulmonary disease, Dave, we know. What my granny called emphysema.'

'Sorry, sir. He was struggling to breathe. Probably died in seconds.'

'So how did he end up on top of...' – Lucy fumbled for the name – 'Mrs Eileen Lamb? Was that before or after pillow-time?'

'I think Dr Sally might suggest it was our job to find that out, Lucy,' Knox said. 'It shouldn't be hard to work out who our suspects are, though. We have the CCTV corridor footage from last night and we can surely narrow our list down. How's that going by the way?'

Over in the corner, a young uniformed constable had been given the soul-destroying job of staring at computer screens and noting all the people who had gone in or out of the room where the murder was committed. He spoke in the present tense, as if giving a running commentary on the CCTV video.

'It's remarkable, sir. All the patients have been visited just after ten o'clock by Dr Wolstencroft and two nurses – at least they're wearing nurses' uniforms and are with the doctor. They stay for ten minutes or so, then they come out. So far no one else has gone in.'

'How far have you watched?'

'About an hour and three quarters thereafter, sir. Whoever it was had better hurry up, because I'm pretty sure that nun woman appears in a few more minutes.'

'Nobody at all?'

'Not one.'

Knox frowned. It made no sense: how would an assailant get into the room other than via the corridor?

'Did anyone check the windows?'

'No signs at all of being opened,' Lucy said. 'Scene of Crime report, page 4.'

'Yet the time of death is definitely after Dr Wolstencroft's doing her rounds... and before Sister Mary arrived?'

'Dr Sally can't say for certain until she's done the PM this morning, but she's 99% sure, yes. By the way, sir, do I understand that you and this Sister Mary Maxwell-Hume have met before?'

Out of the corner of his eye he could see O'Malley pricking up his ears.

'Sister Mary is... used to be my piano teacher,' Knox admitted.

O'Malley coughed. 'Bit mair than yon, Inspector. She's no sae bad at the polis work hersel'. Helped us a' oot a couple o' times. One of them bein' that time when Chief Inspector Plews went an' arrested his ain brither for summit' he didnae dae. Dae yez mind, Inspector?'

'How could I forget, sir?' Mary had solved the crime, made it look as though Knox himself was the clever one, then O'Malley had claimed the credit.

'Aye,' said O'Malley, 'yon's a nice lookin' bird. I hope she isnae the culprit after a' that. When's she due fur interview?'

45

'Tomorrow, 9.30.'

O'Malley's eyes brightened. 'Ah wouldnae mind sittin' in oan that.' Knox didn't doubt it.

The PC in the corner, Andy McFadden, spoke up. 'That's me looked right through the CCTV footage.'

'And?' said O'Malley, irritated to be kept waiting.

'Nothing. No one.'

'Cannae be. Whit about wir demon killer knife – the wan wi' a life o' its ain?'

'Not even a demon knife. Honestly, sir, there's no one or nothing moving in that corridor during that entire two hours.'

'Cannae be.'

'Perhaps you'd like to have a look yourself, sir? The lighting's great, the image is clear as day, but it's always possible I might have missed something.' It was good thinking by McFadden, who'd quickly learned how to take advantage of O'Malley's lack of interest in the mundane aspects of policing.

'Nah, it's OK, son, ah believe yez. But I dinnae unnerstan' how anyone could get intae yon hospital ward and oot agin' wi'oot bein' noticed.'

Not everyone would quite have used quite those words, but everyone was sharing the same thoughts.

FIVE

KNOX HAD ALREADY ISSUED everyone with a plan of the room where Leonard Plews had been found dead. Everyone already knew that it was a mixed area, with eight beds, four each on each side of a double swing door. Nearest the corridor were the four male beds, although of course only three of the beds were occupied. Ian Mould had heart and chest problems; Myles Cherry suffered from emphysema; Alan Smith had lung cancer, and Leonard Plews himself had Alzheimer's Disease. Through the double doors, in addition to the dead body, were four more women. Two, like Plews, had dementia, including Eileen Lamb and also the woman directly opposite, Martha Ramsay. Louise Gray was suffering from liver failure while Robina Wallace had cancer in a number of areas.

'The thing is,' Knox explained, 'that we can't quite rule out any of the patients.'

'I presume we can rule out old man Plews, Inspector?'

Knox understood that having O'Malley present was going to make it a long day. 'I was working on that basis, sir, but I suppose good policing never rules out anything, does it?'

O'Malley chuckled. 'Ah wiz windin' yez up.'

'You can't be too careful, sir,' Knox said, referring both to the police work and dealing with his superior officer. He forged on in the hope of silencing him. 'It appears that each of the patients actually spends part of the day upright. I suppose any of them could have done the deed but, then again, I'm not sure which of them would have known what they were doing. Even Dr Wolstencroft couldn't say for certain.'

'Surely it would take some strength to hold Mr Plews down?' Lucy said.

'That depends on the victim's own condition at the time. If he was asleep, it seems…'

Izzy was sitting near the front. 'Are we really saying this could be anyone?' she asked. 'And how about the nun? Or any of the staff? Or an intruder?'

'Except for the CCTV footage, Izzy,' Knox reminded her. 'Only the eight patients were inside the room at the time provisionally set for death.'

'Perhaps that's wrong.'

'In which case anyone could have done it. The patients, any of the medical staff, Sister Mary, even the postman early in the morning.' Knox realised he was in danger of getting irritated, although in general he usually managed to conceal any annoyance he was experiencing. 'I think we should provisionally work on the basis that we have eight potential witnesses. Nine if we include the duty nurse,' – Knox consulted his notes – 'Magda Czeslawska. She will have been just down the corridor.'

'And only the nun and the nurse are definitely capable of being interviewed,' Lander reminded them all.

'In which case, they're the ones we start with,' Knox conceded. He wasn't looking forward to a formal interview, although it was unavoidable. 'I've already warned both Sister Mary and the nurse that we'd need to interview them properly.'

'Doon here at the station, son?' O'Malley asked.

'Of course, sir. Let's do this correctly.'

'Sooner the better, then, eh?'

***

Before that, Knox had a post-mortem to attend.

Without giving it much thought, he jumped into his car and drove towards the car park exit, to be greeted as he left by a shifty-looking man of around his own age wearing an open-necked shirt and calf-length coat. The man's hands were buried deep in the coat pockets. As Knox stopped the car and wound the window down, the security guard came across to check that everything was in order.

'It's all right, I know this man,' Knox reassured him. 'It was my misfortune to be at school with him.' The security guard withdrew a little but kept an eye on proceedings, unsure if the stranger had entirely innocent motives.

'What brings you here, Billy?' Knox said. Last I heard you were stirring it up at a far-right demonstration down in London. The British League or some other tosh like that?'

The other man grinned. He had a curious habit, which Knox remembered only too well from his schooldays, of stretching his neck out before he spoke.

'Defending the nation. Doing your job for you, PC Plod.' He produced a business card from his coat pocket.

'"W. Montgomery Bishop – Communications Expert and Freelance Journalist",' Knox read. 'You're trying to use your posh handle these days, are you, Billy? Trying to re-invent yourself? And by the way, it's Inspector Plod to you.'

'Inspector? Oh my word. How you've risen in the world, Knox.' Knox was suddenly conscious that Bishop was taking the mickey out of him in exactly the way Mary had, but that his old school colleague did so much less pleasantly. Bishop had always been odd at school, often picking arguments in class, deliberately taking controversial positions in debates and generally trying to be as difficult as possible. He enjoyed the protection of a restaurant-owning father who thought 'Monty' could do no wrong, and had made numerous complaints against teachers on his son's behalf. The lad had effectively been given the freedom to do whatever he liked. But early on in high school Knox had made an enemy for life when he'd discovered that there was a cheese called Stinking Bishop... and coined his school nickname, 'Cheesy'. They'd gone their separate ways after school and it was only through social media and a couple of chance appearances on television that Knox realised that the same Billy Bishop of his childhood had turned into 'Montgomery Bishop', professional right-wing racist rabble-rouser. In short, Knox loathed him, and he could almost touch the contempt that Bishop had for him in return.

'So what brings you back to Edinburgh, Cheesy?' Knox knew that Bishop hated the nickname.

Bishop stretched his neck, then gave a slow, deliberate nod, as if to say, *you want to play it that way, then?*

'The British League's been proscribed. For your benefit that means 'banned'. So they don't exactly need a communications officer at the moment.'

'I'm glad to hear it,' Knox said. 'But you'll just re-emerge as some other bunch of scumbags.'

Bishop's sly smile never left his face. 'I'm sure we can arrange that, Knox. But in the meantime, a man needs to work to live... well, unless you're one of those illegal immigrants who land on our shores and scrounge money from people like you and me, Knox. Anyway, I'm currently working as a freelance journalist.'

'Who for?'

'Anyone that'll pay me. The *Daily Mail*, the *Express*, the *Guardian* – '

'The *Guardian*?'

'Oh, they're not as fussy as you'd imagine, Knox. None of them are. They all go for the cheapest option. I have my own company – Warlock Media – and our news service undercuts everything else.'

'Presumably you don't pay the official union rates.'

'Officially yes. Unofficially, of course not. But then their one employee isn't going to complain, is he?'

'I thought you said you needed the money,' Knox said.

'Sort of… I need a job for the sake of appearances. I still get… paid by my former employers.'

'Even though they don't exist?'

'It's only the British League that doesn't exist any more, Knox. You're not very bright, are you? Keep up. All the people who were in it still exist. Especially the wealthy ones.'

Knox exhaled. 'Such as Justin Pearce.' Pearce was a multi-millionaire who bankrolled any number of right-wing, anti-immigrant, anti-trade union organisations. 'You're still Pearce's mouthpiece, then?'

'His media spokesman, please. Show some respect.'

Knox was becoming impatient. 'Look, Cheesy, what do you want? I'm due somewhere.'

'That's what I'm wondering, John.' The reptile's use of his first name made Knox's skin crawl. 'You suddenly seem to be very busy right now. You've been in and out of that care home an awful lot lately – what's it called now, remind me?'

'It'll be the British League that you're thinking of,' Knox replied. 'It's full of sick people.'

The sly Bishop smile became even slyer.

'Very good, John, very good.'

'Look, Bishop, I need to go. I have somewhere to go,' Knox said, starting the car. Bishop was slow to move out of the way, and the security guard called across.

'Are you sure this man isn't being a nuisance, sir?'

'Now that you mention it, he is,' Knox called back. 'Arrest him, please. He's planning a terror attack on a police station.'

The security guard looked perplexed; Bishop's sly smile turned into a broad grin. As Knox began to wind his window up, he heard the latter call after him, 'Careful, Knox. It's dangerous to fall out with the Fourth Estate.'

***

The encounter with Montgomery Bishop at least had the effect of making his attendance at the post-mortem relatively more bearable. He'd attended one or two and was amazed at how much damage was casually done to the cadaver, and equally amazed by the way all the 'bits' were piled back into the body again and the whole thing stitched up. The body became its own 'body bag'. He was expecting John Laithewaite, the senior pathologist, to do the job and was therefore unprepared for the appearance of Sally MacIntosh. Once more she was dressed in scrubs, blue ones this time. She greeted Knox with a cheery smile.

'Good morning, Inspector. Are you well?' MacIntosh was around Knox's age, perhaps a year or so younger. She was tall – probably five foot ten – and had a lean, athletic build, no doubt the result of her regular cycling. She wore her hair fashionably short, which somehow added to her allure. Most of all, Dr Sally was approachable and understanding. She knew this was the part of the job most policemen hated.

'As well as can be expected in the circumstances,' Knox said. 'And it's 'John'.'

Knox caught a brief glimpse of a wide smile just before it disappeared behind a face mask.

'Presumably better than Mr Plews here,' Sally said.

Knox wasn't surprised that gallows humour came with the pathologist's job. Surely some sort of defensive shield was legitimate. He decided to make a little small talk.

'I've never really had a chance to speak to a pathologist before,' he said. You're a doctor, is that right? I mean, do you have any patients?'

'Not really. I examine tissue most of the time. Lots of cancers, a few other things besides. Now and again I get called on to do a sudden death. Like this one.' She looked down at Plews thoughtfully. 'It makes a nice change from the general run of things.'

Dr Sally had an assistant whose name appeared to be Luke and whose job appeared to be a general combination of dogsbody and sound engineer. Luke was older than Sally and seemed even less concerned about the prospect of carving up a body than she was. But to begin with, his job seemed to be to check that Sally's recording equipment was functioning – she was wearing a clip-on microphone, he was wearing some sort of in-ear headphones..

'All go, Sally. It's picking up everything. The Inspector included, by the way.'

Suddenly it dawned on Knox that nothing was secret in the world of the dead body. Every conversation, every nuance, would be noted in writing later as Dr Sally wrote up the report of the autopsy.

'Even the recording is stored – for evidence, of course,' she said, answering his unspoken thoughts.

'And therefore anything I say is stored, too.'

'But of course,' Sally grinned. 'Were you going to ask me out on a date?' Technically, Knox couldn't see much of her smile behind the mask, but the wide eyes and lines around her face were more than enough.

'Definitely not if you're recording. My three wives might find out our dirty little secret,' Knox said, fighting fire with fire.

The conversation suddenly went quiet as Sally closed her eyes for a moment. It suddenly dawned on Knox that she was saying a silent prayer for Plews, and immediately he wondered why he'd never heard of anyone doing something so obvious before. He wasn't sure that everyone was capable of redemption, or was even worthy of the opportunity, but he admired anyone who thought they were.

Then, almost without being noticed, Knox realised that Sally was into her work. Measurements were taken and noted, along with comments on things like rigor mortis that he vaguely understood along with a great deal more that he didn't. Then she moved on to the knife wound, pointing out some marks around the insertion, together with a more surprising fact.

'Of course you have the knife, Inspector.'

'As you know. You were there when we found it. And it's John, remember?'

'Of course, John. It's interesting. The knife played no part in Mr Plews death, I'm pretty sure of that.'

'Because of the lack of bleeding?'

'That, and something of greater interest. This knife has been inserted into the victim's back slowly. Just once. There's no real violence in the wound, no bruising. It's not been removed then pushed in a second time. The killer – if indeed it was the killer who put the knife in – did so methodically, purposefully, and with no resistance from the victim. Since instinct would have made Mr Plews reach out to lessen the pain, I think we can fairly safely say that he was dead already.'

'Why would anyone do that?' Knox said, although he already knew what answer would come back.

'I don't know, John, you're the detective.'

'What about the nicks... around the groin? You mentioned them in your preliminary report.'

'The nicks on the testicles, and in and around the anus? They look to me like pressure cuts. The knife was held there against the victim as a threat. Nothing life-threatening, just a means to discourage him from moving.' Sally added, without looking up, 'Would it discourage you from moving, John?'

Knox chuckled. 'I'd say so. I'd not move a muscle.'

'Unless someone was trying to suffocate you with a pillow.'

Knox considered what he was being told for a moment.

'So you're saying the knife definitely had nothing to do with his death?'

'I'd say a knife in a dead body rather definitely had something to do with it. But it played no part in the actual death, no.'

'So what did he die of?'

'Myocardial infarction. Heart attack.' Sally held up a lump of material which Knox assumed was the heart in question. 'Loads of clogged arteries, there's a couple of clots in there, and in any case the initial chemical analysis I'd done already warned me to look for it.'

'So you're saying Plews died of natural causes?'

'Eh... no, not quite. I think our Mr Plews probably had this heart attack because he was being suffocated with a pillow.'

Knox took a deep breath. He liked Sally and didn't want to offend her, but he was looking for clearer answers. 'So was he suffocated or did he have a heart attack?'

'Or was he stabbed to death with a Sabatier fish knife, perhaps?' Sally asked rhetorically. Knox could see she was laughing at him. 'No, John, I think someone tried to suffocate the victim by holding him face down into a pillow…' – she lifted an arm and pointed out some marks – '…but his heart gave out before they finished the job. You'll see the bruising on the arms. Those little marks on the back of the arms are thumb marks, the ones on the inside of the arm are finger marks. The victim was held from behind, and there are some more marks on his neck. I think there are even some on the back of the head. Different marks, interestingly. But all suggest he was held from the back. The head and neck makes me think his face was pushed into a pillow. But the heart attack meant that they didn't have to hold him down as long as they might have expected otherwise.'

'Are you saying there might have been more than one attacker?'

'Definitely. Two at least. Maybe more.'

'Wow. What about the fish knife?'

Once again Knox could see the signs of Sally's grin poking out from the side of her mask. 'Oh, that's a complete red herring,' she said.

Knox groaned. 'I should have seen that one coming.'

'It played no part in his death, I'm sure of that,' she said. 'For the avoidance of doubt, Inspector: cause of death myocardial infarction, brought during an attempted asphyxiation of the victim with a pillow. Almost certainly involving more than one assailant.'

'Splendid,' Knox said miserably. 'Throw in a Sabatier knife in the back for no good reason and the picture's complete.'

'I can also see from the state of his brain that the victim had quite advanced Alzheimer's Disease. Something like that, anyway,' Sally added. 'And the early stages of prostate cancer, although he probably didn't know he had it, like so many others. Whoever killed him might have done him a favour, to be honest.'

'I don't suppose the Procurator Fiscal's Office will see it that way.' In Scotland, decisions on how to proceed over any sort of crime would end up being taken there, not by the police. Sometimes it was the most frustrating part of the job. This time, Knox wondered if the Fiscal might try to make a case simply because of the knife. One way or another, though, this was a truly bizarre case, and Knox found it deeply disturbing that Sister Mary Maxwell-Hume of the Sisters of Mary of the Sacred Cross was mixed up in it at all. Not least of all because he'd thought she'd been consigned to his past.

SIX

SUPERINTENDENT O'MALLEY was never going to pass up on the chance to interview Mary Maxwell-Hume. He remembered her well – what man wouldn't? – and had enjoyed the way she wrapped him around her little finger. He pulled rank to ensure that he'd be sitting in with John Knox as his inspector led the interview: O'Malley simply wanted to watch, almost voyeur-like.

Mary turned up precisely two minutes late for her 3.30 appointment at the police station. She'd had to travel by taxi that afternoon, because O'Malley had insisted that no police car be deployed to bring her in: he wanted to see if he could put Mary out of her out of her stride a little. She, for her part, had purposely waited in the taxi for a few minutes to reassert herself.

When Knox showed her into the interview room, O'Malley was already waiting, standing leaning against the wall.

'Nice tae see yez, Sister Mary.'

'I've no doubt it is, Superintendent. I suspect you'd probably like to see more than you will, however.'

'Ah, yez are a funny wan,' O'Malley chuckled. 'But yez're probably right enough. Anyway, the Inspector here'll be conducting the interview, no me. Ah'm just here fur a wee listen in.' Only then did he sit down and switch on the tape recorder. Mary smiled quietly as she studied the two quite senior officers across the table, one of whom was trying to conduct the interview as correctly as possible, while the other didn't give a damn.

John Knox took Mary through the essential introductory details for the sake of the tape, reassuring Mary that she was attending of her own free will. O'Malley remained silent as Knox began to put his questions, though. Given Mary's opinion of him, the Motherwell detective was intelligent enough to stay out of trouble.

'Should I have a solicitor, Inspector?' she asked, eventually.

'You're not a suspect,' Knox said. Then after a moment's hesitation he added, 'Do you feel you need one?' He didn't want to sound so formal, but he didn't want to be accused of favouring her either.

'I think you'll agree I'm not a common criminal, gentlemen.'

Knox ignored her and asked Mary to describe everything she saw inside the room on the day of the discovery of Plews's dead body. Rather as he'd anticipated, she was precise and to the point, recalling as much detail as she could of her movements, what she saw and heard, the temperature, and even what she could smell. Only twice did O'Malley see a need to interrupt her for further clarification: first, to establish in his own mind who was in which bed; on the second occasion he wanted to know exactly what the state of Plews's pyjamas were. As he asked, Knox was reminded how good a police officer O'Malley was. It was an important detail.

'It's a good point, Superintendent,' Mary said. 'Now that I recall, Mr Plews's pyjama trousers were neatly pulled down below his... behind, and his pyjama top was actually quite neatly rolled up. It might even have been folded.'

Knox glanced at the scene-of-crime photographs.

'That's correct, yes.' Not only that, he thought, but O'Malley had spotted it before him.

'Which all goes to suggest that Mr Plews's assailant had plenty of time to do the deed, I suppose,' Mary said. 'Do you think he was drugged first? Do you think he suffered?'

Suddenly, Mary was asking the questions.

Knox hesitated, as he wasn't sure if his superior officer would allow him to give away any details. But O'Malley had no such qualms.

'Would yez have liked Mr Plews tae have suffered, Sister Mary?'

Mary was undoubtedly caught off guard, but she quickly recovered her composure.

'Why... surely no one deserves to die in agony, Superintendent?'

'So Mr Plews wiz just like any other patient as far as youz were concerned?'

'We are all God's children. And Our Lord Jesus suffered on the cross so that we might not.' She gave O'Malley the mysterious smile that Knox himself knew only too well from past encounters. She added, 'Equal in the eyes of the Lord. And we are all capable of redemption.'

'Even me?' O'Malley asked.

'Even you, Superintendent.'

O'Malley continued to probe patiently. 'Would ye say Mr Plews wiz any more in need of redemption than any of the other patients in that room?' Knox noted that O'Malley's grammar was improving slightly for some reason, but it was starting from a very low point. Either he was concentrating, or perhaps speaking to Mary was having a positive effect. It was also a clever question, but then Knox had always admired

O'Malley's abilities as a police officer. Colleagues, suspects and defence lawyers underestimated O'Malley at their peril.

After a moment, Mary simply said, 'I'm not in a position to judge a man's conscience, Superintendent. That's for a higher authority. And of course Mr Plews had Alzheimer's Disease, which itself is a cross to bear.' Mary turned towards Knox. 'You're very silent, Inspector. I thought you were supposed to be leading this investigation.'

Knox smiled quietly. 'I think the Superintendent is asking all the questions I would ask myself. Perhaps more. I'm content to listen for the moment.'

O'Malley seemed keen to continue. 'Yez've never been married, Mary?' he said.

Mary sat up. Eventually, she said quietly, 'Is that a question, Superintendent?'

O'Malley said nothing in response, choosing to keep eyes rooted to the file in front of him instead. Knox could almost feel the tension between them. Mary blinked first.

'I'm guessing you probably know that the answer's 'yes, I was married once'.'

O'Malley's tone didn't change. 'What was his name?'

'Duncan.'

'Full name. Duncan What? Maxwell or Hume?'

'Both. Duncan Maxwell-Hume.'

'Which means you married a man called Duncan Maxwell-Hume. And became Mrs Maxwell-Hume.'

Both policemen could clearly see that Mary wasn't comfortable talking about her marriage. 'That's correct,' she said, after some hesitation.

'What happened?'

'He died. Suicide.'

'Ah. Ah'm sorry. Were you and your husband happy together?'

'Oh yes. I didn't know until after his death that he'd gambled all of our money away. That might have... soured the relationship a little. But I don't know. He gave me so much while he was alive. And gambling is a disease, isn't it? Like cancer. It gets a grip of you then it doesn't really let go. Even if you stop, I suspect you're only ever in remission. It's such a horrible phrase that, isn't it, Superintendent, 'in remission'? It's like the big bad bogeyman's going to come back and get you one day.'

'I never thought of it like that,' O'Malley said. 'But if your husband's name was Maxwell-Hume, what was your maiden name?'

'Spicer.'

'Really?'

Mary drew herself up sharply. 'Do you doubt me?'

O'Malley tapped the file. 'It says here that you were in foster care for a bit. One of the carers was a Mrs Spicer.'

'That's right. I think she was the only woman that was remotely kind to me, but they took me away from her because she was in trouble with the police.'

'Yes, she ran a brothel, I understand,' O'Malley said. 'But that's a bit of a coincidence, isn't it? Your name being Spicer and ending up being fostered by a Mrs Spicer.'

Mary said nothing.

'What name were you born with, Mary?' O'Malley said it surprisingly tenderly. His grammar was perfect.

'I think you know the answer already, don't you, Superintendent? I was born Mary Plews. I take every opportunity to put it out of my mind.'

'Because you were abused by yer faither?'

'My father never touched me. Never once.'

O'Malley looked up in surprise. 'That's what he was convicted of.'

'Not on my evidence. Others lied to deflect the blame from themselves.'

'So you *were* abused?'

'Very much so. Every way you can imagine, and probably a few you can't.'

'So who…?'

'My mother died giving birth to me, Superintendent. The man who took me in afterwards used me for his personal needs.'

She had O'Malley's attention completely. 'Go on,' he said quietly.

'Leonard Plews. Uncle Lenny.'

O'Malley sat back in his seat and looked at Knox sitting to his right. 'You knew all this, didn't you?' When Knox didn't reply, he added, 'I'll take that as a 'yes', then.'

'Does it change anything?' Mary asked.

O'Malley grunted. 'Well it changes things a little, doesn't it?'

'Does it?' Mary asked. 'I didn't kill him, although I had every reason to. I was the person who found him with a knife in his back and who reported it straight away. I'd been there for almost twenty minutes, too, and I saw no one else anywhere near him. And do you really think I would waste such a good knife on someone as unpleasant as Lenny Plews?'

O'Malley chuckled. 'Yez're some wumman, Sister Mary. But yez had the motive a' right and yez might hae had the opportunity 'n a'. It's a powerfae coambinashun.' Knox could see Mary wince at the distortion of the English language.

'I had the motive,' she acknowledged. 'But I've had that for over forty years so why should I wait until the man was on his death bed to kill him? And it was a slow, lingering death, the sort that a man like Uncle Lenny deserved. Why should I put him out of his misery?'

'I think yez are needin' somethin' a bit mair coanvincin' than 'why wid I boather', Sister. An' if it wisnae youz, whae wiz it?'

Mary sat back in her chair and gave first O'Malley, then Knox, the broadest of smiles, before she turned back to gaze at the Superintendent.

'Is that a challenge, Superintendent?'

***

They let Mary go. In truth, they couldn't get close to placing her at the scene of the crime at the time of death, and she seemed genuinely unaware that Plews had died of heart failure. In any event O'Malley had fallen temporarily under Mary's spell as much as Knox, so he was an intrigued as his colleague to see what would happen next. Mary Maxwell-Hume certainly didn't seem a danger to the public. They took her fingerprints and her DNA 'for elimination purposes', but they were sure that would only prove she hadn't been involved in the suffocation process.

O'Malley ordered Knox to follow him into his office. Ready for the worst, Knox got his apology in first.

'I'm sorry, sir. I'm sorry I didn't tell you but I honestly didn't know what to tell you.'

'How about the truth, son? I wis bound tae find out eventually, fir cryin' out loud. Dave Lander had found the file we had on her, and the very first thing he showed me was her birth surname. Of course quite a bit o' that stuff has been destroyed because she wis under age. But your Sister Mary has history, that's for sure.'

'The truth is that I don't think she did it, sir. She's never been a violent woman. She uses other charms on people.'

'That's certainly true,' O'Malley conceded. 'She could probably have persuaded old man Plews to commit hara-kiri if it suited her. But it's no excuse for you, John.'

'No, sir. If I'm being honest with myself, I often feel a bit out of my depth with Sister Mary Maxwell-Hume. On the rare occasions when she's let her guard drop a little to talk about her past, it's almost felt like a privilege to be listening.'

'That might be an example of the wumman's charms, son. Just how close are yez, anyway? I mean, have yez...?'

'No, sir. Although once or twice she made it clear that she was available.'

'Why didn't yez? What man could resist an offer like that? Were yez tied tae a ship's mast or what?'

Knox chuckled. The Motherwell accent might sound coarse to Edinburgh ears, but the reference to the Sirens of the *Iliad* reminded him that there was nothing wrong with O'Malley's education. And an O'Malley joke probably meant that his reprimand would be limited.

'In fact I haven't seen her for a couple of years. It seemed a good idea to stay away from her if I could,' Knox said, adding, 'what with Alice and so on.'

'I can imagine. Still...'

'I know. I can only apologise again, sir, although I suppose my mind's been spinning a little since coming across Mary – of all people – at such a bizarre murder scene.'

'I was gonnae tell yez no tae dae it again, John, but I cannae imagine yez'll see tae many things like that in yer future career. But I dinnae think there's any harm been done. All the other people in that hoa-spit-al pit her in the clear. Mind you, ah'm telt wan o' the patients there died this morning. There was a note left on ma desk here a couple o' hours ago.'

'Which one, out of interest?'

O'Malley looked down. 'Eileen Lamb. Which one's that?'

'Jesus. That's the poor woman that Plews was found on top of. What a way to spend your final hours.'

'Her fingerprints were on the knife, that's right?'

'Correct, sir. Despite being comatose throughout.'

'Then I dinnae think she's our wumman either, is she?'

'No, sir. And of course Plews actually died of a heart attack.'

'Brought on by bein' suffocated wi' a pillow.'

'And he was in the late stages of Alzheimer's.'

'Well, John, maybe a murder conviction might be tricky, but I'm leavin' it tae youz tae find out whit happened here.'

'Thanks, sir.'

'But keep me informed. Of everything. Understood, John?'

'Understood, sir. Perhaps the Polish nurse will be able to shed some light on what happened.'

'Let's hope sae. She wiz the wan wi' the glasses?'

'Magda Czeslawska. She was the nurse on duty, although she claims nobody either entered or left the crime scene, and the CCTV footage bears that out. I found her a bit strange to talk to. She didn't seem as affected by Plews's death as I might have expected.'

'Naw, ah couldnae make anythin' o' her at a'. Ah ken her frae somewhere, mind. We need tae hae her in for sure.'

***

Knox returned home reasonably promptly, arriving just twenty minutes after Alice. A primary teacher, she got as prepared as possible for the next day before she left the building each evening. Yes, she brought work home – what teacher didn't these days? – but Alice felt that she worked harder on her work-life balance than her lover did. She stepped into the shower immediately she came home and as Knox entered the flat he was greeted by a dripping wet woman of thirty wrapped in a towel. Alice was fully six inches shorter and she had to put her arms around his neck and pull him down to her to kiss him. It wasn't a short embrace, and the towel gradually slid down in the process.

'You like me when I'm wet,' she said. 'What about now? It's Friday, let's celebrate the start of the weekend.'

Knox peeled away, briefly noted that his clothes were a little damp now as well, and hopped around for a moment.

'Sorry, I'm desperate for a pee. Can you wait?'

'I think I'll have to,' she said. 'But don't keep me waiting too long.'

As he stood beside the toilet bowl, Knox caught a glimpse of himself in the mirror. He looked exactly the way he felt: tired, drawn, exhausted. Here was a rare moment when Alice seemed aroused, but this time he was the one who was struggling a little. He knew he needed to make the effort, though.

When he eventually reached the bedroom, Alice had indeed made an effort and was in one of her favourite positions. She'd placed a couple of pillows on the bed, and lying face-down with her legs spread and her bottom perched in the air, she was instantly available. Her head was turned away from the door, but as she heard him arrive she simply said, 'Take me now, John. You know I need you.' And as it transpired, she did: tired as he was, he was still able to satisfy her easily. Alice, for her part, was irresistible. It was the best sex they'd had in ages.

But later, as they lay talking, she said to him, 'So you saw your Sister Mary today?'

'She's not my Sister Mary. But yes, I did. How did you know?'

'I can smell her Chanel No.5 on you.' Then Alice added, 'Was she good?'

'Good? What do you mean?'

'Was it nice to see her?'

'She's a witness to a case, Alice.'

'A witness, not a suspect?'

'As far as know, just a witness. But it's complicated.'

'Isn't it always where Mary's concerned?'

Knox said nothing.

'John. Can you be honest with me for a moment?'

He looked at her, wondering what was coming. 'Go on.'

'When we make love, are you ever thinking of Mary?'

Knox hesitated too long before replying, then eventually said, 'What a question. Do you ever think of George Clooney?'

Alice shook her head, then turned away from him. After a few minutes' silence, she got up, saying, 'I'll go and do something about our evening meal.'

SEVEN

I T WAS GOING TO BE NECESSARY to take care over statements from any hospital witnesses. By far the most pressing issues regarding the patients were (a) that they could die any moment and (b) that even those who were alive were of questionable frame of mind to be reliable witnesses. The staff were simply very busy, but they needed to be interviewed, too.

Lucy Grant had taken over the organisation of interviews at St Ninian's and had come up with the imaginative idea of sorting out the patients into order of projected lifespan. As O'Malley had pointed out, the first two, Leonard Plews and Eileen Lamb, had rather beaten them to it already. Lucy was extremely doubtful if any of the remaining six would be fit enough to help either. But when she and Izzy Bryce arrived to conduct some follow-ups, Helen Wolstencroft – who had just returned to work after taking the previous day off – had a surprise for her.

'How are you?' Lucy asked.

'Better thank you,' Wolstencroft said. 'I needed to take yesterday off, though, after the previous night.'

'You did the right thing. It must have been a shock.'

'Yes it was, but it would have been a shock for anyone. It must have been a shock for you as well, surely?' When Lucy nodded agreement, the doctor went on, 'But we all have jobs to do, don't we? You get on with yours, I get on with mine.'

'Perhaps I'm a bit more used to sudden deaths, though,' Lucy said, before realising her mistake. 'Sorry, of course you deal with death all the time. Not violent death, perhaps.'

'No, not any more,' Wolstencroft said. 'When I worked in Accident and Emergency I saw my fair share of sudden and violent deaths. Murders, road traffic accidents, domestic fires. In some ways the murders were the easiest – they were often the most recognisable as human beings.'

'You like this job better?'

'So much more satisfying. These patients are dying on their own terms. We try to give them a little control over their own lives right to the end.'

'That sounds like assisted dying,' Lucy said, quickly adding, 'I don't mean that in any sort of critical way.'

'Assisted dying, assisted living, it all merges into one at this stage. What matters is that the patient is getting what they want. That will certainly include pain relief. Sometimes the dose required to alleviate pain comes close to the lethal limit. You can't be sure how any individual will react.'

The doctor straightened up and tried to look businesslike. 'You'll want to interview as many people as possible, I presume?'

'Yes, please.'

'In which case I'd suggest you interview as many of the patients as possible first.'

Lucy couldn't conceal her surprise. 'They're capable of being interviewed?'

'Not all of them, obviously, although most are worth a try. But the patients with a physical illness such as cancer or heart trouble, definitely. It's perfect distraction from their troubles. Believe me, if they can help, they will. Be gentle with them, though.'

'I promise. I doubt if we'll get any signed statements, but I'll bring a tape recorder and we can at least get down as many facts as possible.'

'If I can help, I will.'

Wolstencroft then conveniently listed the patients in order of 'priority' – by which she meant the order in which they would probably die.

'You'll get nothing out of Martha Ramsay, I suspect. She might tell you something, but I wouldn't think it would be very reliable even if she could get the words out. She thinks every day is Christmas. But her breathing's hard now and she's stopped eating. I feel sorry for people in her situation.'

'Does she have Alzheimer's, too?'

Wolstencroft shook her head. 'Not all dementia is Alzheimer's, although it's the most common and it's what both Leonard Plews and Eileen Lamb suffered from.'

Lucy nodded her understanding. 'What about the others? I'd assumed they'd be lost causes.'

'Because they're on their way out? Not necessarily. You should be able to tell if a patient's lucid or not. Ask them the odd basic question to test how with it they are.'

Lucy smiled. 'Like – 'Who's the current Prime Minister?' That sort of thing?'

'I think that's a little obvious,' Wolstencroft said, taking Grant rather more seriously than the detective had intended.

'It's OK, I get the idea,' Lucy said, keen to move on. 'So – who should I speak to next?'

'Louise Gray looks not too bad apart from her skin colour, but she's nearing the end. That skin is due to liver damage, one of several organs that are simply packing up. She's quite happy but I doubt if she'll be here this time tomorrow.'

'Really? They can go downhill that quickly?'

Helen Wolstencroft looked up directly at Grant. 'Isn't that what we all seek at the end of our lives, Sergeant?'

Lucy could offer nothing in response. 'I suppose so. So Louise Gray is my first port of call. Who's next?'

'Ian Mould has good days and bad. He can hardly breathe sometimes, then we give him steroids which improve his condition but compromise his heart. So we reduce the steroids again and his breathing worsens. It's not a nice way to go, actually. Personally I'd choose cancer over that any time. But if we've just put him back on steroids again he can actually seem in quite good shape. Catch him at one of those points and he'll be only too glad to talk. A bit free with his hands, too.'

'You mean – ?'

'Forever touching up the female members of staff. I've experienced it myself, to tell the truth,' She smiled. 'Don't get too close.'

Lucy was shocked. 'Does that happen often? How do you cope?'

'Not often, but sometimes,' Wolstencroft said. 'I cope by telling myself that these patients are dying and that I'd rather be in my place than theirs. He'll be dead soon. Anyway, try not to tire Mr Mould out, please.'

'Noted.'

'Those two patients are the most urgent, I'd suggest. Of the others, Myles Cherry will probably linger longest. He's got COPD.'

'Chronic obstructive pulmonary disease. Mr Plews had that, too.'

'Indeed. In Mr Cherry's case, his good old-fashioned emphysema has almost certainly brought on by a lifetime of heavy smoking. He's only 62 as well, it's a shame. But if people insist on smoking eighty cigarettes each day, it's going to catch up with them sooner or later. He's actually completely aware of what's going on, and what's going to happen to him. He'll be an excellent witness and he'll want to help. The problem with Mr Cherry is that he's all but unable to speak.'

'That's a bit of a problem for many of these witnesses.'

'Well, he can speak, but his voice is so weak that you'll struggle to hear him. And the slightest effort seems to leave him breathless.'

'OK, but I'm getting your message – worth a try, but don't push it.'

'Exactly. As for the other two, they're quite compos mentis but morphine takes its toll. They're in a lot of pain, so we sedate them a lot.'

'Would they be able to get out of bed?'

'I suppose so. Only if they were awake. We do try to get them out of bed every day to help with circulation and so on.

Lucy thanked the doctor for her help, then began to ask the medic about her own recollections of events. Wolstencroft pointed out that she'd already given a statement but the detective explained that she wanted her colleague to hear it for herself. Privately, of course, she wanted to check that Wolstencroft's version of events remained consistent. Izzy Bryce – who had so far remained silent – had been taking notes without comment. But the doctor's statement was as detailed and measured as on the first occasion, without any sort of deviation from the night of the murder.

Wolstencroft had reached the end when Izzy spoke for the first time.

'Tell me, Dr Wolstencroft, I'm interested in your security measures. What do you have at the front door?'

'I'm sorry. What do you mean? CCTV?'

'Well, yes. How do visitors sign in? Do you search large bags? Any sort of metal or drugs detection system? How do ensure drugs don't get stolen, for instance? There must be a street demand for some of the stuff you have in here.'

Lucy Grant tried to contain her smile. She had to give Izzy credit for slipping it in so neatly.

'We don't search bags, no. The relatives are stressed enough already. But there's a metal detector system at the front door. All of our drugs containers have a magnetic strip which would set off the alarm if anyone tried to remove something.'

'Is it sensitive?'

'Up to a point.'

'Would it detect a knife?'

'I don't know. I'd have to try it out.'

'I have a Sabatier knife in the boot of the police car. It's my own one from home, a bit bigger, perhaps. Can I try out?' Lucy Grant looked at the doctor and shrugged her shoulders. Izzy wasn't short of initiative, it seemed.

A moment later a quiet alarm could be heard going off in reception as she returned.

'We keep it quiet so that the patients won't be disturbed. But that would be noticed,' Wolstencroft said. 'Was that your knife?'

Izzy produced a fairly serious-looking kitchen knife from inside her jacket. Lucy shuddered as she thought what might have happened if she'd tripped and fallen on the way in.

'That suggests the knife didn't come in to St Ninian's through the front door,' Grant said.

'I'm afraid there are quite a few other ways in,' Wolstencroft said, apologetically. 'It's not really that secure a hospital if someone wants to get in or out. The drugs are kept under safe lock and key, but the patients themselves are quite easily accessed.'

'The corridor is easily accessed, doctor,' Lucy corrected her. 'But we have all that CCTV footage and no one actually went into the room from the corridor during the period when we think Mr Plews died. And whoever did the deed, did so with at least six witnesses present. Someone in there must know something. All we have to do is to find a way of getting them to tell us.'

***

'OK, ma'am, where do we start?' Izzy Bryce asked Lucy. The pair had taken their leave of Wolstencroft and were making their way back down towards Reception.

'What would you suggest, Izzy? I'm sure you've got some ideas but you're too polite to say it.'

'OK. Why don't we start by asking the Polish nurse what she saw? Has she given a statement yet?'

'Not a proper one. And that's exactly where we're going, too. The Inspector and the Superintendent both think we should bring her into the station for formal questioning.'

'I gather it didn't work too well on the nun,' Izzy said, wondering at the same time why Lucy had bothered to ask her opinion.

Meanwhile, Lucy noted how fast word about an interview could spread around the station. 'No, but the Superintendent is hoping that, being a foreign national, Ms Czeslawska might be more likely to panic if she's hiding anything.'

'Sounds a bit mean. Do you think she is, ma'am? Hiding anything, I mean?'

'Somebody is, Izzy.' Then she added, 'Izzy, when are you going to call me 'Lucy'?'

Izzy smiled. 'Sorry. It's instinct. It's how things were before I packed it in to have my kids. Things seem to have changed a bit. I'll work on it.'

At the reception desk, Lucy asked if Magda Czeslawska was in St Ninian's, and if so, was she available to speak with. The woman on the desk looked at a computer screen, and was about to reply when Grant and Bryce heard a thick accent behind them.

'You urr looking furr me?'

Bryce hadn't met Magda before, and was slightly thrown by her glasses and expressionless gaze.

'We were hoping to interview you, Ms Czeslawska. Formally, preferably.'

'Do you think I culled Mr Plews?'

Lucy tried to put her at ease.

'No, it's a formality, honestly. But we'd like to do it properly and it would be better if we interviewed you at the police station, and we could turn that into a signed statement.'

'It sounds like you urr urresting me.'

Izzy suspected that her own silence might not be helping. 'Ms Czeslawska, we're not arresting you, I can assure you of that,' she said. 'But we do need your help to be sure that we've got all of our facts right. You're certainly not under arrest, and we can interview you at your convenience. When would be the best time for you?'

'In ten minutes.'

Surprised, Lucy looked at her watch. 'In ten minutes?'

'I finish my shift at four o'clock. You can give me a lift. I live not far from your police station.'

Izzy chuckled. 'You'll have to go in the back seat – it'll look like we've arrested you after all.'

'I don't mind,' Magda said. 'And I'll save a bus fare.'

Magda might have minded a little more if she'd spotted the shifty-looking man taking pictures with a telephoto lens from the open window of a small white car parked on the other side of St Ninian's car park.

Meanwhile, back at St Leonard's, for a man who had just lost his father, Chief Inspector Maximilian Plews was in the strangest mood. He didn't seem particularly upset that his father had died, but was extremely bothered that the investigating officer hadn't found the culprit yet. He was particularly angry that the chief suspect, as he saw it, was walking the streets scot-free.

'Knox!' he called. 'My office, now!'

Knox sighed as he rose from his desk. Dave Lander gave him a sympathetic smile as he passed. Arriving in his superior's room, he made to close the door until Plews yelled, 'Did I give you permission to close my door, Knox?'

Knox left it open. It might be useful if others could hear the conversation anyway.

'If you're sure, sir.'

He didn't sit down. That would have been another mistake.

Plews looked him straight in the eye and asked, 'Why is that woman at large?'

'Sister Mary? We don't think she killed your father, sir. It's the wrong time frame.'

'Wrong 'time frame'?!' Plews screamed. 'Talk in English, man!'

'The PM – sorry, sir, post-mortem – suggests that your father was already dead when she arrived.'

'These pathologists can get it wrong, you know.'

Knox was well aware that Plews would love to have been able to put Mary 'in the frame' for his father's murder. Or any sort of crime, for that matter. But Knox also knew to say nothing. Plews was left to change tack.

'Any progress on my brother's Jaguar?'

'Nothing yet, sir. Nor on any of the other five. I'm working on the assumption that they've all been taken by the same gang.'

Plews sat up straight in his chair. He was dressed as usual in a smart three-piece suit with a dark striped tie that might have showed off his membership of a prestigious Edinburgh golf club. He and his brother Theodore both enjoyed belonging to the club in question, although neither of them could actually play the game to a standard anywhere beyond 'embarrassing' level. In practice, Maximilian and Theodore only ever played golf with each other, and late in the day when no one else would see them. It had actually been from the golf club that 'Teddy's Jag' had been removed, while the car park was deserted.

'I suppose it's possible that all six Jaguars have been stolen by the same gang.' Then he added, 'My brother's would have been the pick of them.'

'Of course, sir.'

'Well, hurry up and find the culprits. Not that my brother really wants his Jag back now, you understand. Some drug addict will have sat in it and contaminated it.'

'Where was your Jaguar at the time, sir?'

'Mine was the only other car in the golf club car park – don't you read the files?'

'It's just good police work, sir. I seem to remember you once saying that you can never have too many witness statements.'

'Did I say that?' Plews asked. After a moment, he said, 'Well, perhaps so, but there's a limit,' leaving Knox completely baffled.

'I wonder why they didn't steal your car, sir?' Knox wondered aloud.

'Indeed. You'd think my car would be more desirable than my brother's,' Plews said, with no justification whatsoever.

'I don't know enough about cars to make a judgement, sir.'

'You will, Knox. Trust me, you will.'

***

In the event, the interview with Magda Czeslawska at St Leonard's was a major disappointment. Lucy and Knox took her through the night's events, but Magda's version of what happened exactly matched her movements on the CCTV. Magda, it seemed, was obsessive about facts, and when she said she'd sat down or stood up at 22.34 hours, she meant it: she even kept a log. She'd even brought the 'log' in question – a large lined notebook along as corroboration. Not that either of the police officers could understand a word, of course, as it was all written in her native language.

Magda confirmed that no one had entered the Murray room before Sister Mary, who in turn had arrived at her usual time, just before the stroke of midnight. No, she'd no idea why Sister Mary came then, but Sister Mary was a strange woman. (Later, Lucy and Knox were to agree that was an amusing observation coming from Magda herself.)

Magda had heard nothing, seen nothing, until Mary herself had alerted her that Mr Plews was dead. Once again Knox and Lucy had hit the buffers of a dead end.

***

Knox arrived home shortly before 7.00 in the evening, and was surprised to find Alice not yet at home. Looking at the kitchen calendar, he noticed that she written 'Chilli', which reminded him that they would be making enough not only for tonight's meal, but for two more to go in the freezer as well. Aware that if he sat down, he'd struggle to get up again, he began chopping three onions and some garlic. The meat – minced beef and chorizo – was in the fridge and the other ingredients were in the store cupboard, and so Knox was hard at work when, around a quarter to seven, he became aware that he was no longer alone in the house.

He peered out of the kitchen to find Alice going through the mail.

'Hi,' he said.

'Hi.' She didn't look up, although she sounded cheerful enough.

'You're late home tonight.'

'I wasn't sure when to expect you home, so I thought I'd get a bit more done at school.' If she'd simply left it at that, he'd have given it no further thought, but then she added, 'Is there a problem?' There was no aggression in her voice, but then Alice was never aggressive.

'No.'

But of course there was a problem. Knox could sense it, but waited for what was coming next.

'I just thought that, if you were going to be late home from work, I might as well be, too.'

Knox looked round at her. 'What made you think I'd be particularly late home tonight?'

'Well, you've been late home quite a bit lately.'

'Twice.'

Alice said nothing for a moment, then said casually, 'How's the murder investigation going? Is Mary in the clear?'

'I think so. Lucy's trying to interview the patients, although I'm not sure how much success she'll have there. I said I'd leave her to it, though. The doctor in charge apparently gave a pretty well identical account the second time around, and in any case Dave Lander's had a team on the CCTV footage and no one goes in or out of the room where old man Plews was.' Then he added, 'You still seem to be interested in Mary.'

Alice hesitated for a moment, then said.

'Aren't *you*?'

EIGHT

CHIEF INSPECTOR PLEWS was in a foul mood the following morning, and went to vent his spleen first at Knox. When he couldn't be found, he turned his ire onto his superior officer Superintendent O'Malley.

'This is outrageous!' Plews was a reasonably neat man, even if he carried a little more weight than his dapper older brother Theodore. But when he became angry, he was inclined to spray spittle in all directions. O'Malley patiently wiped his cheek before replying. The man had just lost his father, after all.

'Chief Inspector?'

'Knox is idle and incompetent – he's found out nothing so far. I demand that you take him off the case.'

O'Malley sighed. He didn't want to cut Plews any slack, but knew he had to.

'It's a difficult case. I dinnae really understand how the culprit done it masel'. The CCTV footage shows nothing, and naebody seems tae have gone in or out – '

'I'm not talking about Daddy's murder!' Plews spluttered again. 'I don't really care about him. He was gaga anyway and the world's probably a better place without him. I'm talking about the theft of the cars. Specifically, brother Teddy's car. How Knox hasn't managed to solve that case is a complete mystery.'

O'Malley sat back in his chair, amused.

'So, Chief Inspector, how would youz go about things?'

'I'd find the cars and then arrest the person or persons who owned the property where the cars were found.'

'Good idea, Chief Inspector. I think Inspector Knox might agree wi' yez. Where dae yez suggest he starts?'

'Isn't that *his* job? Or is he too busy chasing after this nun he's so infatuated with?'

Privately, O'Malley was also a little concerned about the relationship between Knox and Sister Mary – he might even have been a little jealous – but he wasn't admitting that to his odious little colleague.

'Ah dinnae think the nun has anything tae dae wi' the car thefts,' he said. 'Dae you?'

'Has she been ruled out of enquiries?'

'For the moment. Ah'm rulin' her out, even if Knox disnae. Ah ken yer under strain the now, Plews, but when it comes tae yer polis work yez does need tae be a bit mair dispassionate.'

Plews bridled visibly. 'Are you suggesting that I'm not up to my job simply because my father has recently died, sir? I hope not.'

'That's not what I meant.' Of course he was suggesting just that. It wasn't really what he was thinking, though. He was thinking that Plews was an overbearing, incompetent fool. But saying that might not look too good given the man's recent bereavement.

O'Malley sighed, then motioned to Plews to sit down in an attempt to lower the temperature.

'Leave Knox to do his job, Plews. He's a good copper. One day he'll be a very good copper. As far as your dad's death, though, I doubt we'll ever manage a conviction for any sort of foul play. We might find out what happened somehow, but that's about as far as it'll ever get.'

'So a man dies with a knife in his back and the culprit gets off scot free?'

'Your father seems tae have died of natural causes, albeit that he might have been helped along a bit by parties unknown. The witnesses are mostly gaga and each claims to have heard nothing. The knife had nothing to do wi' his death. I'm not even sure what the crime would be, tae be honest wi' yez.'

'How about desecrating a corpse?' Plews said, indignantly.

O'Malley looked at him, and began to count to ten. Plews quickly got the message.

'Will that be all, sir?'

O'Malley just carried on counting, and Plews was out and the door closed before he'd made it to ten.

***

Lucy Grant sat in the corner of the canteen reading her newspaper. Few of her colleagues could be found poring over *The Times* at work, but then not many of her colleagues came from her comfortable middle-class background. Educated at the same Fife boarding school as her mother, Lucy's year had nevertheless been the last before boys were also admitted. Neither of her parents – James Grant was a retired Navy Admiral – approved of the move to co-education. But then Lucy's parents didn't approve of much that happened in the twenty-first century: sex, clubbing, drugs and – worst of all – mobile phones were all evidence of decadence. Living away from the family home, though, Lucy was able to find out about life for herself, which suited her nicely.

In her last eighteen months at school, one thing Lucy certainly managed to learn about was her attitude towards the other sex. The absence of boys in Lucy's year at Loudon Academy meant that relationships between girls, while strictly forbidden, were nevertheless fairly common. In addition, in their final two years, Loudon Academy and a nearby all-boys' school got together for a number of classes, for musical and dramatic productions and for some general socialising. That had predictable results.

For Lucy, therefore, her school experience gave her early opportunities with both sexes. At the time, she couldn't really make up her mind which she preferred and in the nine years since, she'd not really managed to come to any firm conclusions one way or another. She'd been through a number of partners roughly in the proportion of two women for every one man, but was still no nearer a decision. Currently, she shared her flat with a primary teacher of her own age called Amy. Amy worked hard and their lifestyles fitted together; she also had nice curves and was excellent in bed first thing in the morning. But Lucy knew Amy wasn't the answer. Amy was too anxious about their relationship and wanted to make things more permanent. Lucy was still open to the idea of a full-blown consummated marriage to a man, complete with children. She just didn't know what the future held.

Lucy's parents would have disapproved if they'd realised that their daughter was bisexual, but she never had to tell them, because some years previously they'd decided to emigrate to the Bahamas to live off James's ample pension. They definitely did not approve of Lucy being in the police. No, that was for too lowly a job for a woman of her social breeding and upbringing. They threatened not to speak to her, to which Lucy said, fine, and carried on her life exactly as she wished back in Edinburgh.

All of which meant that Lucy Grant was one of those people who saw no reason to judge people for how they conducted their private lives, so long as they did their job well. Generally, she didn't comment on other people's affairs and she expected them to respect her privacy, too. It made her seem a little aloof to those who didn't know her well, but she didn't mind that either. However, deep in her innermost soul she still found it hard to shake off the last remains of her family tradition, and *The Times* was a silent point of contact she had with her absent parents.

'Mind if I join you?'

Lucy looked up to see Knox standing across from her at the table with a cup of coffee and a KitKat biscuit.

'Be my guest.'

'Six down,' said Knox. 'Intrepid.'

Lucy smiled. 'Interesting. 6 down is 'Drum rolls MP in at one'. Seven letters. Intrepid doesn't quite fit. But you got one thing right.'

'I did?'

'There really is a 6 down.'

'Well, that's made my day,' Knox said, triumphant. 'Anyway, Ms Smartipants, have you solved it?'

'Of course. Timpani. It's simple – '

'I'll take your word for it, Lucy.' He waved his KitKat at her. 'Split it?'

'I'm not going to snatch food from my boss's mouth.'

'That's actually a yes,' he said, breaking two of the four fingers and passing them across, foil wrapper included. 'I meant, have you solved the murder of the good Chief Inspector's father?'

'Oh that? No. Have you?'

Knox sighed. 'I've ruled a few suspects out. The St Ninian's CCTV says it can't be a member of staff or a visitor. And we can't exactly question the woman that Plews was found sprawled on top of.'

'Not if she's died since, no.' Lucy hesitated. 'I know your connection with Sister Mary makes this awkward, but are you sure…? Perhaps the time of death isn't quite right?'

'I'm sure, Lucy. Dr Sally never gets the time of death wrong, I'm told. Never once in her entire career.'

'Never once?'

'It's a standing joke in the pathology department, it seems. And in any case, there's plenty of footage of Mary on the way in street and in public transport CCTV, and she's nowhere near St Ninian's until around fifteen minutes before she herself reports the murder.'

'And our Dr Sally says that although victim was probably being held down and being suffocated with a pillow, he actually died of a heart attack,' Lucy pointed out.

'Correct. We're not going to get a conviction on this, I'm pretty sure of it.'

'Perhaps not. It would be nice to find out what happened, though.' Neither of them said anything for a moment, then Lucy added with a bright smile, 'Maybe they all did it together?'

Knox chuckled. 'Like *Murder on the Orient Express*. All the culprits had good reason in the book. I doubt if many of the patients knew what day of the week it was in this case. And they didn't know Plews.'

'Although I hear that Sister Mary knew him.'

'Ah. News travels fast, it seems.' Knox looked down at the table. 'I'm sorry I didn't let you know beforehand, Lucy. I just felt it would… complicate things.'

'John, your business is your own. You don't have to tell me anything.'

'Except in a murder case.'

'Except that it's not a murder case, and Sister Mary's not involved.' There was a moment's silence. 'Is she?'

'Not as far as I know.'

'Well that's fine, then.' Lucy took a sip of her coffee. 'But you can always share things if you want to. Like about who that guy was you were speaking to at the car park entrance yesterday. Ron Flockhart said he looked like a journalist.'

'Is that all over the station as well? Jeez.'

Lucy grinned. 'No, don't worry, I happened to be looking out of the window and took the opportunity to ask Ron when I bumped into him at the coffee machine. Was he right?'

'Sort of. Freelance. But more of a general low-life that I was at school with. He was asking questions about St Ninian's, but I said nothing.'

'We'll surely have to make some sort of press statement eventually, won't we?'

'About what? A murder that didn't happen? About the death of someone who was expected to die but no one cared about. Is that worthy of a press conference?'

'Perhaps not yet, but you know what the press are like, John. Never let the truth get in the way of a good story.'

'I know, I know. And you're making me feel bad again, because I regard you as a friend as well as a colleague. Alice knows about you, but she isn't jealous of you.'

Lucy looked up in surprise. 'You've told her, then? About Amy and me?'

'Yes. I hope you didn't mind. It made things easier. She's neurotic enough about Mary. And Alice doesn't gossip. But she knows Amy professionally a bit and Amy had said she had a new girlfriend called Lucy who was in the police. I thought it was better to get that part cleared out of the way.'

Lucy seemed a little irritated. Knox caught her glance.

'Did I do wrong?' he asked.

'No, no, it's not you I'm annoyed about, it's Amy. I wish she could keep her mouth shut sometimes. It's not as easy being in the police.'

'Sorry. I didn't mean to upset you. Is everything OK?'

Lucy explained that her feelings for Amy were a little conflicted, but that Amy didn't want to hear and assumed that Lucy and she were set for life. Even when one night Lucy had mentioned children, Amy had immediately volunteered to carry an IVF child herself.

'I'm just not ready for that sort of commitment just now. Simple as that.' She sat up. 'This is all beside the point, John. Who could have arranged that Leonard Plews could have had a heart attack by holding his head down into a pillow. Could a group of patients have done it together?'

'You're keen on this *Murder On The Orient Express* idea, aren't you?'

'Some of these patients are apparently capable of getting about not too badly even although they'll be dead in a week or two, the Dr. Wolstencroft said. It's all about summoning energy and limiting pain. And Plews was a small, thin man, wasting away and near the point of death. Not much more than forty kilos, it seems. Not a lot to carry or drag.'

'You've got it all worked out, haven't you?'

'Have you got any better ideas?'

Knox laughed. 'You know, that's the craziest thing about it. Yours is the best idea so far. The only one, in fact.'

Lucy grinned.

'When you have eliminated the impossible, whatever's

left, however improbable, must be the truth. As a girl, I read and re-read Sherlock Holmes avidly. Still do, sometimes.'

'Sherlock Holmes? You really are quite an unusual woman, Lucy Grant. But I'm still not rushing to the bookies' shop to place money on a gang killing by a group of about-to-die care home patients. I reckon we're missing something.'

'Maybe we should concentrate instead on solving the spate of Jaguar thefts instead,' Lucy suggested. 'I gather that's the crime that Chief Inspector Plews is really bothered about.'

'I think he's more bothered that thieves regard his brother's Jaguar as more valuable than his own. For the Chief Inspector, that's the real mystery.'

'So perhaps we should arrange to have the Chief Inspector's car stolen?' Lucy suggested with a mischievous grin on her face.

'The way I feel about Chief Inspector Plews at the moment, Lucy, I wouldn't even want to make him *that* happy.'

NINE

'WHAT HAVE YOU GOT ON TODAY?'

Three days had passed with no sign of a breakthrough on either the 'murder' or the spate of car thefts. His team had interviewed everyone, in some cases more than once.

Knox pushed the cereal packet away. He was an inveterate breakfast reader and anything – a Corn Flakes packet, leaflets put through the door, even credit card bills – was fair game. But a mouth full of toast meant that he couldn't reply to Alice's question immediately.

'Sorry,' he said eventually. 'To answer your question, the same as yesterday. And the day before. The same two cases just won't go away. I seem to be Plews's personal detective at the moment.' Then after a moment he added, 'I know I shouldn't say this about a grieving man, but he really is horrible. I had to ask him some questions about his father and he accused me of meddling around in affairs that had nothing to do with me. I knew old man Plews was an abusive father, but it was hard to get our esteemed Chief Inspector to talk about it.'

'How did you know he was abusive?'

Knox immediately realised his mistake. He'd never told Alice about Mary's connection with Plews; he'd felt it was a breach of her privacy. Now, though, he decided that letting a little out was the least bad option.

'Mary told me. A long time ago. She's actually Plews's niece and was raised by him for a while. It wasn't a happy home.'

'So she knows the Chief Inspector? Doesn't that make them…?'

'Related, yes. Very related, and in a complicated way. But Plews doesn't know who Mary is. Not yet, anyway. It's one reason she carries on using her married name.' Alice did however know that Sister Mary was actually a widow. 'Listen, Alice, that has to be confidential. It could materially affect the case, but if it doesn't it would mess up Mary's life a bit.'

'You know you can tell me stuff and I won't blab. Does O'Malley know?'

'He does now. He'd worked out already that something was going on, actually. He's a bright guy, is our Superintendent. Gets a lot right.'

'I know you like him. I think he likes you, too.'

'Yeah, he's a good policeman. He seems rough around the edges but he plays on it a bit, I think. People let their guard down, thinking he's stupid because of the way he speaks.'

'Folk can be really snobby,' Alice acknowledged. She hesitated, then said, 'So if she's no longer under suspicion, you won't be interviewing Mary again.'

'Oh, I'm sure we will be speaking to her again. She was first on the scene. She's the chief witness and she found the body. Lucy Grant still thinks she could have done it – you know, perhaps the pathologist got the time of death wrong.'

Alice looked up, surprised. 'Is that possible?'

'Not really, no. The pathologist, 'Dr Sally' as everyone calls her, did a lot of tests and they all indicated that the deceased was dead at least thirty minutes before Mary arrived at St Ninian's, and probably a good deal more. But Lucy's as suspicious of Mary as you are.'

Alice bridled slightly. 'I'm not suspicious of Mary.' She rested her hand on Knox's. 'Not even suspicious of anything between you and her either, John. If you say there's nothing between you, then I believe you.'

After a moment, Knox said, 'There's nothing.'

Alice took a deep breath. 'What about the Jaguars? Can I ask about that?'

'There's absolutely nothing to report there at all. Six thefts, all Jaguars, all new, all vanished completely. We've no idea whether they're still in the country or not. I rather doubt it, personally. They've probably been resprayed different colours in some backstreet Estonian body-shop by now. It's a lost cause, I think.'

It had been a while now, fully three years Knox reckoned, since he'd last made his way up the quiet street in Trinity. It was even more difficult to park there now, and as had so often been the case then he'd taken to leaving the car on the main road and making his way up to the front door on foot. Red sandstone terraced houses ran the length of Trinity Loan on both sides, and No. 21 was halfway up on the left.

Sister Mary Maxwell-Hume and he had met by chance while he was out in his patrol car. Knox, relatively newly started on the university trainee scheme and a raw police constable, had performed a simple act of kindness for Mary on a hot day. Well, to be accurate, several acts of kindness. Taking him under her wing, Mary began to assist Knox in some of his work, but never once herself taking any credit. Knox began to be noticed by the 'big-wigs', a young man with initiative who never seemed to lose his cool and who seemed able to get results in extraordinary situations. With his star in the ascendency, there was little doubt that PC John Knox would rise through the rank of sergeant and to inspector in absolutely no time whatsoever. And so it proved.

In addition, Mary had stumbled across the fact that Knox had once taken piano lessons and had even inherited a very good grand piano from his parents. She insisted, rather against his will, on giving the young constable piano lessons either at his flat or, more commonly, at her own house. Knox smiled as he recalled times he'd made his way up the little crazy-paved pathway to Sister Mary Maxwell-Hume's front door, still surrounded by that clematis that always seemed to be in flower. His hands would be sweating with fear at the prospect of yet another piano lesson with her, whereupon he'd be greeted by a tall, slim, elegant woman, exquisitely dressed in some long figure-hugging dress, and liberally-applied Chanel No.5. Always, too, she wore a mysterious smile that lured him in to his fate. He knew that Mary had other students – strangely enough all men – but from early on Knox knew that he was her favourite. For a start, she didn't charge him.

But the lessons had eventually ceased and they'd drifted apart. This visit was professional and he'd decided to call on Mary without an appointment; Knox knew there was a decent chance she wouldn't even be in. The delay that followed his ring on the doorbell could mean anything, though, because it had never been audible from outside. And it was as he glanced all around for signs of life, and it was at that moment that he caught sight of the familiar little brass plate on the wall. Bending down to squint at it more closely, he read:

Sister Mary Maxwell-Hume
Piano Teacher
Private Detective

The last two words had been added more recently, perhaps less than a year ago, Knox reckoned. He smiled, wondering what sort of clientele this new rival to Sam Spade might have acquired.

Knox was so wrapped up in his thoughts that he failed to realise that the door had opened and he was being watched.

'Well... this is a surprise. Is it going to be a pleasant surprise?'

Sister Mary Madeleine Scarlett Maxwell-Hume towered above him. It wasn't that she was very tall – although she was around five foot nine – more that she happened to be standing three steps up just inside her door, while Knox was still bent over.

'Hello, Mary. How are you?'

'I'm well, John. But I presume you're here to ask me more questions, not for a piano lesson.' She stood aside to usher him in, but once the door closed it was Knox's turn to stand aside and allow her to lead on. The brief dance in a confined space was enough to stimulate all those past memories of his former visits, memories of Chanel No.5 and those dresses. Try as he might, he couldn't help himself as he followed her into the living room, past the grand piano he knew so well from the past, and towards two sofas which he thought might have been recovered. Mary didn't hurry. Today, she was wearing an unusual colour, a light grey calf-length knitted item that as usual revealed everything and nothing.

She motioned Knox to sit down on the sofa at right angles to a French window leading to the garden, positioning him so that the daylight flooded his face. Meanwhile she sat at the other end of the same seat, her face in shadow. As she did so, Knox realised that, with the light behind her, the dress revealed even more than he'd first expected.

'You came to ask questions,' she said with a mischievous smile. 'Am I right in saying that one of them has been answered already?'

Knox looked away in embarrassment, but could think of no reply.

'The Sisters of Mary of the Sacred Cross believe that – ' Mary said, but Knox interrupted her.

'I know, I know. You should wear only as much clothing as is necessary for due modesty.'

'Do you think I'm fulfilling my vow?'

'That depends on how modest you think you're being.'

Mary smiled broadly. 'Very good answer, John. My, how you've come on in these last few years. But to answer your question, I suppose I wasn't expecting anyone, so what need was there of any form of dress?' Again, Knox didn't respond, so she continued, 'In which case, perhaps my vows suggest that I should have removed it. Should I remove it now, do you think?' She reached behind her neck for a zip.

'No, no,' Knox said, hurriedly. 'You're immaculately dressed, as ever, Mary.'

Mary's smile returned to 'mischievous mode'.

'I'm so glad you think so. How is Alice?'

Once again, Alice. He could sense the antipathy.

'Fine, thank you. She sends her regards,' he lied.

'Hmm,' she replied, with an obvious note of doubt in her voice. 'And you're 'Inspector Knox' now. How's that going?'

'Busy. Two big cases going on at once.'

'Two?' Mary replied. 'Two murders?'

Knox couldn't see what harm there would be in sharing the information. 'What happened at St Ninian's is one of them. The other is a spate of Jaguar car thefts.'

'Oh well, there's no doubt which of those is the more pressing, then. Property trumps violence every time,' Mary said, without a hint of sarcasm.

'Indeed. Especially when Chief Inspector Plews and his brother both drive Jags.'

'Oh my! Have Teddy and Max had their Jags stolen? How frightful,' she said, sarcasm fully in evidence this time. 'Crimes against the police trump crimes against property.'

'It's not as simple as that.' Knox explained that only Theodore's car had been stolen.

Mary sat back in her chair.

'I see. Teddy's angry that his car has been stolen, Max is angry that his Jag's not deemed to be worth stealing. No wonder Max wants the case solved.'

'That's about it. Meanwhile the mysterious murder of their father gets pushed to one side.'

'Well it's not very important, is it?'

Unsure if Mary was being serious or not, Knox decided that now was a good time to get some questions in. Explaining that he wanted to be sure that they had all the details correct, he patiently went through her evidence while, equally patiently, she repeated her version of what she'd seen. It was standard technique, they both knew, to see if her story was consistent, and to see how good she would be when – as was virtually certain at some stage – she was required to give evidence in court. But Mary was rock solid.

'Tell me, John, and tell me truthfully, please. Am I a suspect?' she said eventually. She looked deeply and sensuously into his eyes, probing away at his inner core. 'I can tell if you're lying to me, you know that.'

Knox sighed. 'Not really. The Chief Inspector would like you to be a suspect, in fact he'd like you to be found guilty and sentenced to death by slow torture. Fortunately he's not allowed to be on the case, and all the rest of us reckon you were miles away at the time of death. The pathologist is particularly competent – you've met her, actually, she declared old man Plews dead at the time.'

'Oh, that young woman? Do you like her?'

'She's good at her job.'

'I said, 'Do you like her?"

'As a person, yes.'

'Do you find her attractive?'

Knox said nothing for a bit, then said, 'Why ask when you know the answer already?'

'Because I want to hear you say it, John.'

'She's attractive. I'm attracted to her. Is that good enough?' he said, irritated, as much at himself for allowing Mary to get under his skin. 'Look, Mary, I'm faithful. I don't cheat on women.'

'No, John. You cheat on yourself.'

'Why are you so jealous of Alice? Don't you want me to be happy?' Knox snapped. He wanted to avoid stating the obvious, that Mary was 25 years older than him, albeit that he still found her stunning.

'I promise you, John, I'm not jealous of her. I just want you to be happy.'

'You think I'd be happier with you than with Alice?'

'Perhaps. Perhaps not. I'm too old for you, we both know that.'

They sat in silence for a moment, then Knox said, 'Look, can we change the subject? I came on police business and I have a crime to get to the bottom of.'

'So why don't we get on with it?'

'We?'

'Why not? I can help you solve the real crime here, the Jaguar thefts. Remember the name-plate? I'm a private detective these days, too.'

'What sort of work do you do?'

'Oh, the usual things – domestic stuff, tracing lost relatives, collecting evidence of adultery and so on. I'm pretty good on fraud, too.'

Knox smiled, relieved to have moved onto safer ground. 'I'll bet.'

Mary stiffened. 'I'll ignore that, John. That was beneath you. I get results because nobody expects a piano-teaching nun to be a private detective.'

'I don't suppose they do, no,' he chuckled.

'Would you believe that I've twice been giving piano lessons to children while a parent has been upstairs with an illicit lover? The women are the worst, by the way. Their excuses are always the same, too. They're convinced the husband is having an affair when all he's actually doing is working all the hours God sends to earn enough to allow his wife to spend a fortune.

'But it can be satisfying, too. Sometimes one parent tries to hide a child from the other in a custody dispute. I do like tracing them by giving the children piano lessons. I can ask the child if they're happy or not. If the child says they're being kept against their will, I tell the police and I get a nice fee. If the child says they're happy, I keep quiet but I ask the parent that's taken the child for the fee instead to keep quiet.'

'That sounds like blackmail, Mary. Should I be getting told this?'

'It sounds like me getting paid my dues. Meanwhile, the child gets to be happy. What your problem with that, John?'

Knox sighed. 'Probably nothing,' he said, fingers crossed behind his back that he could ignore what he'd just been told. He tried to take control of things again. 'Anyway, business is all right, is it?'

'It pays the bills,' Mary replied, sourly. It was unusual for Knox to see her like this. 'Not so many adults take piano lessons these days. Even fewer are interested, like you, in being prepared for examinations.' Suddenly, she brightened. 'I assume you're still playing that beautiful grand piano regularly?'

Knox had inherited a wonderful piano when his parents had emigrated to Australia; for a while, Mary had been his teacher.

'Well, you know…,' then he hesitated.

'Alice doesn't like listening to you playing the piano?'

'She says it's too loud. She can't hear the television. *Eastenders*, *Strictly Come Dancing*, that sort of thing.'

She took a sharp intake of breath, and Knox was reminded how, when she had given him piano lessons, Mary could express her disapproval without so much as saying a word.

'Well, I have to say I'm disappointed in Alice. Your piano playing wasn't that good, John, but surely any piano playing is better than *Strictly Come Dancing*.'

'Don't you approve of ballroom dancing?'

'That's not ballroom dancing, John. That's public vertical fornication.'

'Goodness me, Mary. You do surprise me. I didn't have you down as a prude.'

'A prude? Not really, I don't think so, anyway. I just happen to believe that the act of love is better as a privately shared experience. Those people on television are just strutting around like peacocks, hinting at having sex without actually doing so.'

In any other person, this would all have become a rant. But Knox knew it was best to say nothing when Mary went off on one of her 'lectures' and, sure enough, she petered out.

'Anyway,' she said, 'do you still practise the piano, or not?'

'Yes and no,' Knox replied.

'What does that mean?' she said, sternly.

'It means yes... but not very often.'

'How often?' she growled.

'Perhaps twice a week.'

Mary looked a little startled and Knox wondered if he'd let her down. But Mary's reaction was slightly different.

'In the circumstances, John, I'm actually quite buoyed to hear that you fit even that much in.' But then, just as he had decided that the danger had passed, she added, 'But now I want to hear you play.'

'Well, I'm not really prepared...'

'Come now, John, if you play twice a week, you must be playing something. Or do you just imagine you play twice a week?' Ominously, she began to eye the Steinway that took pride of place in her living room. Knox had played it many times before when she'd given him piano lessons, and he could already read what was going through her mind.

He hoped that silence would protect him, but he was wrong.

'Now, John,' Mary said seductively, sounding like a cross between a schoolteacher and Ingrid Bergman, 'I want you to play something for me.'

'Really, I can't.'

'Really? I think you can, John.'

'Honestly, I think I'd disappoint you.'

Mary smiled mysteriously. Knox knew that smile well: it meant resistance was futile.

'Play something for me,' she repeated. 'What about that piece you once played in public, the Satie *Gymnopédie*. Do you remember?'

She wandered across to the piano stool and within seconds had produced some sheet music.

'Here we are, John. *Gymnopédie No.1*. Play it, John. Play it for me.' She spoke like Ingrid Bergman in *Casablanca*. His first response was to laugh but he managed to contain himself.

'Play it, John.'

He was reminded of the old days, when she would encourage him to play, to overcome his nerves, by using her personal charms. These days he was older and wiser, though, hardened by life and police work to be less susceptible to the soft tones of an attractive woman.

'Play it for me, John.'

And she was, after all, more than twenty years older than he was, even if she remained extraordinarily attractive, sensuous, desirable even. As she took his hand and led him to the piano stool, he was reminded of her soft touch on his skin, soft yet firm. Following close behind her, he had enough time to take in the contours only barely concealed by her dress. Either the dress had shrunk slightly in the last few minutes, or she herself had grown somehow. She turned to smile at him, a smile that commanded as well as encouraged.

'You like my dress, John?'

Caught out, Knox found himself unable to reply at first.

'You're not a voyeur, John. Don't feel guilty. I want you to look at me and enjoy what you see. And I want you to play the Satie for me.'

'It's a lovely dress,' he managed, eventually. 'You have wonderful taste and choose dresses that complement your figure beautifully.'

Mary gave him a wide smile that he'd seen often before.

'Why, thank you, John. That's a lovely thing to say.' Then she looked a little more serious and said, 'But I need you to do something for me.'

'Anything.'

'I need you to massage me. Slowly. All over. Every last square inch of my body.' She refused to let go of his hand.

'Mary, I can't...'

'I mean, massage me all over with Satie's *Gymnopédie No. 1*. Caress my body. Please, John.'

Suddenly it dawned on Knox that there was no way out other than to play the Satie piece for her. Secretly, he'd continued to play it as part of his private little 'at home' repertoire anyway, so there was a chance that it might not sound too bad. But Mary set high standards, and he had to be ready that she would pick holes, however well he performed.

Mary laid the music on the Steinway's music stand as he sat on the stool. Normally in the past, she would have retreated to the sofa on the far side of the room, but this time she remained standing beside him. He could feel himself tense with nerves.

'Wouldn't you be more comfortable sitting down, Mary?' he asked her, hopefully.

'I'll be your page-turner.'

'There are only two pages, Mary. There aren't any pages to turn.'

'I'll make sure you don't turn any, then,' she said firmly. Then her tone changed yet again. 'Play for me, John. Massage me all over with the piano.'

Defeated, he sighed and began to play the opening bars. Nervous, he wanted to play well for her, not to let her down. Mary had invested a lot of herself emotionally in him, he knew that, and had been a wonderful piano teacher. But he stumbled.

'Start again, John. Relax. I know you can play, remember.' She gently laid her hand on the back of his neck and massaged it with her fingers. 'Go on, start again,' she commanded, as she continued to allow her fingers to gently caress his skin. 'Play the Satie for me.'

He began the opening chords again, trying to put her out of his mind. But he stumbled again and stopped.

'Mary, what you're doing is lovely but it's difficult to concentrate on the piano.'

'When you're playing the piano, John, you shouldn't be thinking about it at all. I want you to concentrate on me. Massage me with the music, remember? I know you're good enough. I've heard you play this many times before. I know you can still do this.' Then she added, 'And I'd like you to play this for me, please. In fact I want you to understand that I need you to play it for me.'

She moved around so that she was directly behind him, and placed both hands on his shoulders.

'You're wearing a tie. Take it off and open your shirt a few buttons.'

He was beyond the point of resistance and placed the tie on top of the piano.

'Relax,' she said. 'Now start again, but don't stop this time. Keep going, no matter what. I'll help you.'

As he began to play, he felt Mary lean against him as her fingers softly probe down to stroke his shoulders. Her own body began to flow against his back, and he could feel her gently moving in time with the music – Knox could tell immediately that Mary was experiencing something deeply physical. Rather than worry about what was happening behind him, he decided to carry on playing the music as best he could, and in truth the rhythm against his back matched the tempo of the Satie perfectly. Mary had been wonderful for him in the past, after all, and her life must be a lonely one. What was the harm in letting her enjoy herself, he thought? The *Gymnopédie* really consists of two separate parts, but Knox reckoned that there would be no harm in adapting the second a little so that he could repeat it. If Mary wanted him to stop, she would tell him, after all. She was in command. But she didn't tell him to stop. Instead, as he played the extra bars through to the end, he felt the faintest change of rhythm to match.

At first she said nothing, then she leant forwards, put her arms around him from behind, and kissed his right ear.

'Thank you, John. I told you I needed you to play the Satie for me. Thank you so much, particularly for those extra bars. It's been a long time.'

'Are you all right, Mary?' Knox asked, still not entirely sure he'd been party to what had happened a minute earlier. 'You don't want me to play any more?'

Mary smiled. 'Oh, that's so kind of you, John. But no, thank you, I'm fine. Anyway, you've got work to do and I think I need a shower.'

'Would you like me to let myself out?'

'Yes, please, I think so.' Suddenly she said, 'Have you finished interviewing me?' It was as if she were asking the time.

'Eh… yes, I think so,' Knox said. 'I might have to come back.'

Mary smiled. It occurred to Knox that it was possibly the most happy, relaxed smile he'd ever seen on her. 'I do hope so,' she said. 'Perhaps more piano lessons one day in the future? And of course we have some work to do together,' she reminded him.

'Work?'

'The Jaguar thefts, John, the Jaguars. How could you forget them?'

Knox chuckled.

'Of course. I can't imagine what made me forget them, Mary.' Now it was his turn to kiss her, demurely on the cheek, before seeing himself out without another word.

TEN

THE OPERATIONS ROOM at St Leonard's police station was a mess.

It was hardly surprising that John Knox found working there so frustrating at times: an open-plan area to cover a number of different investigations was bound to lead to trouble from time to time. Files ended up in the wrong zone, 'hot-desking' forced officers to sit wherever they could find somewhere free, rather than with their investigating colleagues, and paper notes lay everywhere. O'Malley didn't like the set-up either, but his main concern was that something of value would be destroyed or, worse still, misfiled, and he'd ordered the cleaners to touch nothing. So touch nothing they did. Priceless case files sat on the floor beside desks, dangerously close to rubbish bins filled with sandwich wrappers and empty yoghurt cartons. At least the contents of the laptops were properly organised, and Knox walked in and grabbed his laptop to check out the latest progress on his two main cases.

On the Jaguar thefts, nothing new. But there was an email from Helen Wolstencroft to say that another of the St Ninian's patients had taken a turn for the worse overnight and that if he wanted to interview Louise Gray he should come soon. But it was timed at 9.25 in the morning, and when he went to phone the doctor, he was reminded that he'd switched off his mobile during his visit to Mary's house. Switching it on, he found another version of the same message as a text at 9.25, followed by another an hour later, then one at noon to say that Louise Gray had died. Knox cursed under his breath. Louise Gray had been very ill, but at least she was lucid. There might not be too many more opportunities to interview patients.

And yet the more he thought about what had happened to Leonard Plews, the more Knox began to believe the impossible: that answers lay inside the ward rather than outside. True, there was the curious feature of the gutting knife, but that hadn't been the murder weapon, if indeed the old boy had been murdered at all.

'What are you thinking?' Lucy Grant was nearby, close enough that they could talk quietly without being overheard. She smiled at him. 'I know that look. There's something going on in there.'

'Your idea, the one you mentioned yesterday about Sherlock Holmes. Once the impossible has been eliminated…'

'…whatever remains, however improbable, must be the truth,' Lucy said. 'I was joking.'

'Perhaps about *Murder on the Orient Express*, but I'm beginning to think that the solution to the mysterious death of Leonard Plews lies inside that room and nowhere else,' Knox said. 'No one went in, no one left.'

'It seems hard to believe, all the same. These are all people at death's door.'

'And some have popped through the door already since, of course. Is someone physically capable of murder at that stage of life?' Knox wondered aloud.

'I don't know,' Lucy said, 'but I know who to ask.'

'Dr Wolstencroft? Didn't you ask her when you interviewed her?'

'Not then. It seemed a crazy idea at the time, and in any event everyone seemed rather shocked. Even Sister Mary seemed dazed.'

'People can be good actors,' Knox pointed out. 'I've seen Mary Maxwell-Hume in many different disguises. She can be quite unrecognisable.'

'But she didn't appear to be trying to hide her shock this time. Anyway, Sister Mary is definitely eliminated from our enquiries, she wasn't around at the time of death. End of story, I'd say.'

'Which brings us back to that room, and those patients. We need to work out what was possible if we're to eliminate the impossible.'

'Time to pay Dr Wolstencroft another visit?' Lucy asked.

'I think so. I probably need to acknowledge her attempts to call me last night.'

Lucy was about to say something, then changed her mind.

When Knox and Grant arrived 45 minutes later at St Ninian's, a small group of reporters had gathered outside. They knew that it was only a matter of time before the media managed to pick up the story, but they'd hoped to contain it as long as possible. Helen Wolstencroft seemed a little put out. She was in her office, sitting at her desk, and greeted the pair of police officers with a tired sigh of resignation.

'What is it this time?'

'Sorry to disturb you, Dr Wolstencroft, but there's something we need to clear up, and we need your help to do it.' Knox waited, gazing at the two seats in front of Wolstencroft's desk until she got the hint and invited the pair to sit. The brief stand-off allowed her a little time to regroup.

'I'm sorry, I don't mean to be rude. I was called in twice here during the night and I've had less than an hour's sleep. Now I have the paperwork to catch up on. Neither of the patients made it. But then of course you know about Louise Grey. I did try to contact you, Inspector Knox…'

Knox shifted slightly uncomfortably. 'Yes, I know, I'm sorry about that. My phone was switched off, unfortunately.'

Lucy glanced at her boss.

'I'd love the luxury of being able to switch my mobile off when I'm on call,' Wolstencroft said quietly. 'Perhaps you haven't seen the *Evening News* today, either?'

Knox and Grant exchanged puzzled looks and glanced at their watches: it was only 11.00 a.m..

'The *Evening News* is 'evening' in name only – the first editions are on the streets by nine in the morning,' Wolstencroft pointed out. 'I thought you'd have known that. Presumably so that the journalists and printers can get home from work nice and early,' she added, with more than a touch of bitterness in her voice.

'Is there something we should be aware of?' Knox asked, anxious to move the interview forwards.

'St Ninian's is on the front page. They seem to have made their minds up what happened already.' She passed a copy across her desk for her visitors to read.

Knox and Grant exchanged horrified looks.

POLICE INVESTIGATE SUSPICIOUS DEATH
AT EDINBURGH CARE HOME

The report – under the by-line of 'W. Montgomery Bishop' – stated that detectives were investigating the 'suspicious death' of an elderly man at St Ninian's Haven, and that a 32-year-old Polish nurse, named locally as Magda Czeslawska, was being questioned in connection with the incident. The rest of the report was padded out with the details of some historical cases where medical staff had been convicted of killing patients – and Bishop had been careful to include only those where the villains were foreign nationals. Also included was a photograph of Magda getting into Lucy Grant's car in St Ninian's car park.

'Bishop must have been watching us all the time, John,' Lucy said. 'Sorry.'

Knox shook his head. 'It's hardly your fault. It's amazing how much he implies from so little.'

'Who is this 'W. Montgomery Bishop', Inspector?' Wolstencroft asked.

'He's a very unpleasant piece of work who's been hanging around your car park for a couple of days. He's working as a freelance journalist at the moment, selling stories to whoever will buy them.'

'Is Magda a suspect, Inspector?'

Knox shook his head. 'Not as far as we're concerned, doctor. Is she here, by the way? We need to put her mind at ease.'

'She was understandably very upset. I sent her home, and I'm glad I did before the posse arrived. She managed to avoid everyone except the Bishop chap. I saw it from the window – whatever she said to him, he seemed to think it was funny.'

'That might not be good news. Bishop has a very warped sense of humour, I'm afraid. Lucy and I really ought to pay her a call.'

'Is that wise, Inspector? At the moment no one knows where she lives – we don't give out that sort of information of course – and your visit might simply make things worse.'

Knox nodded. 'You might have a point. Perhaps you could telephone her and pass on that message on our behalf until we get the chance ourselves?'

The suggestion seemed to soften Wolstencroft. 'That seems reasonable. What did you want to see me about, by the way?'

'DS Grant and I came to ask some information about the physical and mental capabilities of your patients.'

'There's such a thing as patient confidentiality, Inspector, even at this point in life.'

Knox smiled reassuringly. 'I'm just looking for generalisations. What sorts of things are the patients here capable of?'

Wolstencroft sat up and stifled a laugh. 'You're surely not suggesting…?'

Knox tried to ignore her. 'I know they're all very unwell, but are they so unwell, say… that they can't get out of bed?'

'Look, Inspector, you need to understand two things. First, each patient is a separate human being. We don't make generalisations here. Second, some of them are physically in not too bad shape, the ones with dementia, say, but have no idea what they're doing. Others are essentially bedridden but have all their marbles. For some, it's a combination of both.'

Lucy took up the questioning. 'Are the patients separated according to their state of health in any way?'

'You mean… as in 'psychiatric' and 'physical'? No. Their various needs are too complex to make such distinctions.' She added, 'We haven't got the space to do it anyway.'

'Tell me how patients qualify for a room to themselves. Is that on medical grounds?'

Wolstencroft looked at the floor, slightly embarrassed. 'They pay for a separate room.'

'So the eight patients in that communal room couldn't afford single rooms?'

'I suppose not. Or, more likely their families couldn't, or wouldn't, pay.' Knox and Grant exchanged glances, each wondering how two Jaguar-owning sons couldn't spare the money to fund decent end-of-life care for their father. Knox at least had some sort of idea, but he kept it to himself.

'I see,' he said. 'I understand your position, Doctor. But we need to check a few things out. Can I try asking you some questions in another way?' The doctor shrugged her shoulders: no harm in trying. 'Which of the patients could get themselves out of bed unaided?'

'I suppose if they were desperate, most of them. Not Eileen Lamb, I suspect. As well as being the victim she was effectively in a coma, as you know. That's not conducive to going for a stroll,' she added, her voice laden with contempt and irony in equal measure.

Knox wasn't warming to this woman. 'That's one. What about the other seven?' Out of the corner of his eye he could see Lucy taking notes.

Wolstencroft raised her eyebrows a little. 'Well I suppose Mr Plews himself was perfectly mobile. Sometimes we had trouble keeping him in bed, to be honest.'

'And how did you 'keep him in bed'? Sedation?' He tried to say without sounding judgemental; anyway, he knew he hadn't any right.

'If necessary. He wasn't a nice man, I don't think. Even in his lucid moments he could be very unpleasant. Sedation was often the only answer to ensure Mr Plews's safety, to say nothing of the other patients. I'm quite relieved he's no longer with us. Perhaps you feel it's not nice to speak ill of the dead, but there we are.'

'We'd rather you gave us an honest assessment. Are you able to give us a similarly honest assessment of the others?'

'Some of them would be quite mobile, actually. Louise Grey, who died this morning, was sitting up and able to move with a little assistance, although she was getting a bit confused. It can be an issue with liver failure. But I don't think she could have moved unaided.'

'Someone advised me to ask who the strongest person in the room was,' Knox said.

'Good advice, I suppose. Alan Smith has lung cancer, but he's got a week or two yet in him at least. His breathing is bad when he lies down at night, but we can manage his condition reasonably with steroids. He can certainly get up and move about. He's really here because he has nowhere else to go, Inspector. He used to be a good footballer, I'm told, played for a couple of top-division teams, but just before footballers got really rich from the game. Now look at him. It's all a bit sad – they go from living alone in some sort of low-cost housing to dying alone in St Ninian's.

'Physically, there's nothing wrong with Martha Ramsay, but she has dementia, too. Not Alzheimer's, though, so her decline has been slower. She's quite happy, but she couldn't tell the Prime Minister apart from Tuesday. We did have some problems with Martha and Mr Plews, I should tell you…'

'What kind of problems?' Knox asked. The question was out too quickly. 'Ah, you're saying that…' Knox looked to Lucy, who couldn't decide whether to smile or be shocked. Rather than invite further description, he suggested they move on.

'Myles Cherry was an English businessman who has been in trouble with the law – fraud, I suspect – and had lost everything, his family, his house and all his money. Quite recently, I think. He smokes, even although his emphysema was actually caused by his smoking. I know he can get about because he still goes to the front door several times a day for a cigarette.'

'No one tries to stop him?' Lucy asked.

Wolstencroft bristled slightly. 'What can we do? It's a free country, and he's dying, the poor man. Sister Mary didn't much take to Mr Cherry, actually – she claimed he was always trying to fondle her. Mind you, our visiting nun brings some of that on herself, don't you think?'

Knox said nothing, so Lucy was left to respond.

'We couldn't comment on that. There haven't been any complaints, have there?'

'Not about Mr Cherry, no. The bully of the room was actually Mr Plews himself.'

Lucy noted that down, indicating that she was ready for Knox to take up the questions. The remaining patients, Robina – 'Ina', of course – Wallace, and Ian Mould, were each mobile enough at times during the day, and at a pinch, the doctor surmised, either might have summoned up the strength to stab the victim. Grant and Knox both noticed that the doctor had forgotten that the Sabatier knife had nothing to at all to do with the cause of death. Wolstencroft added a little personal detail on each. Ina Wallace was a difficult patient who complained a lot about St Ninian's and was generally unpleasant, but although her tongue was sharp, she'd never been violent. Ian Mould was actually a retired minister of the Church of Scotland, from which Wolstencroft inferred that he was a peaceful man. Knox responded by saying that, in his experience, the relationship between organised religion and peace was complex, to say the least. The doctor reconsidered her opinion and said that for a man of his calling Ian Mould's sense of humour and language could be quite colourful, especially when addressing Plews.

'So there was no love lost between them?' Knox asked.

'Dying patients have their own social dynamic, Inspector. Sometimes the prospect of death brings a collective strength, but more often they each rage, rage individually against the dying of their separate lights. Mr Plews was certainly not one to care about others. I'm not sure if others such as Ina Wallace are really so very different but each of them has his or her own individual capacities. We try to understand, not to judge.'

'That's our job, too, Dr Wolstencroft,' Knox said. 'We simply try to identify what's happened. The law takes care of the rest.'

That produced a puzzled look from Wolstencroft, followed by a rather patronising smile. Her disdain of Knox was apparent, and he realised that he didn't much care for the woman either. Briefly, he wondered if he'd started off on the wrong foot with her, but then he reminded himself that building personal friendships with witnesses was hardly a feature of the work of police officers. Especially detectives investigating a murder. All the same, he was annoyed with himself for letting the doctor get under his skin. They were each just doing their job: hers was to look after her patients. Thinking on the three who had died in the last couple of days, he smiled quietly at the irony. Wolstencroft spotted it.

'Something amusing you, Inspector?'

Knox shook his head, which made things worse: Wolstencroft misinterpreted it as a further insult. Unaware of what was going on, Lucy Grant nevertheless sensed they should keep going.

'We really could do with any help you can offer us, Dr Wolstencroft. Have you any ideas yourself?'

The doctor drew in a deep breath, looked away, then back at her. 'Isn't that your job?'

Any further questions were obviously pointless. Lucy produced a card from her pocket and said, 'Well, if you do think of anything, could you please telephone us at the station? Either of us will do,' she added, throwing a massive hint to Knox that he, too, should be providing a business card with his details. Eventually, he realised what was expected of him and handed one over.

Knox was wondering if their visit had told them anything at all when a nurse knocked on the door and peered round.

'Doctor,' she said, 'I think you should come quickly. Mr Smith is breathing very poorly.'

'You'll have to excuse me,' Wolstencroft said. 'Can you see yourselves out?' And that was it, she was off.

Back at the visitors' car park, Knox was about to get into the car when he stopped and spoke to Lucy, who found herself discussing the case over the roof of a Police Scotland standard-issue Audi 2.

'The longer this goes on, Lucy, the more I'm convinced that the killer was one of those patients inside that room.'

'If it was a murder,' she reminded him. 'And either way, we're racing against the clock here. They seem to be dying like flies in there.'

'It happens in care homes, I understand. Still, you're right, the witnesses all seem to be slipping through our fingers like dust. Already I feel that we're never going to find out what happened unless we get incredibly lucky.'

'If we decide there's nothing to investigate, will there even be a Fatal Accident Inquiry?' Lucy asked.

Knox confessed that even he was unsure. If there was, it wouldn't find anything out anyway and he wondered if there was really much point in spending so much state money on such an empty gesture. Just another 'open verdict'.

Lucy smiled at him. 'Fancy some lunch, John? Take our mind off things? I fancy a nice bridie and a macaroni pie from Greggs.'

Knox laughed. 'That's my girl – guaranteed to remind me of life's true priorities. Let's go to the one in Great Junction Street. The bridies are always a bit special there.'

It took them around fifteen minutes – five tracks from a live Springsteen album – to get there. They were about to get out and head for the queue when Lucy's mobile rang. Not recognising the number, she raised her eyebrows in surprise before answering, then Knox had to sit and wait while she listened, acknowledged with a 'yes' or 'no' at a few points, then finally finished with a 'Thank you, I'll let him know."

'What was that about?' Knox asked eventually.

'That was Dr Wolstencroft. She made some excuse about not being able to talk to you, sorry. Anyway, Alan Smith died just after we left.'

Knox sighed. 'Jeez. That's four down already.'

'Four down, four to go. We need get going here, John.'

'Great idea, Lucy,' Knox said, managing to remove any trace of irony from his voice. 'So where do we start?'

'With a macaroni pie.'

ELEVEN

I F ST LEONARD'S POLICE STATION could be a crowded place at times, one man, Chief Inspector Maximilian Plews, had the capacity to empty it. He was actually supposed to be on compassionate leave, of course, but he insisted that he was too indispensable to be allowed such a luxury as time off: that was for the weak and indolent. Privately, of course, he really didn't care about his father at all. On the contrary, Leonard Plews's death meant that, at long last, money wouldn't be haemorrhaging from his inheritance into the black hole that was keeping his father alive needlessly. And there had been a serious surge in the crime rate to get to grips with urgently, a spike entirely down to the theft of a series of Jaguars, not the least irritating of which was that of his own brother, Theodore. Theodore had taken to telephoning him morning and night to ask why his 5.0 V8 Petrol 510PS supercharged long-wheelbased XJ – top speed 155mph – hadn't yet been recovered, making it clear that he held his brother personally responsible for the collective incompetence of the Keystone Cops police force to which that idiotic Scottish Government at Holyrood had entrusted the nation's security.

Maximilian, meantime, couldn't decide whether to be relieved that his car – a normal-length XJ, and two years older – hadn't been stolen, or insulted that it wasn't deemed worth stealing. Either way, he was in his normal foul mood.

Although not quite as dapper as his slightly older brother, Maximilian was still in decent shape. He and his long-suffering wife regularly walked two cairn terriers that would snarl at other dogs and at human beings, but never, strangely, at Plews himself. Maximilian enjoyed strutting along behind at a smart pace. Plews loved his dogs more than anything else in the world, almost certainly because they actually loved and respected him back. Joan Plews held a certain sympathy for her husband, but even she privately admitted to some of her friends that she wished she'd listened more carefully all those years ago to her mother who had warned that Max would be hard to live with.

To his credit, one thing Maximilian did not generally do was bring his work home. Plews worked a full shift – he was always one of the first in and one of the last to leave – but once he'd left the office that was the end of his day. Going home, after all, meant driving his beloved car. A relatively small man, Chief Inspector Plews was one of the few people who still found it easy to get in and out of a Jaguar, and apart from his dogs, his greatest pleasure lay in listening to Mozart on the car's glorious sound system.

Plews had his own parking bay in the police compound. He didn't really have a parking bay to himself, he wasn't senior enough for that, but his space was the second on the left directly facing the front door. Now and again, other officers tried to park there, either accidentally or to annoy him, but it didn't pay to fall out with Chief Inspector Maximilian Plews. Remarkably lacking in talent as a policeman, Plews had been allocated much of the administrative work, the most powerful of which was the task of drawing up shift rotas. Fall out with Plews and you were working on Christmas Day, New Year's Day, or the day your child started school. A favourite way of making a colleague's life miserable was to give them interrupted night shifts – one every two or three nights. Of course it was possible to get out of one or two bad rota assignments, but there was a limit to the number of swaps you could ask for. Plews just wore his enemies down.

John Knox had often been given poor shifts, but his promotion to Inspector had come at the same time as Plews's to one grade higher. O'Malley and the Chief Constable had made it clear that Knox was not to be targeted – a suggestion that had brought an 'angry and innocent' reaction from Plews. But Plews got the message. Knox made it clear that he was prepared to do his 'fair share of bad rotas, just the same as every other officer' – the clear implication being that Plews himself would have to take some rubbish if he wanted to inflict it on the 'heir anointed', as he sometimes referred to Knox.

Nevertheless, Plews spent many of his working hours trying to think of ways of bullying junior staff. Dave Lander was given a formal dressing-down for having an unkempt beard. Lucy Grant was told off for only being fifteen minutes early for work. Inevitably, only Izzy Bryce – with the least at stake of all her colleagues – was able to stand up for herself. When Plews had given her a verbal warning for 'only working the hours she was paid for', she'd simply requested a written warning instead. That, she explained, would make it easier to make a formal complaint about his bullying. When Plews refused, she confused him still further by taking out her notebook and noting the time, date and details of the meeting where the Chief Inspector refused to give her a written copy of a verbal warning that she didn't understand. Plews stayed away from Izzy Bryce after that.

In fact, it was Izzy Bryce who was on his mind as Chief Inspector Maximilian Plews approached 'his' parking space. She'd had to rush off in a hurry that evening because it was her older boy's final concert at school and she needed to get home to grab a bite to eat, shower and change in time for a 7.00 p.m. start. He had a guitar solo, probably only ten seconds or so as she confessed, but nevertheless it was his moment in the limelight and Izzy wasn't missing it for anything. Even by her standards this was a fast exit from work, and Plews was irritated. A little Mozart might have calmed him down.

There was to be no Mozart.

Arriving at his usual space, Plews was somewhat taken aback to see that it was empty. Confused at first, he racked his brain to try and recall if he'd had to move it during the day, or even if Joan had given him a lift to work. Briefly, he even wondered if he was losing his mind. But then he remembered parking his Jaguar XJ Portfolio and enjoying a little more massage from the seat as he listened to the end of the *alla turca* from the A major Mozart piano sonata. Surely no one would have the temerity to move his beloved car? But wandering around, he could see no sign.

Eventually, Plews marched up to the compound gate to address the security guard.

'Has anyone moved my car?' Remarkably, he was too bewildered to be abrupt.

'Yours is the Jaguar, sir? Yes, it went for its service, don't you remember? A couple of constables ran it to the garage for you. You'd given them your keys.'

Under normal circumstances Plews would have erupted. Under normal circumstances Plews would have railed at the poor man, ending with a promise that the security guard would be guarding nothing from now on and should be considering what his next employment might be. But these were not normal circumstances. He simply stood, bewildered.

***

'You're saying someone dressed as a policeman just walked into the compound and was allowed to drive Plews's car out?'

The news was charging round St Leonard's, and it was Dave Lander's turn to enjoy being informed as Izzy Bryce took advantage of a rare moment when the two of them were the only ones currently in the office.

'It seems the guy actually showed some sort of warrant card, convincing enough to persuade George Spence that it was genuine,' Izzy said. She herself had just heard it from a WPC in the canteen. 'And of course the guy had a key. The key probably didn't actually do anything, but somehow or other he was able to get into Plews's Jag, start it up and drive off in no time at all.'

'Presumably had one of these RFID scanners, you know the ones that can replicate the signal from the remote locking. I think you can get the car moving pretty quickly if you have one of those things. Couldn't have happened to a nicer guy,' Lander added.

'Not the most popular in the neighbourhood, is he? All the same, I wouldn't wish a car theft like that on anyone. Not even Plews.'

'Not even Plews?'

'He's not a nice man, but he's not a lecher. He keeps his hands to himself, unlike that guy in traffic.'

'This must be Carter you're referring to.'

'Is that his name? A wee short red-haired guy?'

'That's the one. And that's why he's in traffic, and only ever working with men. His driving partners have strict instructions to report everything ever since that woman in child protection, of all places, complained about Carter touching her up. I suppose Plews is better than that sleazebag, right enough.' Then Lander added, 'But Plews will make everyone's life hell, all the same. Apparently poor George

Spence has been told to expect formal disciplinary action, although the Police Federation might have something to say about that.'

'We could do with solving that case.' By now Izzy was midway through her lunch. 'Finding the cars would be handy, too.'

'If we only had time to devote. We're too busy with the murder that isn't a murder. Those folk are dead or dying whatever happens. We'll never find out what happened in there. We've got a chance with the Jaguars, though. I hate to say it, but Plews might be right.'

'Typical man. Petrol-head.'

Lander looked at Izzy suspiciously. 'Are you talking about me or about Plews?'

'You, silly.' Then, just as he was about take mock offence, she added, 'Whatever Plews has in his head, it's more unpleasant than petrol. Otherwise someone would have turned him on his side, lit a match, and set fire to him long ago.'

Lander laughed. 'When you take against someone, Izzy, you do it in style. You should go on stage.'

'There's only so much about this job you can share with the general public, I'm afraid, or I'd be tempted. Mind you, most female comics seem to tell jokes about being fat, or slimming, or diets, or all those other things middle-aged women have to put up with.' She stopped for a moment, then turned side on. 'So, does my bum look big in this uniform?'

Lander was nonplussed. 'Em... am I supposed to reply to that?'

'Yes and no. Yes, if you think my bum looks fine in this God-awful police-issue pair of trousers, no if you think I look enormous. Judging by the fact you've said nothing, I assume you think the latter.' She gave him a sly smile.

'Silence should be taken to mean, 'I'm saying nothing until I have a lawyer,' Izzy. We men aren't allowed to comment on a woman's appearance these days.'

'Quite right. Men should be seen and not heard. And only seen if they look like Daniel Craig or Brad Pitt.'

'Not Dave Lander?'

'Definitely not Dave Lander,' she said, but as she moved away past him towards her desk she took the opportunity to ruffle his hair like a little boy. As she walked away, Lander couldn't help but look to see what answer he would have given, much as he tried to resist.

'Well,' Izzy said, without looking round.

'Well what?'

'What would you have said? You get a free answer. Be honest. I won't hit you.'

'These days it's too dangerous, Izzy. Especially with pocket dynamite like you in the office.'

'Pocket dynamite! Wow – that's pretty sexist, isn't it?'

Lander was filled with embarrassment. 'Is it? Sorry. I didn't mean to be offensive.'

Izzy laughed. 'I was joking, you dummy. I asked for a serious answer. And I suspect there's some sort of compliment mixed in there along with the clear statement that my bum's too big, and presumably my boobs are, too.'

Lander sighed.

'Izzy, you haven't read me my rights.'

Izzy took a deep breath. 'You do not have to say anything, but if you fail to mention…'

Lander interrupted. 'Your bum and your boobs are both bigger than – say – DS Grant's. It's not a bad thing. I happen to like you the way you are. There, happy?'

'So I don't need to go on a diet?'

'Is that what this is about? Jesus. No, a diet is not required.'

'Great,' Izzy said, and opening a Tupperware box on her desk. 'I can eat some of this cake that was left over from my daughter's birthday party. Want some?'

'I thought you'd never ask.'

'Let's eat it quick before the boss sees us,' she said.

'The Inspector?'

'No,' Izzy said. 'He'd not make a fuss. But Plews would be a pain in the arse and O'Malley would insist on having a share.'

'Another example of police corruption?'

'Sadly. Mind you, there's probably enough here to go around. It was a big cake.'

'I think I could get outside of some more, all the same.'

Izzy cut each of them a large slice.

Thanking her, Lander casually added, 'What do you make of this friend of the boss?'

'The scarlet nun?' Izzy said. She still had some Smartie-topped sponge cake in her mouth, which she washed down with her coffee.

'She wears those red dresses a lot, right enough,' Lander said. 'She's an attractive woman – do you think John Knox…?' He added hurriedly, 'I mean, I know it's none of our business and so on.'

'That's none of our business, right enough. Fancy her yourself?'

'She's in good shape for a woman of 57.'

'She's a nun, Dave.'

'She's a helluva strange nun, Izzy. Even you would have to admit that.'

'I'll admit I've never met any other nun like her, nor have I ever heard of that religious order she belongs to. And I'd like to have her figure at the age I am now, far less at her age. I wouldn't blame any man – Knox or anyone else – for allowing his eyes to gaze at her a little longer than was politically correct. Especially in those dresses she wears.'

'Look, Izzy,' Lander said, 'once and for all, I like you the way you are.'

'Oh, Dave, you say the sweetest things.'

'Anyway,' Lander said. 'About the nun. I've heard that she and Plews might have history.'

'Which Plews? Our one, or the brother, the one that had his car stolen earlier?'

'Both. And of course both the Plews brothers have had their Jags nicked.' Then he added, 'I find it a little hard to feel sorry for someone who has a posh car nicked myself. Serves them right for spending silly money in the first place.'

'When there's so many homeless and hungry people around, I know, I know,' Izzy said. 'But they're victims of crime, just the same.'

'It'd be a crime to leave what remains of that cake, Izzy.'

'Do you ever think about anything other than your stomach, Dave?' Then – seeing his mischievous smile, she quickly added, 'No, on second thoughts, don't answer that.'

They were halfway through two more slices of cake – washed down this time with cups of water from the dispensing machine in the corner – when they were caught in the act. The office door opened abruptly and Chief Inspector Maximilian Plews slowly entered. Looking all around and discovering no one else to bully, he strutted over towards Lander and Bryce, and stopped. For a moment, no one said anything, and the two junior officers even stopped chewing. Then Plews spoke very quietly.

'Are you the only ones here?'

Dave and Izzy looked at each other, which was a mistake to start with, even although it was self-evident that no one else was present. Their second mistake was that each of them surreptitiously tried to swallow what remained of the cake in their mouths. But Izzy made one further, fatal mistake: she began to laugh.

That was too much for Plews.

'What do you find funny, Constable?'

'I'm sorry, sir, I was simply struggling to finish my mouthful of my daughter's birthday cake.' In desperation, she added, 'Would you like some?'

Plews simply ignored her. Instead, he asked her, 'Bryce, why are we here?'

Utterly thrown, Izzy said nothing.

'I said, why are we here, Bryce? I demand an answer?'

Still bemused, Izzy wondered if Plews was seeking some sort of philosophical answer.

'Sir, I don't know – '

'You don't know why we're here, Bryce? You don't know what your job is?'

'Ah, sorry, sir. Our job is to prevent and solve crime, and to catch criminals who commit them. To help the public.'

Plews drew himself up to his full five feet six inches. From behind, Dave noted how much larger the man's bald spot had grown in the last year or two.

'So tell me, Constable Bryce, which of these have you managed to do today? Prevent a crime? Solve one? Catch a criminal? Or even help the public?'

Izzy hesitated, then said, 'Despite our best efforts, neither of those so far today, sir. But we're giving it our best shot, I promise you. I'm sure we'll find out what happened soon.'

Plews studied the what was left of cake inside the box.

'Would you like some?' Izzy added. 'It's my daughter's birthday cake.'

The Chief Inspector said nothing. Then he picked up the box and turned its entire contents into the nearby waste paper bin. There was nothing either of the two constables could say.

'Solving crimes. That's your job. In case you'd forgotten,' Plews sneered, then turned and made his way back towards the door.

Izzy Bryce was furious but managed to say nothing. It was left to Dave Lander to try and ease the tension.

'I promise you sir, we're doing our best. And we're sorry for your loss.'

'Why does everyone say that exact phrase?' Plews replied.

'We'll do our best to find out what happened to your father,' Lander added.

Plews suddenly stopped in his tracks and looked round, bemused.

'My father? Oh yes, I've lost my father, too,' he said, then resumed his journey out of the door.

TWELVE

A N EMAIL WAS WAITING FOR KNOX when he returned to the office. It was from Mary Maxwell-Hume.

Dear John

Could you please come round to my house when you have a moment? I might be able to help you.

Yours sincerely

Mary

Knox smiled at the formality of her 'Dear John' beginning. He knew Mary must know more about the death of Leonard Plews than first suggested, but hadn't wanted to press things. Mary, after all, was entitled to be in shock, too, no matter how cool and calm she always seemed to be. That night in the ward, she'd seemed all of her 57 years. Now, perhaps, he might be able to prise something from her, although it would be better if she came to the station to make any formal statement. But there would be little point in bringing her in if she had nothing to say.

He grabbed his packed lunch and announced that he was off to 'interview a witness' and would be back in a couple of hours, not that anyone paid any attention to anyone else during the lunch hour at St Leonard's. Conversation turned to the three Fs, food, fashion and football, and crime didn't begin with an 'F'.

Once again, Knox was forced to park his car on the main road and walk a couple of hundred yards down the dead end street towards Mary Maxwell-Hume's house. He realised that he was looking forward to seeing her and had decided that, to lighten the occasion, he should take his packed lunch with him and ask permission to eat it there. They'd eaten together several times in the past, even spent Christmas together once, but a year or two had elapsed since the last occasion. It hadn't been so easy recently, partly because of his new promoted status as a police inspector, but partly also because he knew Alice was a little jealous of Mary. Nothing had ever taken place between them, but even Knox had to admit that Mary Maxwell-Hume had once had something of a hold on him. What he was counting on was that he'd be protected from the siren by the official nature of his visit – albeit that here he was trying to make it less formal. It was only as he approached Mary's front door that he suddenly wondered why he was doing that.

He rang the bell, although as usual it couldn't be heard from outside. Starting to get cold feet, Knox began counting seconds aloud, deciding that if there was no reply by the time he reached thirty he should turn tail and go back to the station. He got as far as twenty-seven when the door opened.

'Why, what a pleasant surprise!' Mary said. 'I could have sworn I could hear you counting there, John. Were you hoping I wouldn't be in?' A familiar faint smile played on her lips.

Knox didn't reply. Couldn't reply. He'd been caught out trying to escape, and he was transported back to the very first occasions when he'd gone to her house. Those extra years he'd seen at St Ninian's had fallen from her again.

And then there was her dress. He was used to tight-fitting dresses that showed off Mary's figure to the maximum, but they were almost invariably self-coloured, or very occasionally contained the faintest pinstripe. This one, though, in her favoured crepe material, was dark green in colour, but with gold lightning flashes across the front – Mary wasn't in the habit of choosing patterned dresses. The dress itself dazzled almost as much as the woman wearing it.

'Are you coming in, John, or are you just going to stand there? It doesn't cost any more, I can assure you. And wouldn't you rather examine me inside?' She opened the door even wider and stood aside to let him in.

Knox, still confused by Mary's offer to be 'examined inside', hesitated.

Mary studied him curiously, but the smile was broader. 'John?' Then she added, 'John, it is a lovely surprise to see you. And if even if you prefer to examine me on the doorstep, I think I'd prefer it to be done internally, thank you.'

'I'm sorry, Mary, you must be getting cold.' As he made his way past her, Knox reminded himself that Mary enjoyed playing with words at men's expense. 'I'm not used to seeing you in such an eye-catching dress.'

Mary arched an eyebrow.

'John, you of all people should know what our order requires of the Sisters in the way of dress. I simply follow the rules.'

'I know, you only…'

'…wear as much as preserves due modesty,' she continued. 'Doesn't this fit the bill? I'll take it off if you prefer.'

'No, no,' Knox said hurriedly. Mary was barefoot, and the dress was close-fitting enough to suggest that it was, as usual, the only item of clothing she was wearing. 'I've not seen you wear any sort of pattern before, that's all.'

By now they'd made it through to Mary's living room – dominated, of course, by that grand piano. More memories flooded back.

'Patterns are permitted if it's all we can find that fits, John. I prefer plain dresses myself. Last time I was in Murrays Department Store, what I'm wearing now was the only thing they had that fitted perfectly. That shop has really gone downhill in recent years. Would you believe it, they actually had some of that horrible piped muzak playing in the changing room?' She shuddered at the thought.

Knox smiled. 'I'm sure Murrays' piped muzak is higher-quality piped muzak than most shops have, Mary.'

'It was actually that ghastly electronica "music". Fatboy Slim. I simply had to ask the shop assistant what it was.'

'Fatboy Slim? In Murrays' changing room?'

'I think it was someone's idea of a joke, John. I tried to listen to a little of his music on Spotify. It was all utterly unbearable. Next time I'm in Murrays I'm going to suggest that they play Bach's *St Matthew Passion* instead.'

'Over their heads, I'd suggest, Mary. How about letting them have a copy of your Collected Piano Pieces?' Mary had once made a CD of her own piano playing and given Knox a copy. 'Very calming.'

Mary's eyebrows rose again. 'Are you suggesting that my piano playing lacks life, John?'

This time, Knox wasn't rising to the bait. 'You know I'm not, Mary. Behave yourself.'

'My, John, how masterful promotion has made you.' She motioned to towards the sofa. 'Please join me.'

They shared the sofa, but only in name. They each occupied their own section, with a clear gap between them.

'You invited me to call round,' Knox said, eventually breaking the silence. 'I presume you meant that you can help us with the case.'

'Well… to be honest, I'd rather hoped you would have come before now. I'm sure we can work together, John.'

'Does that mean you have information to share with us?'

'No. Why would I have information for you?' Mary looked slightly confused.

Clearly the pair were at cross-purposes. He began to fear the visit had been a waste of time.

'I thought you had some information to give us about the death of Leonard Plews, Mary. Wasn't that what you meant?'

She paused for a moment, sat bolt upright, then – possibly for the first ever in his presence – began to laugh out loud, putting her hand over her mouth as she did so. Even she did so, Knox was aware of Mary's intense grace and femininity. Nothing the woman ever did was crude or indelicate. Eventually, her laugh subsided into a quiet giggle.

Meanwhile, Knox still had no idea what the joke was.

'Oh, John, I'm so sorry,' Mary said, for the first time reaching across to his side of the sofa to take his hand lightly. 'If I misled you, I promise that wasn't my intention. I was offering my help with the real crime. The car thefts.'

'More important than a murder?'

'The world is a better place without Leonard Plews, John. You know that as well as I do. And unless you count the man's descent into dementia, then if the truth be told he escaped justice. No, he was evil through and through, and from beginning to end. Possibly better than almost anyone else in the world, you know that story.'

Knox did indeed: Mary's mother had died giving birth to her; her father had accepted his brother Leonard's offer to help bring her up but Leonard had begun to abuse her mentally, sexually and physically; then somehow turned the blame onto her father using his sons Maximilian and Theodore as witnesses. She never saw her father again: he committed suicide in prison a year or so later.

'Why don't you blame Maximilian and Theodore, Mary? They know they lied in court.'

'Uncle Leonard was an evil, manipulative man, John. They did and said whatever he told them to say. They were beaten, too, of course, but only if they disobeyed. I was simply thrashed with that dreaded belt every morning and every night. He had a selection of them, you know – he was a teacher, of course, in those days nobody questioned why a teacher would look for an extra heavyweight tawse that would inflict lots of pain.'

'I'm still surprised you didn't say anything.'

'I told you, he was manipulative. And Uncle Lenny was nice to me to start with, actually – any occasional punishment was just the odd smack with his hand. It only really started to get bad when I reached puberty. By then I'd stayed with him for ten or eleven years. I admit I was an awkward difficult teenager. I probably deserved what I got sometimes.'

'I doubt that. People would have listened if you'd said something.'

'That's looking back on it from a modern viewpoint, John. Why should I trust my teachers? They hit people in class, too – it wasn't banned then.'

'I suppose so.'

'I was so scared and cowed that I was actually a really timid girl in school. I felt particularly dirty and ashamed because of the sexual thing – please don't ask me about that. I never said very much to anyone. That's one reason why I liked music so much – it did my speaking for me. And in any case, look what happened when I did eventually speak – I wasn't believed, Uncle Lenny pinned the blame on my father.'

'Didn't you tell your father?'

'Dad said that these things just happen sometimes, and I should be glad that Uncle Lenny could care for me. But I heard he and Uncle Lenny arguing about me more than once. The worst was just before I finally told the school. Actually, the school noticed, I didn't tell them. It was a swimming lesson, and I'd assumed that my costume covered the bruises on my bottom. But at one point the costume rode up as we were doing a diving lesson and the teacher noticed. I remember that at first I thought that he hadn't seen it, but he went next door and found a female teacher who took me aside and made me pull it up to see properly. And that was when everything just erupted.'

There wasn't much Knox could say. He knew much of the story already but the details just seemed to make the whole scene even worse.

Mary looked up at him with an amused smile. 'It's where the no underwear thing started, you know.'

'Sorry?'

'Uncle Lenny refused to let me wear any underwear. He said he wanted me to think all day about the thrashing to come each night, but of course it also made sure I wore long enough skirts so that nothing could ever be seen. But I got used to it, and later on quite enjoyed the feeling of freedom.'

'I thought you said it was the Sisters who...' Knox wondered if she'd finally let something slip.

'Well, perhaps we're all drawn to groups whose aims we find it easiest to share. It was one aspect of the Sisters of Mary of the Sacred Cross that I had little trouble adapting to. When I was married to Douglas, before I met the Sisters, we often went out into the countryside and if there was a quiet spot I used to love just slipping my dress off and lying there naked for a while. Have you ever tried that, John?'

'I don't possess a dress, Mary. So, no.'

'You know what I mean. You should try it some time. It's liberating.'

'I don't think Alice would fancy doing that. Or having me strip off beside her in the open air.'

'Really? How sad.'

But Knox could sense she'd returned to the present, and he didn't want to enter into a discussion about his relationship with Alice. Mary was a forensic questioner.

'So if you don't care about Leonard Plews, what have you got for us about the Jaguars?'

'At the moment, nothing. What have you got?'

'I shouldn't really tell a member of the public.'

'But I'm not any old member of the public and you're going to tell me anyway.'

Now it was Knox's turn to laugh. It was a relief after the shocking revelations.

'Do you want the official answer or the unofficial one?'

'Both.'

'Officially, our enquiries are continuing.'

'And unofficially?'

'We haven't a clue.'

'How refreshingly honest, John.'

'Unofficially, we've done nothing about the Jags anyway because we're so busy with the murder investigation.'

'Which isn't going too well either. Although I gather from the newspapers that you've arrested Magda, that Polish nurse at St Ninian's?'

'No, we've not, Mary. We gave her a lift into the station to give us a formal statement and a reporter twisted into a piece of racist rubbish.' Knox filled Mary in with the details.

'What an unpleasant man that reporter sounds,' Mary said. 'I'll need to watch out for this Mr Bishop. Perhaps we'll cross paths one day.'

'Perhaps you will. But if you do, be careful.'

'Oh, I think I can look after myself,' Mary said. She looked away and smiled, as if thinking to herself.

'All in all, the fact that Bishop has upset one of our important witnesses has simply made things more difficult for us,' Knox commented.

Mary looked back towards him and sat up, alert. 'Which is where my offer of help comes in.'

Knox had actually forgotten that Mary had left a message for him offering just that.

'Do go on, please.'

'You solve the murder, leave me to lead on the Jaguars.'

'Lead on the Jaguar case?'

'Why not? I can hardly do any worse than you're doing.' Then she added, 'Don't worry, John, I'd give you all the credit.'

Knox was too dumbfounded to answer immediately. He'd trained himself to count to ten inwardly almost every time he heard something that took him by surprise anywhere in his job; Mary took him by surprise almost every time they spoke. It gave Mary enough time to do some explaining of her own.

'After all, John,' she added, 'I'm a qualified private detective. I have a certificate to prove it.'

'You have? You've been on a course or something?'

'Or something.' She pointed to a photo frame hanging on the wall, which displayed a brightly coloured certificate. Peering at it carefully, Knox was amused to read:

The Order of Sisters of Mary of the Sacred Cross
hereby declare that
Mary Madeleine Scarlett Maxwell-Hume
is duly certified as a
Private Detective, Class 1

'How do the classes work, Mary. Is '1' the same as 'beginner' or 'top of the class'?'

Mary pretended to look offended. 'Class 1 means 'First Class', John. I'm good.'

'I don't doubt it. You keep telling me that you set the highest standards.'

'Naturally. It's the only way.'

'It must have been a demanding examination.' Knox tried to look away so that Mary couldn't see him grinning. But he heard her sigh, which caused him to turn round.

'John, I know you don't really believe in the Sisters – '

'Not at all – '

'Please, John, hear me out. I'm aware that you're a sceptic, but I've always hoped that you would at least have the decency to respect what we do. I don't ask you to believe in Jesus, but I hope that you'll respect my beliefs. Don't friends respect each other? Or aren't we friends? You know, I offer my help to you without asking for anything at all in return, apart from your friendship and respect.'

Slightly chastened, Knox sought to undo some of his carelessness. 'I'm sorry, Mary. Of course we're friends, and of course I'm grateful for all the help you've given me over the years, both as a piano teacher and as a friend.'

Mary sniffed. 'In which case, I'm making a formal offer of assistance to you. You deal with the murder of Uncle Lenny, and I'll do my best with the Jaguar thefts.'

Knox hesitated. He wasn't sure if this was likely to lead anywhere.

'Exactly what sort of help do you have in mind?'

'What would represent a good result for you, John? Recover the stolen Jaguars and establish who the guilty parties are?'

Knox smiled. 'That would be ideal. You think you can do as well as me and the rest of Police Scotland?'

'Not better than you, John. You're good. Better than the rest of Police Scotland, surely, though.'

Knox chuckled. 'Why?'

'Because I can do things, get into places, that ordinary police officers can't. Shall I give you a demonstration?'

'Please do,' Knox said, more than a little intrigued.

Mary nodded. Then she stood up and reached out her hand. 'Come on, come with me, I want to show you something.'

She led him by the hand upstairs to her bedroom, reassuring him that he shouldn't jump to conclusions about being shown her sumptuous double bed – although understandably the thought had flitted through Knox's mind. Instead, with the faintest brush of the hand down from his back to his rear, she ushered him through to a tiny dressing room on the far side. Knox was astonished to discover three separate filing cabinets.

'Go on,' she said, 'have a look. I trust you not to break confidences.'

One of the filing cabinets contained – as he had expected – piano music, some of which he recognised from his piano-lesson days. Another contained all of her bills and accounts. The third seemed to contain details of her past cases working as a private detective. Encouraged to go on and look more closely, Knox found himself engrossed in any number of domestic disputes, blackmail threats, accident claims and – most intriguing of all – a whole drawerful of embezzlement, fraud and theft cases which he was suspected had never been reported to the police. 'Surprised?' she said, eventually.

'Definitely. These criminal cases – why do they come to you rather than the police?'

'I'd have thought that was obvious, John. Two reasons: firstly, many of my clients would rather not involve the police because they have something to hide, too. Secondly, because a large proportion of the population has lost all faith in the police. The police never solve anything other than murders.' Then she added, 'Sometimes not even them, of course, but I'm trying to give you a chance.'

'And they come to you instead?'

'Of course. I have a good success rate.'

'Are you going to let me into any of your secrets?' Suddenly, in the severely confined space of the dressing room, Knox became aware once more of the intensity of Mary's Chanel No 5.

'It's not really much of a secret, John. I just seem to distract people a lot. But before I let you work that through, can I ask you a personal question?'

'How personal? I'm standing in a tight little lady's dressing room beside the lady herself.'

'Intimate.' Mary said it softly. 'Then she added, 'It's for your own good.'

Knox breathed in deeply. 'Go on.'

'How are things with you and Alice? Not very good by the looks of things.'

Knox laughed, embarrassed. 'What makes you say that?'

'It's your diary. You've hardly been in at the same time recently, you never seem to go out together, you never spend any money on her. I presume she never spends any money on you either.'

Knox grabbed for his mobile phone, but it was where he'd expected it, in his inside left jacket pocket.

'It's all right, I put it back. But I had a good look first.'

'But it's got a PIN – how– ?'

Mary waved the question away as if it weren't worth answering. Instead, she said:

'Why do you have a condom in your inside right pocket? Do you want to tell me about it? It's been there a while, by the look of things.' She continued, 'I see you shop in Tesco mostly, with the odd visit to Marks and Spencer. And of course you mainly buy your petrol from that petrol station down at Canonmills. You'd get a better deal from the one up on Ferry Road, by the way.'

Knox felt a little violated. 'What have you been up to, Mary?'

'It's all there in your pockets, John. I had a good look through while you were distracted here with my filing cabinets. There are loads of petrol receipts, actually, they're easy. But the most worrying aspect of your life is Alice. You hardly seem to talk – no calls, no texts, not even the odd email. And you hardly ever end anything with kisses. That's a really bad sign for a young couple.'

'The absence of a kiss at the end of a text?'

'Naturally. What couple has sex when they don't even manage a romantic 'x' on their phone when they're apart?'

'We have sex, Mary.'

'How often, John?'

Knox didn't answer. He knew his relationship with Alice wasn't about the sex, but he also knew that Mary had touched something deep down inside that he didn't want to think about. The condom was an old, long-since past joke between Alice and himself: she used to slip condoms into his jacket when he wasn't looking. That effervescence in their relationship had faded a while back.

Mary gently brushed his cheek. 'I'm sorry, John. It's none of my business. I just can't help myself – I'm naturally inquisitive. And in particular, I want you to be happy.'

'Why me?' Knox said. 'I mean, I'm flattered but what do you see in me that you care so much? Now it's your turn to be honest.'

Mary hesitated for a moment. 'Honestly? Well, I can't deny that you're an attractive man, although I recognise that you're not likely to feel the same way about a woman more than twenty years older than you.' They both knew that was untrue, but Knox said nothing. She continued, 'The other thing I like about you is your integrity, your decency. I've told you that before. It's not something you see very often – in a policeman, especially.'

'That's not very nice.'

'It's inevitable, John. The police have to work with the dregs of society. Sometimes they feel the need to do bad things to protect the public.' Knox knew she was right. Too many of his colleagues had come to believe that the end justified the means.

'And you got all of this by raiding my pockets while I wasn't looking?' he said.

She shrugged. 'More or less. Sorry.'

'You'll be telling me what underpants I'm wearing next.'

'Dark blue and light blue striped briefs from Marks and Spencer. Size 30-32.'

'Mary! Did you even manage to dig down there?'

'It's all right, John. I caught sight of a tiny part of the waistband, and I've seen them before in the shop. I got the size from one of the receipts in your pocket.' She paused for a moment, then added, 'Am I forgiven? Did I go too far?'

Knox relaxed and smiled. 'Probably, but I forgive you.'

'At least you know now what I can do,' she pointed out. 'I think you yourself would struggle to find out what underwear your villain was wearing. There things that the police aren't even allowed to ask.'

'That's true,' he conceded.

'So… do you want me on board?'

Knox shrugged. 'As long as no one else knows… why not? It might be dangerous.'

'A lot of what I do can be dangerous.'

'I've never heard you admit that before.'

'It's been an afternoon for revelations.'

Knox squeezed Mary's hand. 'Be careful, Mary. You're precious.'

As he drove back to St Leonard's police station, Knox found himself wondering about Mary. Friends and colleagues alike warned him of the dangers of getting too close to her. Perhaps they were right, but on the other hand she'd never let him down in the past. But was he taking advantage of her? It would be completely unprofessional to enlist the help of any ordinary member of the public in either of these investigations, but Mary was hardly 'an ordinary member of the public'. Perhaps, for once, Plews was right: this was police business and Mary Maxwell-Hume had no business being there. Still...

Knox was so engrossed in his thoughts that he failed to notice the white Fiat Panda in his mirror that tailed him the entire journey.

THIRTEEN

ONCE AGAIN, KNOX RETURNED to an empty flat. There were some leftovers from the Sunday roast beef joint, but he couldn't remember what Alice and he had agreed they should do with it. Briefly, he considered waiting until she got home, but instead he looked in the fridge to see if there was anything else there that might prompt a memory. He was annoyed with himself, though, because he knew this was exactly the sort of thing he'd been neglecting lately, and Alice would be quite right to be fed up. His new job was all-consuming, and it was consuming their relationship, too, he knew that. The trouble was that being a police inspector was exciting and stimulating: it was like a drug.

The fridge revealed a few items – a lettuce and some cucumber that could keep another night or two – as well as some potatoes and carrots. Large baking potatoes, too, ideal for peeling and mashing.

Shepherd's pie. That was it, he was sure. Probably with a green vegetable from the freezer, broccoli or something. Alice and he had made shepherd's pie before quite a few times, and he himself was a passable cook, so he felt confident enough to peel the two baking potatoes, then chop them up and put them on to boil. While they were cooking, there was time to deal with the leftover roast beef, which he decided was best pulverised in the food processor before turning it into a casserole dish. Knox was surprised to discover that there was no gravy left over, but that wasn't a problem as there were plenty of gravy granules in the cupboard above the kitchen work surface. He added a dash of liquid stock and some hot chilli sauce as seasoning would give the whole thing a bit of a kick. Eventually he was able to mash the potatoes and spread it on top of the moistened roast beef.

He was beginning to get worried about Alice – it was almost eight – and he was on the point of phoning her mobile to check she was all right, when the front door opened and in she came.

'You're late tonight,' Knox said. 'You saved me a call.'

Alice bristled. 'You were going to phone me?'

'You're later than usual. Did you have a parents' night?'

'No – I just needed to work late.' Then she added, 'You work late often enough.' There was a sharpness in her tone.

Knox shrugged. 'I was worried. Sorry.' Then, 'Don't I get a kiss?'

Alice smiled an apology, the moved to kiss him quickly on the lips before recoiling.

'Chanel No.5. John, you reek of it.' Alice didn't need to say any more, she knew he'd been seeing Mary Maxwell-Hume. Knox didn't have Alice's sense of smell but he wondered if that was alcohol on her breath. Now wasn't the time to ask, for sure.

'Mary said she could help us.'

'About the murder?'

'Well, I shouldn't really be talking about the case – '

'It's all right, I won't pry,' Alice said sharply.

'But the truth is she wasn't much help today. She does private detective work now, would you believe that?'

'I'd believe anything where Mary Maxwell-Hume's concerned.' Then Alice added under her breath, 'And so would you.' Knox picked it up but decided to ignore it.

'Anyway, she showed me into a store cupboard where she keeps the files of all her cases. More than you'd expect. We were there a while. There wasn't an open window.'

'It's all right, John, you don't need to explain yourself.' Cold. Hard.

'I've prepared the meal,' Knox said.

Alice looked confused. 'What did you have to do? Slice the meat? Did you make some sort of fancy salad?'

Now it was Knox's turn to be confused. 'Shepherd's pie?'

'We're having shepherd's pie? You've turned that lovely sirloin into a shepherd's pie?'

'I thought…'

'Please don't tell me you've used the potatoes…'

'I was trying to be helpful,' Knox said, rather plaintively.

Alice said nothing. She sat down, then pointed at a calendar on the wall.

'Don't you ever read what I write there, John? Salad with the roast beef tonight, baked potatoes tomorrow. Those salad leaves won't be usable tomorrow, they'll just go to waste.'

This wasn't really like Alice at all, but in recent months she'd been getting more and more impatient with him. He couldn't do anything right. Knox was annoyed with himself, realising that he should probably have paid more attention when she was talking, but the truth was that Alice handled the routine of domestic living much better than he did himself. He knew he had become obsessed with his work, or perhaps he was just being plain selfish: he enjoyed working more than any other aspect of his life at present.

And it suddenly dawned on him that police work was more stimulating than Alice at the moment.

'John?' Alice pulled him abruptly back into the present. 'Does your silence mean that tomorrow night's baked potatoes have now become tonight's shepherd's pie?'

Jeez, Knox thought to himself. Baked potatoes – is that where our relationship has reached? But now wasn't the moment.

'I'm sorry, Alice. I really *was* just trying to be helpful.'

And then once again Alice suddenly flipped back into conciliatory mode.

'I know, I know. I'm sorry, too – I was looking forward to that roast beef salad, too. It was a lovely piece of sirloin and it was a bit too special for shepherd's pie, let's be honest.'

'As I said, I'm sorry. I'll get some more potatoes for tomorrow night and we can start again.'

'It's OK. I'm sure tonight's meal will be lovely.'

Alice drew him round to face her and kissed him lovingly. Pointing to the casserole dish, she said, 'That'll need to go in the oven. I need to have a shower. That Chanel No.5 suggests you haven't had one yet either. Do you want to go first?'

'If you prefer. Or you could join me.' Alice might have been quite a bit shorter than Knox, but she was adaptable enough and their shower sex could be surprisingly pleasurable. But on this occasion she simply looked away.

'I think I need time to myself to unwind, John. I'm sorry. Perhaps later. Better still, first thing tomorrow – you're always pretty turned on first thing. We could set the alarm early.'

'That's fine,' Knox said, realising as he said it that he was committing himself to nothing at all. 'You go and have your shower first, I'm not in a hurry.'

Alice simply mumbled an 'OK' and left. The subject wasn't raised again. They barely spoke for the rest of the evening, in fact, watching television or checking the internet instead. Nor did either of them mention the shepherd's pie, which Knox realised suited him but might have been overly spiced for Alice's taste. They went to bed at different times, and Alice was asleep when Knox turned in just twenty minutes later. Generally, they slept naked in bed, and Alice had always said that she didn't mind if he took advantage of her if he needed to. The exception was during her period, when she wore knickers as code. Tonight, she was wearing knickers, but Knox could count and remembered that she'd been wearing them for two or three days only the previous weekend.

***

They didn't speak the following morning, either. Alice had gone, leaving a note to say that she had a lot to do at school, had to go in early, and might be late home again in the evening. The note suggested that Knox just make his own arrangements for dinner, she'd look after herself. There was no kiss at the end.

Knox wondered how it had come to this. Was it her work? Was it his? Was it his relationship with Mary? Was it his relationship with Alice? Most likely a combination of them all, he decided over his slice of toast. Mentally, he thought through each in turn. There wasn't a lot he could do to help Alice's workload; there wasn't a lot he could do – at the moment at least   about his own. In fact his conclusion was rather a stark one: things would probably only get worse in their respective careers so they'd better each get used to it. Mary had entered his life temporarily and would probably leave it again, although he found that thought surprisingly depressing. And at the moment there wasn't much he could do about Alice if she wasn't there to talk to.

Knox found himself deep in thought about their recent relationship. Alice had always had an interesting solution when things were cold between them, or especially on the rare occasions when they argued or actually fell out.

Sex.

It was always Alice's idea. Invariably, she held out her hand and drew him to bed. Perhaps they didn't even get that far. But now it occurred to Knox that, pleasant as her approach might be, it meant they always ended up glossing over things rather than thrashing them out together. Often as not, the following morning did bring a new perspective, but it was really just using sex as a painkiller rather than treating the root cause of the illness. Now, without even that analgesic, the ache was strong and it wouldn't go away.

In fact the only thing that seemed to make the pain fade was immersing himself in his work, even although he knew that his job was also a significant part of his problem with Alice. His relationship longed for steady hours, but the thrill of not knowing what might happen next, day or night, was almost the part of police work that he enjoyed most. Not for the first time, Knox wondered if he and Alice were compatible at all.

He was still deep in thought when the phone rang.

'John? Lucy here. Just had a call from St Ninian's. Robina Wallace is on her way out. The nurse said she had a really bad night and she's unlikely to see out the rest of the day.'

'Jeez. She might be a malicious old crone, but she was at least coherent. Is she able to talk?'

'That's the thing. Her cancer's stopping her from making any sort of noise at all. It seems she's in a lot of pain and St Ninian's actually want to let her go.'

'You mean… kill her off?' Knox was shocked, although he wasn't quite sure why.

'Well, yes. Their point is that we've no right to keep her in pain just because she might suddenly be able to tell us what happened.' Lucy paused, then added, 'I'm not sure they're wrong, John.'

Knox knew that both and St Ninian's and Lucy were right, in fact.

'Can we get over there now? See how she is?' he asked.

'Want me to pick you up from your house?'

'No, no, we'll be quicker if we go separately and meet at St Ninian's.'

Less then twenty minutes later they were standing in St Ninian's discussing Robina Wallace's health with a duty doctor called Dr Cartwright. Knox was relieved it wasn't Helen Wolstencroft he was having to deal with, but this younger man, if friendly enough, wasn't a lot more cooperative.

'The thing is, Inspector,' he was saying, 'Robina Wallace might be your star witness, but my first duty is to her as an individual, and to look after her health.'

'The woman's dying!' Knox said, louder than he intended.

'And she has a right die with dignity, and not in pain. Anyway, the tumour has completely destroyed her ability to speak. The poor woman can barely breathe.'

Lucy intervened. 'Can we ask Robina if there's anything she'd like to tell us?'

The doctor smiled. 'Nicely done, Detective Sergeant. If you respect her right to say no to that, I can't see what harm it would do.'

'We could do signals – thumbs up, thumbs down, that sort of thing. It's not exactly top-quality court evidence, but it would be better than nothing.'

'Well, all right,' said the young doctor. 'But only if I'm allowed to supervise.'

He led the two detectives into a small room where a patient clearly lay behind drawn curtains. Cartwright went in to speak to the elderly woman alone, and Knox and Grant heard him explaining that the police were desperate to talk to her. They heard some sort of gargling noise, then Cartwright seemed to stop her abruptly before asking her to do something again. After a few moments longer, the doctor pulled open the curtains to reveal a frail old woman with tubes attached to many parts of her.

'I'm surprised,' Cartwright said. 'Mrs Wallace here has indicated that she's prepared to write her answers down for you,' and he produced a pen and a small notepad from an inner pocket. He shrugged his shoulders and said, 'Handy sometimes.'

'Thank you, both of you,' Knox said. Then he bent over Robina a little and said quietly, 'Mrs Wallace, we're here about the death of Mr Plews. We could really use your help. Is there anything you can tell us?'

Robina Wallace signalled weakly that there was something important that she needed to say, and made a writing gesture.

Cartwright quickly provided her with his notepad and a cheap ballpoint pen and she started to write. It was clearly laborious, and Lucy went to help her, but Robina covered up the notepad to prevent her from seeing it, to Lucy's confusion. It must have taken the poor woman three or four minutes to write what seemed to be very little. But Knox and she knew the wait would be worth it if they got a name.

Eventually Robina put the pen down, exhausted. Dr Cartwright picked up the paper, studied it with raised eyebrows, then handed it over to the police officers.

'I think her message is clear enough, don't you?'

Knox closed his eyes in despair. The note simply said, 'PISS OFF'.

By mid-afternoon she was gone. Now only three remained.

FOURTEEN

'**Y**EZ ARNAE LOOKIN' EFTER yer witnesses very well, John.'

Knox and Grant had just returned to St Leonard's with the news of Robina Wallace's demise and Knox had been summoned to O'Malley's office. Knox knew that the Superintendent would have something to say, although he was a reasonable man. After all, each of these patients was destined to die soon – that was why they were in St Ninian's after all.

'I'm really not sure what to say, sir. To tell the truth we're getting rather desperate for a break.'

'Yez have tae admire the wumman's spirit, though. I like yon final thrust at life. See yon Dylan Thomas? 'Rage, rage against the dying of the light?' By God she didnae gae gently into the sweet night.'

'The woman herself seems to have been anything but sweet. But she's not going to tell us much now that she's gone, is she? I'm beginning to lose hope that we'll ever find out what happened in there, if I'm honest.'

'Never give up on a case, John. Tell yourself yer big break is just round the next corner. But you have tae learn tae prior-i-tise.' O'Malley pointed his index finger upwards teacher-like

155

and dragged out the word for even greater effect. 'Speaking of which, Chief Inspector Plews has been nippin' ma ear a' day about that car o' his. Are yez makin' ony progress on that?'

'It's in hand, sir.'

Knox hoped that would satisfy the Superintendent but he knew that was unlikely. The man was far too shrewd for that. At first O'Malley simply looked at him, as if waiting for an answer, then eventually said, 'Well, are yez gonnae brief me? I've got tae tell the man something. He thinks yer daein' nuthin' at a', and at the moment he might no' be sae wrong.'

'I've delegated the task, sir. I felt that, so long as the murder enquiry was proceeding, I needed to focus on that.'

O'Malley grinned. 'Delegated? Now that's wan o' ma favourite words, John. Whenever yez delegate, there are two key things tae bear in mind.'

Now it was Knox's turn to grin. He liked and respected O'Malley, knew something was coming, and that he, Knox, would be the butt of it.

'Please enlighten me, sir.'

'First of all, make sure that whoever yez delegate to can actually dae the job. Second, ayeways remember that if they cock it up, it's your fault. Dinnae go blamin' yer inability tae find thae Jags on some wee constable. Anyway, whae is it?'

Knox said nothing. O'Malley usually had incredible antennae and he was slightly surprised he didn't know the answer already. Perhaps he did.

'Come on, John, whae is it? Ah've got a half-eaten cheese sandwich in my office and ah've near forgotten what colour it is. Probably mouldy green by the time ah've got this out o' yez.'

Knox took a big deep breath.

'Sister Mary Maxwell-Hume.'

Knox had been with the force for five or six years now and knew O'Malley well, but this was the first time he'd ever seen the man speechless. He simply stared at Knox, but did nothing more, then Knox saw him start to shake all over while his face went a deep shade of red. Knox even began to worry if the man was having a stroke. But suddenly, the Superintendent's shaking burst out into uncontrolled laughter which continued for fully a minute before subsiding as tears ran down the man's face.

'Are you all right, sir?'

'Sister... Sister... Sister... Mary Maxwell-Hume?' By now O'Malley had staggered back towards his desk and propped himself up while he recovered his composure and mopped himself up. 'Jeez, John, I thought yez had outgrown that woman. Did yez no' pay any attention when I spoke tae yez about her?'

Knox explained that he'd gone round to interview her, thinking she had new light to shed on the murder, but in fact she was really interested in the serial car theft case.

'Sister Mary pointed out that she can go places that we can't,' he added.

'I'll bet,' O'Malley said brightly. 'She can go a few places on me, for a start.' Knox closed his eyes in despair. The Superintendent chuckled. 'No, son, it's all right, ah ken she widnae hae anythin' tae dae wi' me. Just ma little joke.'

'Shall I pass on the message, sir?'

O'Malley's lascivious grin reappeared. 'Cannae see how it wid dae any harm.' He thought for a moment then added, 'Tell you what, John, I'll leave that decision to you. I know ye'll dae what's in my best interests. That's unless ye have designs on Sister Mary yersel'. But then you've got yer Alice? How's that goin', by the way?'

'Fine, thanks.'

'Fine? Really? Anyone call tell things aren't fine, son. And yez are far tae busy for everything bein' 'fine'. Take it frae me, I can spot these things a mile away. Remember me and the missus crashed and burned years ago. Been there, got the tee-shirt.'

'Your police work got too much for your wife?' It hadn't been what Knox had heard.

'Well, that and Mary McGovern, that nice-lookin' wumman frae PR. But my eye only wandered because me and Mrs O'Malley weren't... you know.'

Knox reassured his superior officer that he could fill in the gaps for himself.

'Anyway,' O'Malley said, getting back to the subject, 'what's this nun of yours gonnae dae? You say she's a private investigator?'

'Yes. And I've seen what she can do with a mobile phone or a long-range lens. And I've experienced first-hand her pickpocketing skills. She can mesmerise people while she's finding out all sorts of stuff about them.' Knox told O'Malley about her recent pickpocketing demonstration, missing out the condom part.

'Oh for the ability tae dae that, John. Our job wid be so much easier. Nae warrants, eh?'

'She can certainly flit in and out of places unnoticed or in disguise if she needs to.'

O'Malley nodded. Then a thought occurred to him.

'Em... what are we paying her, John?'

It wasn't a subject John and Mary had ever discussed.

'I'm not sure she'll charge anything, sir. Sister Mary tends to work on a... commission basis. She pays herself, somehow. Or rather, in my experience, the villains usually pay her without realising. So in this case I don't know what her plans would be.'

'Make sure she understands we cannae pay her. There's nae money in the police budget to pay for loose cannon nuns that moonlight as private detectives.'

'Understood.'

'And mind you it's dangerous. There are places a lady shouldnae be.'

'That ain't no lady...'

'Aye, aye. Very good, son. Too dangerous for civilians, then.'

'I'll impress on her the need for safety, although she's a private detective and I'm sure she knows the dangers full well. Would you like to speak to her yourself?'

'I'd love tae speak tae yer Sister Mary, son. But I dinnae think it's a good idea. I need... what was that thing Reagan had?'

Knox looked puzzled.

'Deniability. In the 1980s, President Reagan's staff never telt him anything so if things went pear-shaped he could claim he didnae hae a clue. Which of course he didnae, but no' in that sense. Others went down for the rap instead. The ultimate in loyalty.'

'So you want 'deniability', sir?'

'That's about the size o' it, son. The buck for Sister Mary stops wi' you. This conversation never happened. Understand?'

'Understood, sir. What will you tell Chief Inspector Plews?'

'What he wants to hear. That we've got our best people onto the car thefts. Whatever yez tells him in the way o' detail's up tae you.'

O'Malley made some grunt to indicate that he'd nothing more to add and the meeting was over. As Knox left the office, the Detective Superintendent called after the him.

'Good idea using that nun, by the way.'

Lucy Grant, Izzy Bryce and Dave Lander were in a huddle when Knox returned to the Operations room. Naively, he assumed they were discussing the developments in the murder case, but in fact they were far more animated by Chief Inspector Plews's car being stolen. The three junior officers found Plews's misfortune amusing, and Knox had little sympathy for the man himself. But he found himself having to remind them that the Chief Inspector was a victim of crime, just like any other member of the public.

'I know, sir, but the Chief Inspector himself isn't making it very easy,' Lucy explained on behalf of all of them. 'Every five minutes he complains about the hire car his insurance company has lumbered him with – a Volvo estate, it seems, built like a tank and as fast as one, too, he says.'

'Nice car for a stand-in,' Knox acknowledged.

'Needless to say he keeps asking how the case is going,' said Lander. 'We do suggest he asks you, but of course you've been out of the office a bit on other cases. Especially the murder.'

Knox wondered if any of them knew about Mary Maxwell-Hume.

'I've not a lot to tell him about the Jaguars at the moment,' he said. 'It's only just become my case, actually now that the Chief Inspector's been ruled out because of a conflict of interest. The Superintendent is trying to keep his mind occupied with a couple of cases. One of them is an art fraud case, it seems, so he can work with his brother.'

'Will this be the same brother that had his Jaguar stolen?' Izzy asked. Only recently returned to work since looking after children, she was less up with the station gossip. Lander explained that Theodore Plews, the Chief Inspector's only brother, was the manager of a local auction house. According to those who knew them both, Theodore was an even more odious man than his police officer brother.

'So what are we doing about the Jaguars?' Lander asked.

Knox hesitated. 'I think we need to focus on the St Ninian's case first. I've got some plans for looking into the Jaguar thefts and I'm working on them at the moment.'

'Are we… going to be let into those plans, sir?'

Knox took a deep breath.

'No, Dave, not at the moment. I'd like to keep that to myself just now. I'll let you know soon enough, but in the meantime I'm hoping our thief gets careless and makes a mistake somewhere. I'd prefer him or her to think we're not really trying very hard.' As he said it, he watched Lucy, who studiously kept looking at the desk. It made him all the more sure that she had some suspicions.

'But we're doing something,' Lander said, seeking some sort of reassurance.

'Something.' Knox's tone indicated that the discussion was closed. Then he added, 'Tell you what, Dave, could you please get me the complete up-to-date details of each of the stolen Jags? I'd like something in writing to refer to, if that were possible.'

'How much detail? Chassis numbers, that sort of thing?'

'Why not? Can't do any harm. Meanwhile, we need to get back to the deaths at St Ninian's.'

Knox encouraged Lucy to start by reviewing what they already knew.

'OK, the victim had been found face-down lying on top of another, female, patient who was comatose,' she said. 'He was half-undressed and had a new, unused Sabatier filleting knife in his back, and the knife had the initials 'LP' on the handle. But he actually died of a heart attack, probably brought on by his face being held down on the bed so that he was asphyxiated. The knife-wound was in fact completely post-mortem.

'The body was found by the victim's niece Sister Mary Maxwell-Hume, a nightly visitor to the St Ninian's. Sister Mary actually had motive to do the deed, having been abused by the victim as child.'

'Was she?' Izzy said. 'Wow, that changes things a little.'

Knox glared at Lucy, who suddenly realised that the information about Mary's connection with Leonard Plews wasn't public knowledge.

'Yes, I'm sorry,' Lucy said to Lander and Bryce. 'I'd forgotten that neither of you knew that. She's a victim, too, and also entitled to anonymity.' She turned to Knox and said, 'Sorry, sir, I didn't realise it was confidential.'

Knox was quietly seething. 'You didn't realise that the abuse of a witness while a child might be confidential? Jesus, Lucy.'

'It must be relevant, sir,' Izzy said.

'It's only relevant if the witness in question could have committed the crime,' Knox snapped. 'But she's in the clear, beyond question. Death occurred almost an hour before Mary arrived in the building.'

Lander and Bryce had hardly ever seen Knox angry, and certainly not as angry as he was now.

'Sorry, sir,' Lucy said. 'It was unprofessional.' She knew, all the same, that she'd touched a nerve and that Knox had been desperate to protect Mary.

'Is there anything at all that makes Ms Maxwell-Hume's connection with the deceased relevant to the investigation, sir?' Lander asked, trying to smooth things over a little.

Knox sighed. 'Now that Lucy's spilled the beans, I suppose I should fill you two in on a little more detail. But it goes no further than the four of us, is that understood? O'Malley knows, of course.'

'Does the Chief Inspector?'

'He does now. He was strange about it, like he couldn't absorb it.'

Knox went on to give some limited detail: that Mary had been brought up by her Uncle Lenny, who had abused her for several years before she'd escaped. Knox also said that her mother had died in childbirth but was vague about her father, saying only that he'd died in prison. He said nothing about the trial itself, or Theodore and Maximilian's part in it.

'Anyway, let's get back to the murder, can we, Lucy?'

Lucy nodded. 'Apart from the victim, there were seven patients in the ward, three men and four women. The CCTV shows no one else coming in or going out during the timeframe. Of those seven, four, including Eileen Lamb, the woman on top of whom the victim was found, have already died. But although they're close to death, only Eileen Lamb was totally physically incapable of being involved in any way in Mr Plews's death. The others could all potentially have summoned up enough energy to commit some sort of foul deed.'

'And there's also the possibility that more than one of them might have been involved,' Knox pointed out. 'But the problem with that is motive. There might be one psychotic killer in there, but there's unlikely to be a whole squad of them. And anyway, why kill Plews?'

'We know he wasn't a nice man,' Lucy said.

'Yes, but did any of the patients know? What had Plews done to any of them?' Knox motioned to Lucy to keep going. 'What are our lines of enquiry?'

'Running out fast, sir. We have three patients left. One is the Reverend Ian Mould, then there's Myles Cherry, our businessman, and then finally there's Martha Ramsay who has dementia.'

'Alzheimer's?' Lander asked.

Lucy shook her head. 'No, some other, less common form of dementia. But she's had it a long time and doesn't remember very much. I'm not sure what she'll ever tell us, to be honest.'

'That's assuming they know anything at all,' Knox pointed out. 'Most of them were doped up to the eyeballs on serious painkillers.'

'I don't think we should write off this Martha Ramsay,' Izzy said. 'I had a great-aunt who had some strange form of dementia and she lived for years. Physically she was fine, and she was quite happy. She thought she was Grace Kelly. Kept talking about the films she'd been in. She was quite convincing apart from the fact that Grace Kelly's dead.'

'Are you saying she could provide us with some answers, Izzy?' Knox asked her.

'I'm saying my great-aunt could have stabbed a knife into someone if she'd been told she was acting Scene 28 of her latest movie.'

'Speaking of the knife,' Knox said, 'are we any further forward on how it got in there? I can't exactly see anyone getting onto a 26 bus in their pyjamas and popping into John Lewis to buy a knife like that.'

'That particular knife can only be bought online or in specialist kitchen shops, sir,' Lucy said. 'But we've no idea where it came from apart from that.'

'Anyway,' Knox said, 'how did it get into that room? The place is like Fort Knox. It's got all sorts of metal detectors. And why wait until after he was dead to stick the knife into him? Did any of the patients have a grudge against Plews? We need to find the answer to all of these questions.'

FIFTEEN

THE CAR SHOWROOM of Hoggart & Law – 'Edinburgh's Leading Jaguar Dealer' – was one of the few that could still afford to operate near the city centre. Business rates were soaring and most of the low- to mid-range car franchises had moved out of the city altogether, but Hoggart & Law judged that potential buyers of Jaguars would expect rather better than a soulless complex somewhere beyond the City Bypass.

At half past eleven on a Thursday morning, business at Hoggart & Law was usually dead. The firm employed several staff, all of whom worked at weekends, but during the week there was little else to do other than complete the odd delivery of an ordered car to a customer. Thursdays were especially quiet, and the firm felt it was quite safe to leave the showroom in the care of just one salesman, and their most inexperienced one at that. Young Jason was ideally suited to the role, as he could entertain himself all day on his smartphone checking emails, playing computer games, and of course on social media. Jason was simply addicted to *Megalife*. Jason actually had over two thousand *Megalife* friends. Each of them knew what Jason had eaten for breakfast that morning, his views on whether Chelsea had played well the night before, and in particular if he thought Claire deserved to be evicted from the weekly reality show.

But this Thursday was a little different. Jason was just into his second digestive biscuit when no fewer than seven different potential customers appeared in the space of ten minutes. As the first pair through came the door, a couple in their early fifties, Jason leapt to his feet, dusted the crumbs off his suit and went to offer assistance. They introduced themselves immediately as Mr and Mrs Fox – Mrs Fox did most of the talking, but it was her husband who seemed to be hanging on to Jason's every word. The couple explained that they were looking for a nice car, perhaps not completely new. Mr Fox wanted to know about the in-car hi-fi system, and Jason – now warming to his task – was keen to let him hear the sound quality in each of the used cars on the forecourt. Mrs Fox, on the other hand, wanted to know about each car's comfort levels – heated seats, air conditioning, vanity mirrors. Naturally, the second-hand cars that she liked were different from those that took her husband's fancy. As Jason sat with her showing her each car's features, he was struck by her red dress and, in particular, her liberal use of perfume.

As Jason was showing the Foxes round the Hoggart & Law range of 'pre-owned' Jaguars, two more customers arrived. This time it wasn't quite so clear whether or not they were connected. The first was a man in his thirties, medium height, dark-haired with designer stubble and dressed casually. The second was an older woman, graceful, wearing dark glasses. Confusingly, she too was dressed in red, in her case a bright scarlet raincoat. Jason wondered if the two newcomers perhaps even have been mother and son but he was more concerned that the younger man might be some sort of film or television celebrity: he never liked to miss the opportunity for a selfie with the famous. But in the meantime he still had the Foxes to deal with and so he found himself dancing backwards and forwards between everyone trying to reassure them that he would attend to each of them in turn.

Jason's 'Hoggart & Law Sales Adviser Induction Course' – completed only a few months previously – had stressed that no customer should be left unattended for longer then a few minutes. In his short career, that had been no problem for the young man, because an entire day could pass sometimes with barely so much as a single customer, and even on the busier days most of the customers were happy enough to wander around. But he began to get a little flustered when he realised that the two newer arrivals were nowhere near each other in the showroom. The young man hovered around for a little, but then quickly began to look impatient, forcing Jason to politely take his leave of the Foxes for a moment to enquire if he could be of any assistance. The newcomer responded curtly in a London accent, saying that (a) he and 'that other lady over there' were not connected, and that (b) he was interested in buying a brand new F-type and wanted to compare showroom and online options. That second option had Jason interested, thinking of the potential commission to be earned on a £70,000 sale.

Now that Jason was darting between designer-stubble man and the Foxes, he was relieved to hear the lady in the scarlet raincoat say that she was happy simply to look around. If he, Jason, didn't mind, she'd like to look under the bonnets of some of the cars and take a closer look. Again, he caught a whiff of perfume, but not being an expert, hadn't a clue what it was.

Designer-Stubble Man continued to look familiar. Perhaps he was a local football star? Or someone from a TV series? But Jason didn't want to be too obvious, so instead he played it cool, looking out all the relevant brochures and price lists for each model. Designer-Stubble Man gave nothing away, other than a brusque 'Is that your best offer?', to which Jason replied, as trained, with 'How much were you looking to spend, sir?'

The question didn't go down well. Designer-Stubble glanced at the name-plate on Jason's suit jacket.

'I'm not sure that's any of your business… Jason. Were you trained to make impertinent enquiries about the private financial means of your potential customers? No? I don't suppose so. So how about you just run through a few prices? The real prices, not the ones on these silly little bits of paper.'

He tossed the price lists onto Jason's desk.

'Eh… I'm sorry, sir. I didn't mean to offend you.'

'Shall we just get on with the business… Jason?' Perhaps Jason recognised the man from some sort of true crime television programme.

In the background, Jason could see that the Foxes were looking a little irritated that Designer-Stubble had jumped in ahead of them in the queue. Feeling like a juggler, Jason jumped up and insisted that he'd be 'with them in a moment.' The Foxes looked unconvinced, but Designer-Stubble grunted an understanding that Jason was struggling to cope.

Jason decided that his best approach was simply to get on with dealing with each of the customers in turn, but just as he was finalising some figures for Designer-Stubble, two more customers arrived. He was immediately distracted by the fact that they were both attractive women, neither a lot older than Jason himself, but also because they were each wearing red coats – one dark, one bright. Now convinced that Designer-Stubble was nobody important, he could barely take his eyes off one of them in particular, the blonde in bright red, and once again he found himself infuriating the Foxes.

'I'll be with you in a minute!' he called across the showroom.

The two women came a little closer. Perhaps they were older than he'd first imagined, but still…

'Just have a look around, please,' Jason said.

Blonde-with-the-Red-Coat had immediately clocked Jason's interest.

'I'm looking to buy a sporty number,' she said. Her voice was cut-glass. Jason now realised that each of the women were in their forties. 'Always fancied a Jag, ever since hubby went off with ours after the divorce. Stuck with the Range Rover, which is fine for the shopping or taking the kids to school, but when you're out on the open road you need a bit of oommph.' She turned to her friend in the dark coat. 'Don't you agree, Julia?'

'Oh my, Libby, one must have standards. But I like a little maturity in my cars.'

'Of course. Cars are like men. They need to be run in properly before they're in full working order,' Libby said, which had both women in peals of laughter. Make that late forties, Jason thought, before turning back to Designer-Stubble.

'Would you like some time to think, sir, while I attend to these other customers?'

Designer-Stubble drew out an iPad Mini from an inner pocket. 'Why not? I could sit across there out of the way and check out the online prices. That would give you a chance to chat up those women.'

Jason had said 'Thanks' before he realised that he'd actually been insulted. Still, he thought, at least he could spread himself about now, so he wandered across to the Foxes.

'Sorry about that,' he said. 'How are you getting on?'

Mr Fox's expression gave nothing away. 'I can't quite make up my mind which car I like best. I really need to see under the bonnets to see what condition they're in.'

'I can assure you that each car is fully serviced, sir – '

'Your idea of a service and mine might be different. Of course, if you're not interested in a sale – '

'No, no, I'm sorry. But you'll understand I'm busy just now. Perhaps I could show you the bonnet catch and how to pop the lids, and you check them out yourself? That way I wouldn't be standing over you. I'm here to answer any questions, mind you.'

'That might work,' Mr Fox said. 'And Mrs Fox can check out the interior. I'm also interested in the radio, sat-nav and so on. I notice that most of your used cars are out on the forecourt. I'd like to compare them. Could you make sure that all the cars are unlocked?'

Jason made his apologies to everyone then set off to fetch all of the keys. He'd been told he should be careful with car keys, especially remote keys that didn't actually need to be physically inserted into the ignition system. However he felt had little choice, and in any case most of the cars were boxed in and the entire forecourt was covered by CCTV.

A few minutes later he returned with a batch of keys.

'I'm not sure which key is for which car,' he explained. 'I usually just try a number and wait until the right car flashes.'

Mr Fox smiled for the first time. 'That sounds a good idea. But I could do that and you could go back to serve someone. You know I've got the keys.'

At that very moment 'Julia' and 'Libby' approached, looking impatient, prompting Jason to turn back to the Foxes with, 'OK, I'll leave you to it, then.'

The two women spent fully ten minutes asking Jason all sorts of meaningful technical questions. Meantime, he became aware of a backdrop of rising and falling electric windows, headlights going on and off, wipers swishing to and fro, car bonnets and boots being opened up and their interiors closely examined before being noisily closed again. The Foxes had been joined by Designer-Stubble Man and even the graceful lady with the dark glasses who was still patiently waiting for some sort of attention. Together, they wandered from car to car: Mr Fox took notes on a little notebook while Designer-Stubble was using his iPad to make comparisons and even, sometimes, to take photographs.

Just as Jason turned back to deal with the Julia and Libby, he was interrupted yet again as a courier came into the showroom and demanded a signature for a small parcel – parts, Jason presumed.

Then finally, with the four others occupied and also hardly likely to get up to mischief in each other's presence, Jason finally felt able to give some attention to Julia and Libby. Libby, he learned, was being careful with her divorce settlement money, so she was more interested in cars that were two or three years old – 'perhaps costing no more than forty thousand or so', as she put it. Julia reckoned that she should take them for a test drive, but Jason had to explain that was impossible because he was all alone in the showroom.

'All alone?' Julia whispered huskily in his ear, then both of the women went into hysterics again. Remarkably, they seemed to be wearing perfume as well, so that now there four female customers, each wearing a shade of red and each wearing some sort of perfume. Jason began to feel a little sick. He offered to arrange a test drive but Libby pointed out that she was a woman – something Jason had already noted – while adding that it would be difficult to arrange a test drive anyway if the other customers currently had all the keys. So instead, they offered to look around like everyone else. Doors, boot- and bonnet-lids were opening and closing noisily everywhere, inside the showroom and out on the forecourt. Designer-Stubble disappeared but then Jason saw him emerge from under a car then dive under the next one.

By now Jason was all at sea. He'd considered phoning one of his off-duty colleagues for advice, Mark perhaps, but irritatingly he couldn't find his mobile phone, which he'd last seen while playing computer games. He'd normally have put it in his jacket pocket, but in the general mêlée he'd obviously laid it down somewhere. Meanwhile he was surprised to discover that the courier driver was talking to, of all people, the elegant lady with the red coat and dark glasses. Why hadn't he gone away? Did they know each other? He tried to look on the bright side: the courier wasn't looking to buy a Jaguar. It was all getting too much. He sat down before he passed out.

Now reduced to a bemused watching role, Jason watched ever more doors open and close – Libby and Julia had joined in the general jamboree, too. He closed his eyes and waited for the storm to pass.

Ten or fifteen minutes later – he wasn't quite sure – Jason was awoken by the gently invasive perfume of the elegant lady in the red coat and dark glasses. Opening his eyes, he was surprised to discover that she was alone and that everyone else had left. Had he been asleep? If so, it was something he would want to keep to himself.

Gradually, his eyes focused on the woman standing over him. Close to, she was more attractive than Jason expected, although her age could have been anything from 45 to 65. She'd unbuttoned her coat to reveal a matching red dress that seemed so neat that it displayed her figure to best possible advantage. His mind must surely have been playing tricks on him, but her smile reminded him of that painting he'd learned about at school, that Mona Lisa, the one that was so expensive. The woman in that picture had a smile which might have been friendly, or sensuous, or simply laughing at him. Given that he'd clearly been asleep, Jason guessed it was probably the last of these.

'Don't you want these?' she said.

Only now did Jason realise that the lady was holding a an A4 polythene pocket of the type he himself used to look after valuable car documents. Inside was every single car key, thankfully properly labelled. Belatedly, he jumped to his feet.

'I hope you didn't mind, but I borrowed one of those envelopes off your desk,' the elegant woman said. 'It seemed a good idea to keep all the keys in the one place.'

Jason was still a lap behind. 'I'm so sorry, I think I must have nodded off for a few seconds.' He looked at his watch and realised he'd been asleep for fully twenty minutes. At least his watch hadn't been stolen, but then he suddenly panicked and started picking up everything on his rather untidy desk and checking underneath.

'Have you lost something, Jason?' the woman asked, quietly.

'I've lost my phone… I've lost my phone.'

'Now then… think… where do you normally keep it?'

'In my pocket, but – ' Jason patted his inside jacket pocket and discovered it exactly where it should have been. 'But it's there…'

'That's good, then, isn't it Jason?' She said nothing more, simply maintaining that mysterious smile for a while before going on, 'So what shall I do with these keys? They're all labelled.'

'Thanks.' Goodness knows how much work losing a label or two would have caused, he thought. 'Just give the keys to me. I'll put them all back in the safe.'

'That sounds a good idea, Jason.'

Jason took the keys, but then his sales manners returned. 'I haven't really had a chance to speak with you, madam. What do you feel your needs are?' As soon as he said the words, he wanted to grab them back.

'Now there's a thought,' she said. 'Whatever do you mean… Jason?'

Flustered, Jason tried to explain that he was there to help with anything she needed.

'Oh, how splendid. But I've had a good look and I'm not sure you quite have what I'm looking for,' the woman said. 'I might have to look elsewhere.' The smile remained. 'Perhaps you might suggest something?'

Jason was disappointed to lose a sale, but he couldn't help himself. He reeled off the names of four other Jaguar franchises in the area, and – of greater interest to the elegant woman – three back-street garages who were prepared to repair, service and sometimes sell Jaguars.

She nodded politely, then leant much closer to whisper in his ear. Her perfume was much stronger, and he had an unexpectedly close-up view of the woman's dress. He wanted to touch, to find out more, but she discreetly held her right index finger up to wave 'no'.

'But you've been so helpful, Jason. Thank you so much.'

Jason wondered if she was going to kiss him. But instead, she turned and walked towards the exit, fully aware that his eyes were glued to her departing rear view. But right at the exit, she stopped and called back.

'Did you manage to get his autograph? Mark Kerr's.'

'Autograph?'

'The man with the beard. Mark Kerr, the Scotland football captain. I understand he's quite famous.'

She turned and left. Jason wanted to kick himself. Kerr was his hero.

But at least there was one consolation. He went back to his seat, fired up *Megalife* on his mobile and began to post all about the time Mark Kerr came in looking to buy a Jaguar.

SIXTEEN

THE FOLLOWING DAY BROUGHT more bad news from St Ninian's. First thing in the morning, Dr Wolstencroft called in to say that Ian Mould had died during the night, while Myles Cherry was in serious discomfort and was being heavily sedated. She'd gone so far as to hint that Cherry had passed 'the point of no return', as she put it, which the duty sergeant had taken to mean that pain relief was now the only thing she was concerned with, even if it needed a fatal dose.

Chief Inspector Maximilian Plews had actually been into St Leonard's police station that morning, and had even briefly spoken to the doctor on the telephone himself. He already seemed resigned to the possibility that his father's death would be shrouded in mystery, and certainly cared nothing for the welfare of any of the other patients. On the other hand, the return of his Jaguar was a different matter.

Knox wasn't actually due to start work until early afternoon. However he'd asked St Ninian's to keep him informed of any developments, and Wolstencroft had phoned his mobile with the news of the two patients as well. Conscious that any chance of his eye-witnesses ever telling him anything was disappearing by the hour, and with Alice off to work at school, he felt there was little better to do than head in to St Leonard's early. He arrived just after ten, almost three hours early, to hear Plews bark his name from an open door.

Knox sighed inwardly as he made his way in. This could lead to nothing but grief.

'What's the meaning of this?' Plews demanded, tapping his watch. 'Coming in at this time of day?'

'Sir, I – '

'I'm fed up hearing excuses, Knox. It's shoddy. You're an Inspector now, you're a big boy and you're supposed to set an example. Timekeeping is critical. A late police officer is a liability.'

'Sir, I – '

'You're still on probation, technically, Knox, and Superintendent O'Malley and I will be making a note of this. Consider this a formal reprimand.'

'Sir – '

'Are you arguing back, Knox?'

'No, sir. But perhaps – '

Plews sat back in his chair. 'I see. Perhaps I should put this in writing?'

Knox hesitated for a moment.

'I wonder if that might be for the best, sir, in the circumstances.'

'You want me to put it in writing? Really? You want to take it that far?'

'Only at your convenience, sir. But it might clarify things all round.'

'Well, Knox, this is a poor start to your career. You clearly don't even understand the disciplinary system yet. And of course I'll have to share this with Superintendent O'Malley. You really want that?'

'I understand the consequences.'

Plews growled.

'Presumably, Knox, if you can't even be bothered getting to work on time, you'll have made no progress solving anything.'

'We're working on it, sir.'

'And?'

'The strangest thing about the car thefts is that so many of them have a personalised number plate. In your case, 'MAX 1', in your brother's, 'TED 1E' and so on.'

'So?'

'Car thieves normally never touch personalised number plates – they're too easy to spot. That suggests that the cars are being given a makeover somewhere – a new number plate for sure, and probably resprayed a different colour. That takes a little time. We think the cars could well be hidden somewhere. And if they've had their plates changed, the thieves must know what registrations would look all right as they go through the speed cameras and other roadside checks we do. That's possible, but we don't think it's likely they could get all the missing cars right straight away. These cars would be easy to spot.'

'Fanciful. Impossible.'

'Meanwhile, we're also looking at the all the ways that Jaguars could be moved on. We're checking all the ports at the moment for shipments of cars going abroad and so far it appears nothing has left the country. It's the best we can think of so far, sir.'

'You're saying that my car is being butchered as we speak?'

'Resprayed, sir. And I'm saying that it's one of the lines we're pursuing, sir.'

'Well, get on with it. Don't stand around here all day.'

Plews seemed to have forgotten both the reprimand and the fact that it was he who had summoned the Inspector into his office in the first place.

'If that'll be all, sir?'

'That's all. Back to work, stop prevaricating.'

It was only as Knox was hallway out of the door that he heard Plews belatedly call from behind him, 'By the way, any progress on my father's murder?'

'The witnesses keep dying on us, sir. But we're working on it.'

Plews didn't even look up. 'Well, make sure you don't neglect the car thefts, Knox. I might get the car back but I certainly wouldn't want my father back.'

'What do you reckon to Myles Cherry and the woman with dementia, John? Is it worth paying them a visit?' Lucy Grant asked, as Knox finally made it into his own office. After his encounter with Plews, he'd have quite liked time alone, but Lucy was the least demanding of his colleagues. Lucy's sexuality – and the fact that Knox knew about it – made him feel at times that they were like a married couple, and they could sit silently in the car together without either feeling the need to fill the space with empty conversation. He'd even said as much once, worried that he'd overstepped the line, then been reassured that Lucy took it as a compliment. On this occasion, he had a lot to think about, and he didn't reply immediately.

Lucy waited for quite a while as she watched Knox stare rather vacantly into a blank space on the wall. Eventually she said, 'John?'

'Sorry, Lucy, I was a bit lost there,' he said, coming to a little. 'Yes, I suppose we should. I'm sure we'll get nothing out of them, but we need to be seen to be making the effort. Perhaps we could speak to some of the staff again while we're at it. We've rather concentrated on the patients so far.'

'Given that they're dying like flies, it seemed a reasonable plan of campaign.'

'Well, perhaps it's time to interview everyone who was on the premises again. Even if we know that no one went in or out of the room where the patients were, somebody might be able to shed some light on what happened. For a start, how does a brand new fishmonger's knife find its way into a roomful of terminally ill patients?'

'I understand that St Ninian's have its own internal inquiry under way,' Lucy said.

'OK, so we should ask what progress is being made on that as well. But first we have to see if Myles Cherry is capable of anything. At least if he can speak to us we might get some sense out of him. The other surviving patient – what was her name again?'

'Martha Ramsay.'

'Martha Ramsay thinks every man she speaks to is Elvis. Or Cliff Richard. Her memories are of fifty or sixty years ago. But she doesn't know her own children. Even if she did tell us something important, we wouldn't know whether or not we should pay any attention.'

'You reckon we're wasting our time?'

'We'll go through the motions, but that's all. Mr Cherry might be lucid although he wasn't able to tell us much even when we interviewed him before.'

'I remember. He claimed to have seen nothing, and every sentence seemed to exhaust him. He just wanted to lie quietly.' Then she added as an afterthought, 'Perhaps I should have said, 'He just wanted to die quietly.'"

Neither of them said anything for a short while, as if trying to absorb what Lucy had just said. Then, Knox abruptly stood up and said, 'Well, we'll find nothing out of them if we don't ask them, that's for sure. And who knows, perhaps one of the nurses knows something. We still haven't found out how the knife got in there.'

'You think a nurse put it there?'

'Somebody must have. We're told the patients in that communal room never received visitors, so the only others who ever went in there must have been staff. At least you'd imagine so. And everyone signs in and out anyway.'

'But there's nothing on the CCTV.'

'We have to keep asking, Lucy. There has to be a solution to all of this. Come on, let's go.'

Just twenty minutes later, they were in St Ninian's car park. Lucy had telephoned ahead to let St Ninian's know they were coming and was informed by the receptionist that the doctor meeting them would be Mike Cartwright, the younger doctor they'd met once before. During the twenty minute journey, Knox had confided to Lucy that he was relieved not to be dealing with Helen Wolstencroft, whose coolness he found unsettling. In response, Lucy had suggested that the doctor's response might merely be a defensive protection against outside intrusion into the final days of her patients' lives, and also against being questioned by a male detective in a position of authority. She hadn't meant to give offence, but Knox had taken it anyway, leading to a slightly frosty car journey.

But things were to get frostier still in the car park itself. As they got out of the car, the door of a white Fiat Panda opened and a familiar figure emerged.

'Good afternoon, Inspector John,' Bishop said. 'Or have you been promoted since I last saw you?'

'Still Inspector, Cheesy. And the afternoon has just become a little less good in the last twenty seconds or so.'

Bishop nodded towards Lucy. 'Aren't you going to introduce me, John?'

Knox bowed in fake apology. 'Of course. This is Detective Sergeant Lucy Grant. Lucy, this is W. Montgomery Bishop, formerly communications officer for the British League, now masquerading as a freelance journalist. Montgomery and I were in the same class at school, I'm ashamed to say.'

Neither Lucy nor Bishop offered a hand for a handshake.

'We saw your article in the paper about Ms Czeslawska,' Lucy said. 'It wasn't very helpful, and needlessly targeted an innocent member of the public.'

Bishop grinned, ignoring the jibe. 'Nice to meet you, too, Detective Sergeant Grant. You and John seem to be spending a lot of time here at St Ninian's. Any titbits for the press, John?'

Knox studied him. 'What did you have in mind?'

'How about an exclusive?'

Knox paused to give the matter a little thought.

'OK, Cheesy. I'll give you one bit of information, just one, and that's all. Don't ask for any more.'

Bishop looked interested. 'OK. Go on.'

'Somebody's died in there.'

Bishop chuckled. 'People do that all the time in care homes and hospitals. Is that supposed to be news?'

'I promised you one bit of news. You promised not to ask for any more. I've kept my part of the bargain,' Knox said. 'Sorry, Cheesy, but we're busy,' he added, turning his back on the journalist and ushering Lucy into the St Ninian's Reception area.

Bishop's sly grin replaced the chuckle once more. 'No doubt,' he called after them. 'But busy doing what?' Then he added at the top of his voice, laughing out loud, 'The public has a right to know!'

'You don't seem to like each other, do you, John?' Lucy said, rather stating the obvious. 'Does that go back to school days?'

Knox filled her in with some of the background as they sat in Reception waiting for Dr Cartwright to appear.

Lucy studied Knox closely. 'Does he have the ability to be a pest?'

'He probably does, to be honest. I checked him out. Even if he can't cause trouble himself, he knows plenty of people who can. For a start, he can arrange that anything he writes will be on the front page of more than one newspaper.'

'Is that because of this Justin Pearce character? Why does nobody do something about the paymaster then?'

'Pearce? Pretty well untouchable. He's due millions, perhaps even billions, to the UK taxman. He's effectively on the run, spending most of the year either in West Indian tax havens or on one of his two luxury yachts. That's why he needs highly-paid stooges like Bishop, to represent him in the media. And Bishop is a journalist of sorts, spewing out racist and fascist vitriol in his articles.'

'Wow. You really hate this guy. Should I have heard of him before?'

'You might not have made the connection, but he writes a weekly column for the *Daily Mail* – he's their ultra-right correspondent. Or at least he did until the British League got closed down. At that point the *Mail* told him to lie low for a bit. But he'll be back, for sure.'

'Jesus – that guy? I had a vision of a man in his seventies, but instead he's… he's this old school pal of yours?'

'He's no pal of mine.'

'Whatever… I'm shocked, John. He's evil. He did that fake exposé of cheap illegal immigrant workers on building sites a few months back. Full of stuff about eastern Europeans coming in by the lorryload, 'taking British workers' jobs', that sort of stuff.'

'That's the one. Totally fictitious, but it didn't stop more than a dozen foreign nationals from being put in hospital by vigilante groups. Women like Magda Czeslawska are easy targets for the Montgomery Bishops of this world.'

'So it would be good to avoid making an enemy of him, then?'

'Ah…' Knox looked at the floor sheepishly. 'I'm afraid it's a bit late for that, Lucy.'

Just at that moment Cartwright arrived and both police officers were glad to reach the safer ground of gathering evidence. Cartwright was more cooperative than Wolstencroft, and a good deal more forthcoming about the health of the two remaining patients.

'Of course I understand you'd like to hear whatever these two can tell you, Inspector,' the doctor was saying as they made their way towards the little room where Martha Ramsay and Myles Cherry had now been moved. 'They're together. Company for each other, although to be honest I'm not sure what 'company' means for these two. Martha Ramsay hasn't a clue what day of the week it is, and we've been forced to sedate Myles Cherry heavily. He's in lots of discomfort.'

'We'd heard,' Knox said.

'He might not last tonight. He's really in poor shape.'

'What are the chances of getting any sense from him?' Lucy asked.

'Minimal, I'm afraid. Most of the time, he's pretty well unconscious. Whenever he becomes vaguely aware of what's happening, he notices how much pain he's in. See for yourself.'

By now they were in the room with the two patients.

'Here are two police officers to see you,' Cartwright said. Coincidentally, it transpired that it was Magda Czeslawska who was tending to Martha Ramsay, and she had just pulled back the curtain around the bed.

'Thank you, my dear,' said Martha to the nurse. Then she said, 'Can I have my raincoat now, please? I think I'd like to go for a walk.' She started to get up but the nurse edged her back to bed, but not before revealing that she was wearing nothing on her lower half. Knox and Grant looked away, embarrassed for the woman. Then she turned on the nurse. 'That woman has stolen my pearls! That woman has stolen my pearls!'

'It's all right, Mrs Ramsay,' the doctor said. 'These are police officers. You're safe now.'

'Arrest that woman!' Martha Ramsay yelled. The nurse simply hushed her, and – to Knox's amazement, began to sing a song in some sort of foreign language, at which Martha became calm. After a moment the nurse realised that Knox and Grant were watching her with bemusement.

'It's a Polish lullaby,' she explained in a thick accent that betrayed her own eastern European origins. 'Mrs Ramsay seems to like it.'

'We're sorry to interrupt you, Magda,' Knox said, deliberately using her first name to try to put the nurse at ease. 'We need to try to speak with Mr Cherry and Mrs

Ramsay, but perhaps we can talk to you later if we may?'

'Do I huff a choice?' Magda glared at Lucy. 'Lust time I tried to help the police, I was accused of murder.'

'Not by us, Magda,' Knox said. 'Sorry about that, anyway. But we're really here to try asking the patients questions. Can we have a moment with them?'

Magda said nothing. She merely shrugged her shoulders and left.

The two officers and the doctor drifted instead towards Cherry's bed. He lay on his back, motionless, an oxygen mask across his face. Thinking of the two occupants of the room, Knox wondered at the futility of keeping someone alive in this state of living death.

'Can I ask Mr Cherry a question?'

'You can try,' the doctor said.

Knox leaned forward, more in hope than expectation. 'Mr Cherry, Mr Cherry. I need to speak to you. About the man who died.' Then, realising what he'd said, he added 'I mean, the one who was stabbed,' although that was a bit misleading as well.

No response. Knox asked again.

He was about to give up when Cherry moved his lips and began to say something. Actually, he was singing.

'Sweet talkin' woman... sweet talkin'...'

'It'll be the morphine,' Dr Cartwright said.

'What is it, anyway, sir?' Lucy asked.

Knox and Cartwright looked at each other as if to compare notes. 'I think it's an old ELO song. Electric Light Orchestra.'

She grinned. 'Is that old-timer music?'

'Slow down... sweet talkin' woman...'

'It's the morphine, I'm sure,' the doctor repeated. 'I don't think he knows what he's saying.'

Knox nodded. He hadn't expected much from Myles Cherry, but somehow he still felt disappointed.

'We have to work on the basis that he's telling us to speak to Martha Ramsay. It might be futile, but we have to try.'

Lucy looked at him and smiled. 'You never know. She might come up with something we can use.'

The doctor shook his head in despair, but ushered them across anyway. Martha Ramsay sat up, looking apprehensive.

'It's all right, Martha, these are nice people. They won't hurt you.' To Knox and Grant, he said quietly, 'And I don't want her upset either, please. We can't be sure what's going on in her mind, and she might be terrified of you two. You'll understand I need to stay and check that she's all right.'

Knox tried to be reassuring. 'Of course. And please, you're welcome to stay. You might be able to help us analyse anything Mrs Ramsay says. Perhaps my colleague DS Grant would seem less of a threat to her?' His suggestion was met with hesitancy from Lucy and another shrug from the doctor. Knox wasn't quite so sure he liked him after all.

But Lucy's attempts to ask questions came to very little. Martha ignored most of the questions, only responding once, to look Lucy fiercely in the eye and ask what she'd done with the money Martha had 'won on the horses yesterday'. Lucy was slightly taken aback, but she'd experienced worse. Then Martha turned towards Knox and said, 'Horrible man, horrible man,' which caused him to raise his eyebrows, too. From the corner of his eye he caught a glimpse of Lucy trying to contain a smile, although she was fully aware that Martha's dementia was tragic, not funny.

'I think we've learned all we can here, doctor,' Knox said, before turning back to Martha and thanking her for her help. Martha stared at him, then said nothing. The detectives thanked the doctor for his time and effort, then Knox asked if they could have a quick word with Magda while she and the police officers all under the same roof.

They found her alone in the staff rest room.

'First of all, Magda,' Knox began, 'I'd like to apologise again for the way you've been treated by the press.'

'Do policemen tell reporters what to write in this country?'

'No.'

'Then why are you saying sorry?'

Knox reckoned that Lucy and he had done their best. The woman in front of them was difficult to age, probably in her early thirties. Knox reckoned she might actually be quite attractive, but her tied-back blonde hair accentuated the severity of her cheekbones and her general attitude exuded an almost animal enmity that could even have been mistaken for fear. To top the whole effect off, she wore glasses through which she stared unblinkingly at everyone she spoke to.

'Thank you for speaking with us, then. We won't take up much of your time,' Lucy said, trying to break the ice a little.

'As I said, I didn't huff a choice.'

Knox smiled: no, he conceded, she probably didn't. But he hoped that she wouldn't mind answering a few questions, and promised it wouldn't take long. They already had all the basic details such as her date of birth in their notes elsewhere. To try and put her at ease, he invited Magda to tell them a little bit about herself – where she grew up, her background, what made her want to become a nurse.

They got slightly more than they had bargained for. Magda, it turned out, was a woman with chips on both shoulders, elbows, knees, everywhere. Born in Krakow, she'd trained as a nurse and when Poland joined the European

Union, she'd come looking for work only to find that her Polish qualification wasn't enough to let work in the NHS and so she was forced to look for other sources of income. She openly admitted that she'd made money by having sex with men – and even a couple of women – although she insisted she was neither a 'prusstichoot' nor a 'sux vurker', because she only ever slept with men she liked and accepted their 'gufts uftervurds'. Then her life had taken an extraordinary turn when she'd been persuaded to join up with a boy-band and some 'uld geezers' in a 'pup concert', which had brought Magda two large sums of money. The first was £5,000 as a fee for her performance; the second was a contract to wear and advertise glasses – the very glasses she was wearing at that moment.

'I thought I recognised you. From the billboards and the TV adverts,' Lucy said. 'Are you very short-sighted?'

'No,' Magda said. 'I huff purfect eyesight. But I like the glasses. And I used some of the money to pay for my training course to allow be to be a nurse in this country. Then I got a job here.'

'Magda,' Knox said quietly, 'what do you think happened in that room?'

'How should I know?' She shrugged her shoulders. 'You're the detuckives.'

'Magda, I get the impression that you don't like the police. What's the problem?'

'The police don't like me.'

'What makes you think that?'

'Brrrcxit.' She spat It out. 'You vunt rrid of me.' The nurse's accent seemed to be getting thicker as she became angrier. 'That reporter vunts rudd of me.'

'*We* don't want rid of you, Magda,' Knox said as gently as he could. 'I promise.'

'Thut's vut they ull say.'

'I promise,' Knox repeated. 'Look, why would we want rid of you? You're helping us with our enquiries, you're helping St Ninian's patients in their final days.'

Magda grunted.

'Magda,' Lucy said, 'Did you like the ward patients?'

Magda looked bemused. 'Like them?' It was a strange question, Knox thought.

Lucy went on. 'Who were your favourite patients? You must have had favourites.'

Magda thought for a moment then said, 'I shouldn't spick ill uff the dead, but Mr Plews vus a hurrible man. Hurrible.'

'That bad?'

'Suddly, ve nurses are nutt allowed to cull people.'

Knox was amazed by the change in Magda's accent as she became angrier.

Lucy seemed affected, too. 'Vutt – I mean, what, about the others, Magda?'

'Mr Cherry – he iss sleazy. Dirty hands. I'm glad he vill die soon. The Robina woman complained all the time. The priest didn't approve of suxx.'

Neither Knox nor Lucy could contain themselves.

'The Reverend Mould? How on earth…?'

'I was giving him a bed burh one day and… well… it huppens. Even when they're dying.'

'It's OK, we get the picture,' Lucy said.

'I said that people at the end of their lives should nutt feel guilty about being huppy. He didn't agree, said it vuss a sin. He said it vuss disgussting. I don't think suxx is disgussting.'

'No, I don't think either DS Grant or I think sex is disgusting either,' Knox assured her.

191

'The priest said I was disgussting.' Magda's glasses allowed her face to be almost expressionless during the telling of the story. 'So I didn't like him. I don't have to like every one of my patients.'

'No, Magda, I suppose I don't like everybody I have to deal with,' Knox said, thinking of Chief Inspector Plews. 'But it's part of the job for people like you and me, isn't it?'

'Yuss.'

Changing tack, Knox said, 'Tell me, Magda, what do you know about Sabatier knives?'

'Butter knives?'

'Sabatier knives. It's a brand name of knife – actually, it's a type of knife. Used by cooks.'

'I do nutt cook, Inspector. I get other people to cook furr me. Is that the kind of knife Mr Plews was killed with?'

Knox didn't want to reveal too much about the kind of weapon used, or the exact causes of death.

'You can't shed any light on the knife?'

'No.'

Knox and Grant decided they were going nowhere with the interview, ended it and thanked Magda for giving up time to speak to them. The nurse didn't say anything by way of acknowledgement, but instead merely stood up and left the room.

'Does she really know nothing, Lucy?' Knox wondered aloud. 'Or is she hiding something? I can't tell.'

'It could be her because her English isn't too great, John.'

'It's strange that,' Knox said. 'She's been in the country for several years.'

'I think that's really her accent. I did some research on her a few days ago.'

'Really?'

'I thought she was familiar. Do you remember that she was once involved with that boy-band, the C-U Jimiz? Before the C-Us became famous had those hit singles?'

'Yes. That nonsense with the rock festival? That was her?'

'I'd already done some research online and I found a few videos of interviews of her on TV shows. *Later with Jools Holland...*, *The Graham Norton Show*, that sort of thing. Her English was even worse then. Mind you, I think she understands what's being said to her perfectly.'

'So is she messing us about?' Knox asked Lucy.

'Haven't a clue.'

'Does she know anything at all about the murder?'

'Haven't a clue.'

'We're pretty clueless all round, Lucy, aren't we?'

'Looks like it. Which doesn't look good for a couple of police officers, I'd say.'

'So we're not going to admit it to anyone,' Knox said. 'Least of all Chief Inspector Plews.'

SEVENTEEN

ONE OF THE MANY GOOD TIPS Knox had picked up from O'Malley was to keep revisiting evidence. That particularly applied when they'd reached some sort of dead end. The Superintendent was fond of saying that 'every crime has a solution – yez just havnae found it yet.' So, if only for the want of something else to do, Knox dropped Lucy back off at the station and set off by himself in the direction of Edinburgh Royal Infirmary just two miles up the same road.

On the way he telephoned ahead to check that Sally MacIntosh, the doctor who had attended the scene of the crime – and who was coincidentally the pathologist who had conducted the post-mortem – was on duty. The receptionist insisted on putting him directly through, and he found himself talking on his hands-free as he was driving.

'I'm sorry, Dr MacIntosh, I really didn't mean to take you away from your work.'

'Not at all, I've just started my lunch break. And is your name really Inspector John Knox?'

'I'm afraid so. Look, I was just on my way up. Is there any chance of seeing you right now?'

'You want to see me right now?' Dr MacIntosh said, doubtfully. 'I'm not sure it's a good idea right now.'

Slightly put off, Knox said, 'I'm sorry, if it's inconvenient...'

The doctor chuckled. 'It's all right, I'm teasing you. You'd be most welcome. I'm about to take a shower…'

Knox realised he was being played along. 'No! I'm sorry, that wasn't what I meant.'

'You wouldn't like to see me in the shower?'

'You know what I meant.'

'I know what you mean. And don't worry, I'll be out of the shower and ready for you by the time you've parked and found your way in.'

Sally MacIntosh was as good as her word. By the time Knox had tracked her down, she was back in what appeared to be fresh scrubs, only her slightly damp hair betraying any sign of the earlier shower. She greeted him with a warm smile and shook his hand.

'Follow me,' she said, leading him to her office. Knox found himself lingering a little too long on her rear view. He couldn't help himself, but the fact was that he couldn't help but notice that she was an attractive woman in a very ordinary, straightforward way. Her blonde hair was hanging down, not yet tied back for her afternoon shift, and in the confined corridor he could smell her post-shower freshness. There was something else there, too, but he couldn't place it.

As she ushered him through her office door, MacIntosh turned and said to him, 'Impressed?'

'Sorry?'

She gave him a quiet, knowing smile. 'What do you think?' Knox wondered if he'd been caught, but then she said, 'My little gymnasium.'

In one corner of the room stood an exercise bike and a rowing machine.

'In my dreams I have a treadmill, too, but that would be a bit extravagant.'

'You exercise every day?'

'Twice, at lunchtime, and before I leave work. Standing around being a pathologist isn't great for the posture, so I take regular exercise. It seems strange, because the hospital's incredibly hot, and there am I, making myself perspire even more. But needs must. Other people get sore backs.'

'And at least you can change your scrubs, it seems,' Knox said, nodding at the doctor's fresh clothing.

By now they were sitting at her desk.

'Well, yes,' she said, 'but you don't think I wear them when I'm exercising, do you? That wouldn't be very nice for the laundry staff, don't you think?' Knox was indeed trying to 'think', when she added, 'Anyway, that's what the lock on the office door is for, isn't it?'

Knox was still trying to take all that in when she suddenly changed subject.

'Have you eaten?'

'I'll be fine, thanks. Please don't let that stop you, though.'

'You shouldn't miss meals, Inspector. Look – you're here professionally, but I'm not a suspect, am I?'

Knox laughed. 'No, I can assure you that you're not a suspect, Dr MacIntosh.'

'Which is what I was going to say. Please call me Sally. Can I call you John? Is that too forward to ask of a policeman?' There was a mischievous look in her eye.

'Certainly not. Please call me John.'

Sally looked down at her lunch, which consisted of three bowls of prepared salads which she'd bought in a local supermarket.

'I don't know what I was thinking. My eyes were bigger than my stomach.'

'It looks lovely, I'll give you that.'

'Sure I can't tempt you?'

'I'll survive thanks. I can do with losing a pound or two of weight. Anyway, you've only got the one fork.'

'I don't mind sharing, really.'

'I'll be fine,' Knox said.

Sally began to dip into one of the salads, a cous-cous mixture. 'What did you want to see me about, John?'

'I'm really trying to go over all the evidence again. See if we've missed anything.'

Sally repeated what she'd said about the time of death. In fact, privately she felt she could really be more precise than she could in her report: almost certainly between 10.15 and 10.45, she said, on the basis of digested food, body temperature and the onset of rigor mortis.

'During which time no one came in or out of the room,' Knox said. 'There's nothing on the CCTV at all.'

'There's nothing at all?' Sally shrugged. 'Well, I'm afraid I can't help you.'

'And Sister Mary's in the clear, arriving at midnight.'

'Oh, completely,' Sally said. 'There's absolutely no chance that death took place anywhere near then.' Sally hesitated for a moment, then went on, 'You seem quite concerned about Sister Mary. You know each other, I understand?'

'We go back a few years.'

Knox did like the look of the pasta salad, but he said nothing. Instead, he asked, 'And the knife?'

'Administered post mortem. A complete red herring,' Sally said. She smiled and looked at him. 'Red herrings are your department, I'm afraid. Unless they're in a salad.'

Suddenly, she looked serious. 'John, are you feeling all right, you look a bit pale?'

'Let me feel your throat.' She reached forwards, felt around his neck and said, 'Hmm. Can I look at your throat?' She picked up a spatula. 'Go on. Let me see. Say 'ah'.'

She stood up and examined his throat.

'Say 'ah' again. Close your eyes this time. You're putting me off, staring at me like that.'

'Sorry.'

Seconds later, Knox tasted a delicious forkful of pasta salad with green pesto and pine nut kernels in his mouth.

'Better?' she asked him.

'Lovely. Thanks. I didn't mean – '

'Look, there's loads. Eat, or else it'll go to waste.'

And remarkably, for the next ten minutes Knox found himself being spoon-fed by Sally MacIntosh, while, for amusement, he did the same for her.

'Are you married, John?'

'No, but I live with someone.'

'Would she be jealous of this?'

Ashamed, Knox realised that it was the first time that he'd considered Alice. He hesitated. 'She might, perhaps.'

'Then I'm sorry I put you in that position.'

'Don't be. I enjoyed it.'

'Perhaps we can share lunch again?'

'I'll bring my own fork next time.'

'That wouldn't be so much fun, would it?'

'No. To be honest, it wouldn't.' It was out before he'd said it. 'I'm sorry. That's not very professional of me. Please accept my apology, Sally.'

She studied him, then a faintly familiar smile played across her lips.

'I really wouldn't worry about it, John. It was my idea.'

Knox took a deep breath. 'Still.'

'Perhaps it wasn't such a good idea then?'

'No, no, that's not what I meant,' he said, flustered. 'I just meant… oh, I don't know what I meant…' Then he said, 'Can we get back to talking about the case?'

'What about the case? Or do you mean 'talk about anything other than sharing lunch with a single fork?' Because if so, I'd suggest that leaves quite a wide range of possibilities. We could talk about the weather, or the traffic on the roads, or that new thriller serial that was on TV last night.'

'Let's see if we can exhaust the case in hand.'

'OK.' She sat up brightly with wide open eyes, pretending to be an eager schoolgirl in class.

'Was it murder?'

'Is this twenty questions?'

'I've no idea, Sally. I'm just trying to sort this out. Was it murder?'

'Probably. Almost certainly.'

'Enough to convict in a court?'

'Not a chance. Plews definitely died of a heart attack. I can say for sure that someone tried to suffocate him as well. But I can't prove that someone had tried to suffocate him immediately beforehand to cause him to have a heart attack.' She smiled mischievously. 'That's two questions.'

'Could one of the other patients have killed him on their own?'

'No. It would have required at least two of them, and probably three.'

'What about the knife?'

'Definitely post mortem. As was the… rearrangement of his pyjamas. I'll spare you the gory details, but it's all about secretions. That was just for effect.'

'And you say that death took place between 10.15 and 10.45? No one either entered or left the room in that period.'

'That's when death occurred, John. I promise you that.'

Knox sighed. 'So the killers were definitely patients in that room.'

'You're the detective, John.'

'Not much of one, it seems.'

'That's not what I hear,' Sally said. Knox was flattered, but wondered which of his colleagues might have been talking about him. It was a little unnerving that Sally MacIntosh seemed to know even that much about him when he knew nothing about her. Not much of a detective, right enough, he said to himself.

**

Chief Inspector Maximilian Plews was not a happy man. He sat in his chair, clearly expecting Knox to stand to attention. Knox took the safe option and obliged.

'Where have you been, Knox?'

Knox gave a non-committal response saying that he'd been following up some leads relating to his father's death.

'Knox, I told you before,' Plews barked. 'Nothing's going to bring him back. And anyway, I gather that the knife didn't kill him, he actually had a heart attack. It wasn't murder. So why do you insist on wasting so much time on him?'

Plews was clearly unaware that Sally MacIntosh's post mortem also suggested that his father had suffered the heart attack while being suffocated with a pillow. Knox decided not to enlighten him, and instead decided to keep it simple.

'Don't you think we should be investigating the fact that a dead body was found with a knife in its back, sir?'

'Only if there's nothing more urgent to look into.'

Knox sighed inwardly. 'Such as the car thefts, sir?'

'Knox, I know you're new to detective work, so perhaps I should make some allowances. But even you should be able to see that the spate of car thefts is clearly the work of a criminal gang. These old people in the nursing home were all going to die anyway. Get your priorities right.'

Working with Plews for so long had trained Knox not to argue with him any more than necessary.

'Sometimes I wonder about you, Knox. Perhaps you've been promoted too soon. Or perhaps beyond your capabilities. Just because you've got a degree – what's it in, remind me?'

'History, sir. Glasgow.'

'There you go. Something entirely worthless from a second-rate institution. Just because you have some entirely worthless degree shouldn't give you any special privileges in the promotion stakes. Good old-fashioned spade work, that's what should count. Ask Superintendent O'Malley, I'm sure he'll agree with me.'

'I will, sir. I'll ask him.'

Plews lowered his voice. 'Look, Knox, perhaps I ought to share something with you. I'm under a lot of pressure myself from outside.'

'Is this your brother, sir?'

Plews looked even more disgusted than usual.

'Teddy? Do you think I care about him? All he's concerned about is the reputation of that precious auction house he runs. I keep telling him that one day he'll go to jail for selling on stolen property, but he just laughs at me. Calls me 'PC Plod'. Of course I remind him that I'm a Chief Inspector, but he just laughs all the more. People have so little respect for the police these days, Knox, but one expects more from one's own brother, even someone in the auction trade like Theodore. By the way, brother Theodore really hates that nun you used to be friendly with. I'm relieved you have a girlfriend and don't see her any more.'

Knox said nothing.

'Anyway, exactly what are you doing to catch the car thieves?'

'I've got my best team onto it, sir. My best people.' Behind his back, Knox crossed his fingers, hoping that Plews wouldn't ask for any more details, but, just in case, he drew the Chief Inspector back to what he was saying earlier. 'You were going to tell me about the pressure you were under, sir.'

Plews cleared his throat. 'One of the Jaguars was stolen belonged to Major David MacFarlane.'

Knox looked at his notebook. 'Yes, so I see. Stolen on the 18th of last month, one of the first thefts. Lucy Grant interviewed Major MacFarlane. You know him?'

'MacFarlane is the Captain of the Royal Edinburgh Club. You'll know it as Dirleton, but the 'R.E.C.' is its proper title.'

'Dirleton? The golf course where they play the Open sometimes?'

'There are actually two courses there, but, yes, that's the club. The thing is, I'm not one of the 'in crowd' in the club. Teddy and I don't really have many friends there. Recently, I even accidentally overheard someone suggesting that perhaps black balls should be put in our lockers.'

'I don't understand, sir.'

'No, I don't someone of your background would. It means we're 'not their sort'. They'd ask us to leave.'

'That's not very nice of them, sir,' Knox said, thinking at the same time, *I can quite understand how they feel.*

'Anyway, the day after MacFarlane's car was stolen, I received a telephone call from the man himself, asking me to 'give it my special attention'. Obviously it'll do my status in the club no harm at all if I – you – solve this case.'

'But your own car's been stolen as well, sir.'

'Yes, Knox, that doesn't make me look very clever, does it? So far, MacFarlane doesn't know it. And he mustn't find out.'

Knox said nothing for a moment, trying to take in the full implications of what he was being told.

'OK, sir, I understand. I'll be discreet.'

'Good man, Knox. I knew I could count on you,' Plews said. Then he casually shape-shifted back into his normal mode and dismissed Knox. 'You may go,' he said curtly.

Knox was glad to leave. But as he reached the door, he suddenly stopped and turned round. 'I've never heard you say you play golf before, sir. Have you been playing long?'

Plews looked up. 'Golf? Stupid game. But the R.E.C. is a good place to take one's friends for lunch. Very good for one's career prospects. You should try it sometime.'

Knox trembled with horror as he thought about it.

'I'll bear that in mind, sir.'

EIGHTEEN

JUST NORTH OF THE Queensferry Crossing there is a series of slip roads, one of which leads not into Dunfermline, Inverkeithing, Rosyth or one of the more distant Fife towns, but instead to the South Fife Industrial Park. The Industrial Park – an oxymoron if ever there was one – houses the showrooms and service centres for no fewer than seventeen different car manufacturers, one of which is Jaguar.

Most people who visit a car showroom are just having a casual look around, but when the showroom itself is slightly off the beaten track, there's a greater chance that any passer-by is actually seriously interested in buying. Catalina Dominguez and Franciszka Grywaczewski were employed by McConnell's Motors because as students they would work for less than the statutory minimum wage, and because 'Kat' and 'Frankie' were prepared to work on Thursdays. Business was dead on Thursdays. None of the full-time sales staff wanted to work on a day when there was no chance of a sale.

That particular Thursday afternoon, the weather had been simply dreadful. As usual, Kat and Frankie were on their own. The girls didn't mind: they were good at entertaining themselves, dancing to music on Spotify, played through the showroom speakers. On more daring occasions, they'd even taken photos of each other in their underwear, draped across the Jaguars in seventies-style poses for the benefit of their respective boyfriends. Today, however, was an occasion for their third great distraction: cake. Kat, as it happened, had learned cake-baking skills from her mother and that very morning she had arrived at work with a large plastic tin containing a Victoria sponge that she'd carefully produced the previous evening. The girls only knew each other through working together, but gradually they'd become firm friends, even clubbing together on weekend evenings. Usually they did so with their boyfriends, but it was much more fun when there was just the two of them, not least because it gave them more to talk about as they tried to pass away the time at work during the week. The girls were therefore a little put out when two customers came into the showroom within minutes of each other.

The first was a designer-stubbled man of no more than forty, perhaps less, in an open-necked shirt and a slightly shabby brown suit. Frankie felt he looked suspicious, so she went over straight away to ask if she could be of assistance. To her great surprise the man claimed to be looking for a second-hand Jaguar, perhaps two or three years old, but he had precise requirements. His partner, he explained, was fussy about colour and hated maroon in any form; in addition he preferred a wooden dashboard. Learning that the partner was a 'he' was enough to unsettle Frankie slightly, not because she was homophobic but instead because she realised that unbuttoning her blouse a couple of buttons would have little effect on her chances of selling a car. She'd have to rely on proper sales technique.

The customer, who gave his name as Roebuck, insisted that Frankie look up the McConnell Motors database to see if any of their other eighteen garages across the United Kingdom had anything in stock. While she was doing that, the customer threw Frankie a true curve-ball: he asked her for a complete printout of all the Jaguars available in the entire country. Frankie wasn't sure, but when Roebuck pointed out that he was just interested in the specifications, he understood the prices might be confidential until he came to show an interest, she relaxed slightly and set about the task.

With almost perfect timing, a tall, elegant, silver-haired woman in a red dress entered and began to wander around the showroom looking at the cars on display. With Frankie fully occupied, it was left to Kat to drift across, not that she expected the woman to be seriously interested. In fact, her first approach set things off on the wrong track straight away.

'Excuse me, madam, but are you and that gentleman connected?'

The lady in the red dress said nothing at first, then slowly removed the reading glasses as she turned to face Kat.

'Excuse me, young lady, but do I look as if I'm with that gentleman?'

'I just wondered if…'

'If perhaps…'

'I was his wife? Was that what you were going to say?'

'I'm sorry – '

'You do realise he's gay, don't you?'

'How would I have known – ?'

'Or perhaps you thought I was his mother? Was that it?' The lady in the red dress was calm and clinical. 'You think I'm old enough to be his mother?'

'I'm so sorry, really – '

'Is this how they teach you to sell cars, young lady? Insult the customer?'

'I'm sorry – '

'We're not connected, no. I'm here because I'm interested in buying a car. Isn't that what you sell, young lady?'

'Yes, I'm sorry,' Kat said. 'What kind of car were you thinking of?'

'A Jaguar would be nice. Isn't that what you sell here?'

'Yes, madam, I'm sorry, of course we sell Jaguars here. Did you have a particular car in mind?'

'A cheap one, preferably.'

'I'm not sure if we have any cheap ones, madam. How much were you prepared to spend?'

"Cheap" is a relative term.'

The lady was in no mood to relent.

'Only a few thousand. How about that?'

Kat looked crestfallen. There was no used car in the showroom priced at under £20,000, a fact she wanted to break gently to the silver-haired lady.

'I'm not sure we have any in stock in your price range, I'm afraid. Must it be a Jaguar, madam?'

'Do you sell any other kind of car?'

Kat gulped. 'No.'

'So you're trying to get rid of me?'

'No, madam, I promise you're welcome here,' Kat said rather clumsily, perhaps now aware that two teenage boys had appeared in the showroom and were opening every car in turn and sitting inside. 'I'm sorry. I was merely trying to help you establish what car might best suit your needs.'

'I've told you, young lady, a Jaguar, but not too expensive,' the silver haired woman said. She looked across the showroom pointedly at the two boys, who were climbing in and out of some of the cars on display. 'And a clean one, preferably.'

Kat took that as a cue to attempt to get the boys to leave and approached them. She wasn't entirely successful at first, as the boys ducked and weaved between the cars in order to avoid her. She called after them, threatening to call the police, but the boys responded with 'Back to your own country!' comments of the type she'd heard so many times before during her stay in Britain. Kat, however, was a resourceful woman, and finally her patience snapped. She pulled out her mobile phone and began to take photographs of the boys. Incensed, they railed at her that she had no right to take photographs of them, but now Kat was in full flow and starting to dial the police number. The boys raced out of the showroom, at which she made only a half-hearted effort to pursue them.

By now, the silver haired woman was genuinely feeling sorry for Kat, and apologised for the treatment these Scottish boys had given her. Not all Scottish people were like that, she insisted. Kat explained that she'd experienced a fair bit of abuse in Dunfermline, but she'd become fairly used to it. Relations between Kat and her customer were definitely thawing, and then she added:

'Listen, Mrs…'

'Smith. The name's Smith.'

'Listen, Mrs Smith. If you're looking for a Jaguar that's a little cheaper than the ones we have here, my boss keeps a few business cards for another dealer on the Ferry Road. His name is Jimmy Martin. He repairs and sells all sorts of cars, but I know he particularly likes Jaguars and drives one himself. Perhaps someone like that would be more likely to have something in your price range.'

Kat moved across to a desk in the showroom corner and produced a small business card from its top drawer.

'Why, that's very thoughtful of you. Thank you. I'll look in on him tomorrow.'

'Please don't tell anyone I gave it to you, though. I'd get into dreadful trouble. I might even lose my job.'

'Oh my, that would never do! But who's going to know?' The silver haired lady gazed all around: Kat, Frankie and she were the only ones left – the man in the brown suit who had described himself as 'Mr Roebuck' had departed. 'You've been enormously helpful,' she added, making her exit.

'Would you like tea, John? Earl Grey? Lapsang? Darjeeling?'

Knox hesitated. In truth he'd have preferred a cup of coffee but he didn't want to offend his host. It had been a long hard day but the message had been very insistent: please come round to my house on your way home from work.

'I'll have whatever you're having yourself, Mary. Please don't go to any trouble on my behalf, though.'

Mary glided through to her kitchen, returning a few minutes later with a pot of tea for herself and a cafetière of coffee for himself.

'Mary, I said – '

'People are so transparent when they would rather have coffee, John. I've made it quite strong for you, too. I haven't brought any milk. You still drink it black, is that right?' As usual, they shared the sofa that looked out past the grand piano onto the back garden, and Knox could almost taste her Chanel No. 5.

Knox smiled. 'That's right. And thanks.' He took a sip, then said, 'So, what do you have for me?'

Mary produced one of her Mona Lisa smiles. He could tell she was feeling triumphant. Knox had seen the look often enough in the years he'd known her, enough to wonder if it was truly seemly for a woman of God to look so smug. But, then, as he reminded himself, Mary Madeleine Scarlett Maxwell-Hume was no ordinary nun, and the Sisters of Mary of the Sacred Cross was no ordinary religious order.

From behind her end of the sofa, Mary produced a large folder, roughly A3 in size, in which she had collected a number of computer printouts.

'These, John, are the used car buying and selling transactions from every Jaguar dealer in Scotland. A kind young lady in Dunfermline provided them for me.'

'You travelled all the way to Dunfermline to investigate our missing Jaguars? And how did you – ?'

'It's better you don't ask, John. Remember that I can go to places you can't.'

Knox had no idea whether she was answering his first question or his second. He hesitated, and she carried on.

'Many of these Jaguar dealers actually have branches across the United Kingdom, and they're listed, too. However I don't think that our missing cars have been driven south of the border. They might have been moved there some other way, but I'm pretty certain that they've disappeared off the road up here. At least one of them would have been spotted on CCTV somewhere.'

'OK,' Knox said, pointing at the sheets, 'but that looks like a lot of cars you have there.'

'It looks like it, but it's not. First of all, this is all the used cars that the entire company has sold over the last three years. These companies never seem to destroy any data. We're only interested in anything bought or sold in the last four months.

'Secondly, these garages take other brands of car for trade-in. There are lots of cars on here that aren't Jaguars. Finally, of course, the stolen cars all had personalised number plates.'

'People who drive Jaguars rather do tend to go in for that sort of thing,' Knox said.

Mary continued. 'However it's also true that personalised number plate cars have already had their car registration plates changed once. It's therefore to be expected that it'll happen again. I don't think you can trust all the information you see on these sheets, John.'

'Perhaps not. But the cars also have Vehicle Identification Numbers, VINs. We'd spot those.'

Mary sighed. 'John, for a policeman you're remarkably trusting. A little bit of editing and the VIN can be changed on a car. It's what you change it to that matters.' She paused for dramatic effect.

After a moment Knox took the hint. 'Go on.'

'Someone is creating fake VIN numbers for these Jaguars. The reason that all the stolen cars are so similar is that the replacement VIN identity plates have already been manufactured somewhere. Once that's done, and you produce fake V5 Car Registration documents to match – '

'– And, that's easy, I give you that –'

'It's simply a matter of creating a new number plate for each car.'

'But why does nobody at DVLA spot the fake VIN and registration numbers when the cars are bought and sold?'

'Ah, now that's the hundred million dollar question,' Mary said, breaking off to add, 'Dollars are such a brash currency, don't you agree?' She screwed her nose up in distaste.

'I've never given it much thought, Mary. Do you have any theories on how our supposedly highly-efficient Driving and Vehicle Licensing Agency might be letting these cars slip through the net?'

'I think there are a couple of possibilities, one more likely than the other.'

'Go on.'

'It could be that more Jaguars are being stolen than you know of, or perhaps some scrapped or written-off cars are coming back to life. However, that would require a lot of Jaguar cars.'

'And the other possibility is?'

'Someone has hacked into DVLA and created a whole list of fake registration numbers and VINs. Perhaps they're altering existing records.'

'That's impossible. Nobody could do that, Mary. I presume that's the less likely option.'

The Mona Lisa smile returned. 'You think so, John?'

'Mary, if the combined efforts of the Russians, Americans, Chinese, North Koreans and any number of terrorist organisations can't hack into the government computer at Swansea, how would a cheap car thief do it?'

'First of all, John, a Jaguar isn't a cheap car – '

'Mary, you know what I mean.'

'The answer is simple, John: why would any terrorist hack into DVLA? It's not going to bring the country to a halt. So counter-intelligence agencies pay no attention to anything going on there. I can assure you of that.'

'Why are you so sure?'

'Because I've been… studying the matter for a while.'

It took Knox a moment to catch on to what Mary had just said. He looked at her; she looked away guiltily.

'Mary,' he said, 'have you learned some IT skills suddenly?'

She bristled. 'Just because you've never noticed before doesn't mean to say that I can't find my way around a computer. Is it because I'm a woman? Have you suddenly gone all sexist on me, John?'

'Stop trying to deflect me, Mary. You know that's not true. I'm asking you – have you found a way around the DVLA computer in Swansea? Yes or no?'

She hesitated.

'Do you really want me to tell you the answer to that? After all, you might have to arrest me.'

'I don't want to arrest you, Mary.'

'Then don't ask so many questions.'

'It's what policemen do, Mary.'

'Good police officers ask the right questions, John, I've told you that before.'

Knox sighed.

'So, Mary… suppose you tell me what the right questions might be.'

'Ask me if I know who's hacked into DVLA lately.'

'Lately! You mean it happens a lot?'

'All the time, as a matter of fact.'

'So… do you know who's been hacking in? Can you give me some names?'

'I can provide you with a list of IP addresses, the identity unique to each computer, that's all. And I can tell you that those IP addresses are based here in Edinburgh. The rest would be up to you. All sorts of stuff gets in there, most of it by accident, I should point out. Anti-virus, clean-up software, inappropriate access by the police themselves.'

'What do you mean – 'inappropriate access by the police themselves'?'

Mary explained that in most organisations staff were trained to interrogate a computer database in a particular way, but that very few people actually listened properly at the training sessions. As a result, some of them – accidentally or otherwise – found a different way to use it. Holding down random combinations of keys could achieve almost anything, she insisted.

By now, though, Knox mainly wanted to know if Mary had been breaking the law.

'I told you, John, good policemen only ask the right questions.'

'OK, I won't ask. But could you please make sure you don't get caught doing something illegal, just for my sake?'

Mary smiled innocently. 'John! Me – get caught? How could you think such a thing? But anyway, I'm only guiding you on where to look.'

She then went on to do just that. Opening the folder, she spread its contents of computer printouts on a coffee table in front of them. The printouts turned out to be lists of all the occasions that the Vehicle Licensing computer database had been looked at remotely, either legitimately or otherwise during the past six weeks. To Knox, they just looked like a series of utterly incomprehensible letters, numbers and punctuation marks, but Mary explained how the gibberish could be decoded to reveal the date and time of the computer activity, as well as some of the information being sought each time. Each enquiry contained a request for information about a car's registration plate, age, Vehicle Identification Number, its make and model and colour of course; plus the car's owner, date of birth, address and so on. Most of the time, of course, the activity was legitimate – the police, other government agencies and so on. But Mary had already worked out how to identify those legitimate uses of the DVLA database: they came from a limited number of IP addresses.

'You can guess which ones come from legitimate organisations,' she said. 'They often use servers and a handful of static IP addresses that don't keep changing. They're also the most common ones. Thankfully, because there's an awful lot of them. So it's the others we're interested in.'

Mary had picked out a number of entries with a green highlighter pen. The common feature of each was that they were enquiries about Jaguar cars, including all of the ones that had been stolen recently.

'Are you saying the theft of these Jaguars have been individually planned, Mary?'

'Tell me when DAV 1E was stolen,' she said.

Knox looked up his notes. '3rd March.'

'There are enquiries about it on the 24th and 25th of February,' she said, triumphantly. 'How about MAV 1S?'

'26th March.'

'Searched for on the 6th.'

Knox sat back. 'Are they all like that?'

'I think so. The Chief Inspector's car and his brother's were both researched on the same day, six weeks ago.'

Knox sat in silence for a while, then he said, 'Can I keep this file?'

Mary recoiled in horror. 'Oh, I don't think so, John. Do you want to get me into trouble? There would be so many questions, after all.'

Knox chuckled. 'Yes, I suppose there would. So…'

'You're going to have to pretend to do the entire search yourself all over again. Or perhaps get someone else to do it for you. Why not get the Chief Inspector to order it? It'll make it look as if you're making lots of effort on his behalf. And he'll hardly say he thinks it's not an effort worth making, can he now? Not for his precious Jaguar, can he? And he'll look good in the eyes of brother Teddy.'

'No, I don't think so. But then how do we catch the criminals after that, Mary?'

'Aren't you supposed to be the policeman, John?'

Now it was Knox's turn to smile quietly. 'I thought you said that a good police officer knows what the right questions are.'

Mary smiled back. 'Touché, John.' She reached over and touched him gently on the sleeve, an intimate gesture he found surprisingly pleasant. 'I think we're making progress, though, John. Don't you?'

NINETEEN

WHEN KNOX RETURNED HOME, he found that Alice had been home already and gone out again, leaving only a note to say that she had agreed to go out with some colleagues from school for a drink. She would be late: don't wait up. No kiss at the end.

There was no mention of any planned evening meal. He racked his memory for anything they might have discussed. Knox had no wish to upset Alice again by forgetting the menu, but this time he was fairly sure that nothing had ever been decided. He was cooking for himself. A rummage around in the cupboard revealed a jar of pesto that was close to its use-by date. To go with it he could finish off the remaining odds and ends of a couple of different packs of pasta. He needed a shower before that, though, and he wandered through to the bedroom, intending to take his clothes off but instead collapsed fully-clothed, exhausted, on the bed.

He woke almost two hours later, somehow managing to feel even more tired than when he'd first come home. This time he stripped off, stood in the shower for fully ten minutes, then forced himself to cook and eat. Normally both the shower and food were simple pleasures that Knox enjoyed immensely, but tonight his sole aim was to get them both over with, hang up his suit properly, brush his teeth, then flop into bed once and for all. He only just made it before a long deep sleep overcame him.

O'Malley had told him not to come in until 11.00 – 'Yezur workin' tae hard son' – and Knox was glad of the chance of a long lie-in. But the result was that he didn't hear Alice come home, nor did he hear her leave in the morning. Come to think of it, he asked himself, did she ever come home at all?

**

Next day, the news from St Ninian's was not good.

In a literal sense, the news was awful in that Bishop had been up to his tricks again, penning an article for the *Evening News* that had been widely syndicated to other papers – and now to local television and radio as well. Written in the form of 'unanswered questions about strange deaths at Edinburgh care home', the reports implied foul play in the demise of several patients without actually providing any hard evidence. Part of the problem lay in the fact that whenever a reporter asked the specific question, 'have there been any suspicious deaths at St Ninian's lately?' everyone on the St Ninian's staff had been given strict instructions to say nothing. So Bishop had simply used the highly effective 'what are they hiding?' approach to keep his readers informed. Once again, the journalist targeted 'the immigrant Pole' Magda Czeslawska, but now he was also hinting that Helen Wolstencroft must be orchestrating some sort of cover-up.

The news about the patients wasn't any better. Myles Cherry continued to drift in and out of consciousness, but was saying very little that made sense when awake. Martha Ramsay made no sense whether she was awake or not – she was rambling about a woman she knew. But aware that they had to be seen to be doing something, Knox suggested that Lucy pop in to ask a few more questions – any questions – of the staff. According to the duty roster that the police had been supplied with, both Magda Czeslawska and Helen Wolstencroft would be on duty, they knew, so Lucy could at least speak to the staff who were present on the night of the murder. Knox wondered if Lucy's female touch might be more productive if he weren't present himself. Privately Lucy wondered if Knox was simply trying to avoid the flak, both from the press outside St Ninian's and from the staff inside.

In the event, the visit proved easier than she'd expected. A large van was making a delivery just as she was arriving, and her entry into St Ninian's went unnoticed by the gaggle of reporters until she was sufficiently far enough into the building that she could ignore them.

Lucy's plan had been to speak to Wolstencroft first, but when she arrived the doctor was busy, talking with some recently-bereaved relatives. Instead she asked to speak to Magda, ready to say sorry for yet more media harassment. But the nurse dismissed her apology.

'It is nutt your fault. They urr journalists. They just make up the news. I met that verry hurrible vun, he's the vurrst.' Not for the first time, Magda's accent became heavier as she became more animated.

'That'll be Montgomery Bishop,' Lucy said. 'I'd agree, he's horrible. Thankfully, I've just managed to avoid him.'

'He is a sudd man. Because he is so hurrible, nobody loves him so he is very lonely. That makes him even more hurrible. Last night when I was leaving he asked me in a loud voice if I had once been a prostitute.'

'He did?' Lucy should have been shocked, but she knew how some of the press worked. 'Did… you say anything back?'

'I told him that I have never been a prostitute. I only have sex with people I like. And so I wasn't available to him.'

Lucy chuckled. 'Nice one. How did he respond to that?'

'He said nothing. Tried to luff at me. But the other reporters laughed a lot.'

Magda seemed to be in a talkative mood, especially when Lucy produced a trump card, a large box of chocolate assorted biscuits. Magda, it transpired, could smile broadly when chocolate was involved.

'Thunk you,' she said. 'I like chocolate. Chocolate gives pleasure without usking for anything buck in return. Unlike men.'

Lucy chuckled. 'Perhaps I want something in return, too, Magda.'

'You vunt sucks?' she asked, astonished. 'I vill have sucks with women, but I don't like it so much.'

Lucy laughed. 'I'm sorry, Magda. It was a joke. I don't want your body.'

'But you like women, don't you?'

Lucy's jaw dropped.

'I kun tull,' Magda said. 'It's OK. I dunt mind if you dunt. And thunk you for the biskuts.'

Flustered, Lucy said, 'I'm sorry, Magda, but can we change the subject? I'm here to ask some more questions about the night of Mr Plews's death.'

Magda said she was due a break and suggested that they try out some of the biscuits. Grant decided that building a few bridges would be time well spent, and instead offered to buy Magda coffee and cake in a little café down the road from St Ninian's.

Over coffee, Magda said, no, her night shift didn't take her into the Murray Room unless one of the alarms went off. No, no alarm went off that night. No, she'd no idea how anyone could have got past her desk and down the corridor and enter the Murray Room. Yes, Sister Mary Maxwell-Hume was the only visitor, coming on the stroke of midnight as she always did. She repeated that Plews was a truly horrible man, 'worse even than the journalist'. Lucy asked her about the knife but Magda repeated that she didn't know what a Sabatier knife was, nor where to get one.

Lucy asked Magda where her desk had been in relation to the corridor. Magda's desk hadn't moved at all, it seemed. It sat facing the entrance hall, at right angles to the corridor door. Anyone coming in, like Sister Mary, would simply have to pass right in front of the desk and almost certainly say hello. The far end of the corridor was blocked up by the new building extension work.

'What happens if you need to go the toilet, Magda?'

'Why should I go to the toilet?'

'Well… you know….'

'I don't usually need to go when I'm on shift. I do a pee in my break time. When do you do a pee?'

'We're not here about my toilet habits, Magda.'

'Yuss,' Magda said triumphantly. 'And you're investigating Mr Plews's death. Do you want to know about my number twos, too?'

'No, no, I'm sorry, Magda, I get the picture.'

'You vunt a picture?'

'That's not what I meant – '

'This time it is I who is joking,' Magda said, proudly.

Lucy apologised once more, explaining that she wasn't trying to pry into the nurse's private affairs. But she couldn't help adding that toilet habits, like sexual preferences, were a private matter. To Lucy's surprise, Magda apologised, too, admitting that she had been needlessly rude to a woman who had brought her chocolate biscuits.

Over a second mug of coffee, Lucy discovered that virtually everything that Magda did was motivated by money or sex. She'd come from Poland to Scotland to make money. She'd taken on modelling jobs to make money. Although she insisted she was not a prostitute, she enjoyed being paid for something that she enjoyed doing a lot – namely, having sex. She would never take money for sex if she didn't enjoy it. Women were generally not customers, but she'd 'done it' with a couple of women customers simply to see how nice it could be, and been pleasantly surprised: but that was as far as it went.

Lucy wanted to know if Magda had any long-term partner, but the answer turned out to be no. No man, it seemed, had been anything other than a disappointment to her, which Lucy thought was a little harsh.

'Do you like the man Knox?' Magda asked.

'Honestly? I sometimes wish I weren't gay. But we are what we are, Magda? Don't you agree?'

'Vise vurds. I am Polish, you are a lesbian.'

Still taken aback by Magda's directness, Lucy said, 'Perhaps you should also be the police officer.'

'You get better pay,' Magda replied. 'Meanwhile I clean up piss and shit. Can we swup?'

Once again Grant found herself apologising that it didn't seem a possibility. But she acknowledged that a few weeks in a care home might teach her, Lucy, a thing or two. Including never to take life for granted. Magda nodded.

'I honestly don't think anyone else could have got into the Murray Room where Mr Plews died,' Magda said. As she suddenly became more cooperative, Lucy noticed that Magda's Polish accent softened markedly. She took Lucy through all the stages of the evening rounds, and they studied the activity log for the evening, which involved looking over a couple of pages on the computer screen yet again. Nothing at all between nine in the evening and midnight, when Sister Mary had discovered the victim's body. Unlikely as it seemed, the murderer had to have been in the room: one of the other patients. And both Lucy and Magda had to acknowledge that there was no sign of anyone in the corridor during the period when Mr Plews had been killed. All, in all, it was a mystery, Magda said.

'And then there vurr two,' Magda pointed out. 'Like the murder story. The dirty man and the mad woman.'

'Will Mr Cherry last much longer?'

'No. Days at the most. When will we be able to use the Murray Room again?' The murder room huss been a crime scene for over a week now. 'Our managers say that people who need to come here. Ve need that extension buddly.'

Lucy was once again reminded that death waits for no one. Care homes like St Ninian's did an essential job and the loss of eight beds was almost catastrophic.

'I don't know, Magda,' she said quietly. 'It's not my decision.'

'Nuck's?'

It took Lucy a moment to mentally translate that into 'Knox'. 'Perhaps. I don't know. I'll ask him, I promise.' In truth, she could see little reason not to re-open the Murray Room, for all the evidence they'd turned up in it. But she wasn't admitting that to a witness from St Ninian's. 'I appreciate that there are people waiting to come here. I'm only glad that I'm not one of them.'

Magda didn't reply, not that there was any need to.

'In the meantime, I'm sorry to be rude but I still need to go back to St Ninian's again and speak to Dr Wolstencroft,'

Lucy said, standing up. 'I'm sorry, but I might have to come back again to ask more questions, I'm afraid.'

Magda shrugged her shoulders and thanked Lucy for the coffee and cake. Then, slipping her coat on, she left without another word, merely a quizzical glance through her entirely pointless, but expensive, spectacles.

***

Grant's conversation with Helen Wolstencroft got off to a curious start.

Lucy knew that Wolstencroft was in a same-sex relationship, but the doctor – lacking Magda's sixth sense for these things – was unaware that Lucy herself swung the same way. At the outset, Knox had found her somewhat prickly and defensive, and Lucy wondered if Helen Wolstencroft might relate to a 'sister' better.

'I gather you were here earlier,' Wolstencroft said. 'I'm sorry I wasn't available.'

'I'm aware you're busy,' Lucy began. 'It's very good of you to spare me a little of your time.' In fact, both knew full well that the police could insist on interviewing any material witness to a crime, but a little soft soap rarely did any harm.

Wolstencroft didn't reply to that, but instead said, 'I see that the press are keeping an eye on us. Crawling all over us, to be exact.'

'I'm sorry, doctor. So long as they're in a public area and not breaking any laws, there's not a lot we can do. We'll try and keep them as far away as possible. I hope you'd inform us immediately if they crossed the line or you felt threatened.'

'I think these chaps know exactly where 'the line', as you call it, is, and stay just on the legal side of it and no more.

But my duty is to protect my patients and my staff, and I'd like to get rid of them. These latest headlines are simply not good for morale.'

'I understand, doctor. And we're doing our best.'

'Hmm,' Wolstencroft said, then continued, 'Where's the Inspector today?' Wolstencroft asked. 'Too busy?' Hostility oozed from every pore.

'It's not the only case we're working on, but that's not why I'm here,' Grant said. 'John likes me to look at cases independently from himself, sometimes. He reckons that other colleagues looking at things from other angles can shed all sorts of new lights.' She used her superior's first name deliberately to emphasise how well they got on.

Wolstencroft drew herself up straight on her chair and tried to look ready for business.

'Go on, then.'

'OK. There were eight patients in the room that night, including the victim. Which of them, in your opinion, was physically capable of killing Mr Plews?'

'If they were awake? Any of them. Even Eileen Lamb.'

'The woman who had dementia and on whose body the victim was found?'

'Definitely. She only had to be awake momentarily and think she was being raped. It would just take a well-aimed swipe with a knife, and she wouldn't have to know what she was doing. She would have been very confused. Some people are quite strong in the last moments before they die.'

'There was the problem of how she would get hold of the knife, though.'

'Indeed. But you didn't ask me to do the police work in that question, Detective Sergeant Grant. Doesn't that apply to all of the possible suspects?'

Lucy nodded. Clearly, Wolstencroft had forgotten that the cause of death wasn't the stab wound, and Lucy had no intention of reminding her at the moment.

'What of the others?'

One by one, the doctor took Lucy through the remaining six patients. In each case, the answer was the same – theoretically possible but highly unlikely. Lucy began to wish she'd never come, because she seemed to be gathering suspects, not eliminating them. And most of these suspects were dead, as well.

'Tell me about this new wing that's being built,' she said. 'Where is it to be?'

'At the other end of the corridor where the builders are working. We've lost a couple of private rooms temporarily but we'll gain a dozen more in the end. The second phase is actually to replace the Murray Room itself with three more private rooms, so that each of our patients will have space to themselves at the end of their lives.'

'No more sharing?'

'No more sharing. It'll take a year or two, but it'll be good when it's finished.'

Lucy paused briefly, then asked, 'Tell me about your fire escapes. Isn't there one in the corridor? That seems very dangerous.'

'There isn't one there at the moment. The builders had to block it off. There's a locked door there, though.'

'A locked door? Where?'

'You saw all that plastic sheeting at the back? If you look beyond that, there's a temporary steel double door in the wall where the store cupboard used to be. The builders sometimes use it during the day to avoid trailing through the building.'

'But… we asked Magda at the time. Why didn't she say?'

'If you asked at the time, 'Is there a fire escape?', Magda would have taken you very literally. She's a bit like that. One of our psychologists reckons she has Asperger's Syndrome, but I wouldn't know myself. But it's always locked and alarmed at night, and it was that night. I checked it myself.'

'Someone must have a key, though.'

'Of course. We have a key, but the workmen don't.'

Lucy began to feel she was losing control of things a little. 'I think the important point is that someone else might have had access to the Murray Room.'

'But you'd have been able to see them come in on the CCTV. We do take security and patient safety very seriously,' Wolstencroft said – but then no sooner had the words left her mouth than she realised her mistake, so she added, 'Give or take the odd murder. But I can assure you that Mr Plews is the first patient we've ever had stabbed to death at St Ninian's. I've checked the records.'

'You have?' Grant asked, dumbfounded.

'No, that was a joke. Sorry, black humour. It's a general medical weakness, I'm afraid. But the point is, no one was in the corridor, either. Didn't you say that the CCTV showed that?'

'Fair point. Still, if there was indeed a potential entry point at the end of the corridor, the police should have been told.'

'Sorry. A case of the right hand not talking to the left.'

'How do you know the workmen don't have keys as well?'

'Ah. I can help you there. The builders themselves suggested that we get our own locksmith to fit the lock, so that only St Ninian's has copies. So they can only come and go with our supervision. To be honest, it's more to make sure that the patients can't wander off anywhere, it's not because we don't want the builders to come in. It's just that we don't trust them not to leave the fire escape door open.'

Lucy took a moment to take all of that in, then she said, 'So who has a key for the fire escape door? If it's a fire escape one assumes…'

'The duty nurse would have a key, and there's a spare key kept on a hook in Reception.'

'So someone like, perhaps, Magda Czeslawska would carry a key when she was on duty.'

'Naturally, or else it couldn't be used as an escape route in an emergency. But you said the CCTV had established that no one at all was in the corridor at the time of Mr Plews's death, didn't you?'

Lucy said nothing. A thought had occurred to her: in fact, why hadn't it occurred to her before?

TWENTY

'YOU'RE TELLING ME THAT someone could get in and out of that corridor after all?'

'Well, not perhaps at the time of the murder,' Lucy said, 'but it would be a way to get the knife into the room, wouldn't it?'

Knox sat back and sighed. 'It certainly would. It would need help from inside, not a lot. The knife could be left by anyone just outside that door at the end. Then someone inside could use the key to open the door and bring the knife into the room and hide it somewhere inside where the murder was due to take place. Is there anywhere someone could hide a knife?'

'There are all the lockers, John. Who's going to look in the back of one of those cupboards? Not a patient, that's for sure. They all had other things to think about.'

'Jeez, it brings every member of staff back under suspicion, doesn't it?'

'Of being an accessory at least.'

Lucy hesitated; Knox knew she wanted to ask something but wasn't sure.

'What's on your mind, Lucy?'

She turned to look at him. 'Is Mary back in the frame again?'

Knox found it irritating that Mary was everyone's first suspect. 'I suppose she might be. Her fingerprints weren't found on the knife but I suppose she might have wiped it clean. She'd also have had to be very careful how she inserted the knife so as not to get blood on herself. But we shouldn't rule her out, no.

'But we need a complete rethink on the knife, Lucy. Almost anyone could have supplied the knife, but it still needed help from inside St Ninian's to get it into that room. Poor Dave Lander – he might have to go over that CCTV footage again. I'm not even sure how far it goes back, to be honest. We were only looking for people in the corridor, but now we might be looking for signs of a knife any time in the days, even weeks, leading up to the murder. A real needle in a haystack.'

Lucy said nothing. To her, it was too much of a coincidence that the woman who had discovered the dead body was also the person with the most reason to hate him.

'I know what you're thinking,' Knox said.

Lucy chuckled. 'You do?'

'Well, perhaps not exactly what you're thinking, but I can see doubt written all across your face. But I just don't believe Mary killed old man Plews. It's not… stylish enough for her. I keep saying this – why wait until death was closing in on Leonard Plews anyway? The same applies to the Chief Inspector and his brother. Plus those two have another thing in their favour.'

'Which is?'

'They'd mess it up.' They both laughed this time, before Knox continued, 'Lucy, Mary really is a woman of God, you know. Sometimes her eccentric beliefs seem a bit off the wall, but she honestly believes in a Heaven and a Hell. She prays – genuinely – that Leonard Plews will go to Hell where he truly belongs. And the last thing she wanted was for Plews to gain any sort of 'victim' status at the Pearly Gates by being murdered. Beneath that tough exterior, she's actually quite a vulnerable, damaged woman.'

'You believe that?'

'I know that.'

'Well, somebody sneaked the knife in there,' Lucy said. 'Just like somebody killed Plews, even if we can't prove it was murder. And it's the knife that bothers me. Why bother with it?'

'It's certainly a bit strange,' Knox admitted. 'Perhaps the killer didn't know if old man Plews could fight back or not.'

'Do you really believe that?'

'No.' Knox took a deep breath. 'The knife seems to be a message for us. Somebody truly hated Leonard Plews.'

'Someone like Mary, the Chief Inspector, or his brother,' Lucy said. 'Unless we can find someone else who has a motive.'

***

Dave Lander was none too impressed at the prospect of reviewing a good deal more CCTV footage. The only saving grace was that the disk had been set to wipe over itself after 14 days, limiting his torture. He'd even asked if there was any point, anyway, given that whoever had slipped the knife into St Ninian's surely wouldn't have carried it openly. Knox agreed, but pointed out that Police Scotland needed to demonstrate in court that they were thorough and professional, considering all angles. And it was always possible they might get lucky.

Meanwhile, Izzy Bryce had been invited to turn her attention to the Jaguar thefts. Like any other police officer, Izzy had regarded being taken off the murder case as demotion, but she took it in reasonable part. Knox gave her the printouts that Mary had collected and invited Izzy to look it over with fresh eyes.

'This is quite an impressive collection,' she observed. 'Can I ask how she managed to obtain all of this?'

Knox chuckled. 'Best if you didn't, I'd suggest. Sister Mary Maxwell-Hume reaches into the parts other people can't reach. Or where angels fear to tread. You choose.' He told Izzy about having his pocket picked.

Izzy arched her eyebrows at him. Chief Inspector Maximilian Plews would have taken that as insubordination, not that Izzy would have cared, but Knox didn't mind. Then she made a point he himself hadn't considered.

'Doesn't that mean Mary's quite capable of smuggling the knife in without anyone seeing her do it?'

'Good point. Don't tell Dave Lander, though. I need him to go through that CCTV footage as conscientiously as he can. He might have to be convincing in court one day.' He tapped the printouts and smiled. 'Aren't you checking out the Jaguar thefts?'

'Another needle in a haystack, just like all the CCTV footage?'

'Hardly,' Knox said. 'Eight Jaguar saloon cars don't go missing without leaving a trace somewhere. Why are they all missing just now, for instance? Why is it only Jaguars? No Bentleys, or Land Rovers or even Porsches. What's on earth's going on here?'

'And they're just vanishing into thin air?'

'Seemingly.'

'Perhaps they're a bunch of kids who only know how to break into Jaguars,' Izzy suggested.

Knox was about to reply, then stopped. 'Perhaps you're on the right track there. A very interesting track, at least.'

'I was joking, sir.'

'I wasn't, though. That's worth looking into.'

'If it's kids, how are they getting rid of the cars?'

Knox had to admit that it was a weakness in the hypothesis. He said nothing, which Izzy took as a cue to find some space in the open-plan office area where she could lay out the information on available used cars provided by the garages. Just as he was about to head for the door, O'Malley wandered into the office, coming in the opposite direction.

'Well, son, how are yez daein'? Making progress wi' the crime of the century?'

Not quite sure of his relationship with the Superintendent, Knox decided it was safer to play the role of O'Malley's stooge.

'Regarding the murder, do you want the official answer or the unofficial answer, sir?' he said.

O'Malley chuckled. 'Go on then. Official wan furst.'

'Our investigation is proceeding, sir. We're following a number of lines of enquiries.'

'And unofficially?'

'We haven't a clue.'

O'Malley recoiled. 'Jeez? Yez're daein' that well?' Then he chuckled again. 'Just as well ah meant the real crime of the century, John – the stolen cars. Ye ken whit the Chief Inspector's like.'

'I do indeed sir. Officially, our answer's the same for the cars as it is for the murder.'

'And unofficially? This had better be good, mind, ah've a feeling ah've heard this joke before.'

'We're following a number of Sister Mary's clues.'

O'Malley looked genuinely surprised. 'She's come up wi' somethin'?'

'Oh yes, sir. As she likes to say, she can reach into places that others can't.'

'Did yell yer Sister Mary that she's free to reach anywhere she likes wi' me?'

'I haven't had a chance to pass it on yet, sir.' Out of the corner of his eye both of them could see Izzy Bryce in a corner, desperately trying to suppress a smile.

'Maybe ye'd better no' son. It might no' go down sae well. Anyway, yer sayin' she's managed tae come up wi' a couple of leads?'

'Calling them 'leads' might be a bit strong, sir, but she's done a lot of research on our behalf, and very quickly, too. She wonders if the fact that they're all personalised name-plates isn't part of the pattern.'

'Well, son, ah think that's a decent startin' point, isn't it? Did yez need tae be telt that?'

'She's put an idea into my head – '

'– I'll bet!'

Knox tried to be patient. 'These cars have all had their number plates changed once already. In fact they each began life as a car with a different plate altogether. Perhaps they've gone back to that original plate. Or a new one altogether. Either way, what matters is that no one will be looking for that plate at all. It could be driving around in plain sight.'

"Hiding in plain sight, John?' That's a' the rage just now.' Knox and Izzy laughed. There had been a spate of crime dramas on television where the answer had been 'hiding in plain sight'. 'In ma young days they'd huv just said ye couldnae see it fur lookin' at it,' O'Malley added.

Knox nodded in agreement. 'Meanwhile, we seem to have two related issues, sir. One involves disappearing items, the other one an item that's appeared from nowhere.'

'So we dae, son. Perhaps we're looking fur two magicians.' His eyes lit up. 'Abracadabra!'

For all that O'Malley had his faults, it was hard not to laugh along with him when he was in this sort of mood, and the echoes of laughter were still in the air when Chief Inspector Plews marched into the office. The effect was immediate: a stiffened silence spread across the room, and even O'Malley said nothing. Plews was clearly aware of the change in atmosphere but ignored everyone else and spoke to O'Malley directly.

'Can I ask for a report on progress, sir?'

'About yer faither or about yer jam jar?'

'About my jam – about my car, sir.' If Plews could have saluted, he would have.

'We're following several lines of en-qui-ry,' O'Malley said. He dragged the last word out for effect. He was having considerable difficulty keeping his face straight.

'That means you're doing nothing,' Plews said abruptly.

Now it was O'Malley's turn to take a sharp tone.

'Excuse me, Inspector Plews? Are yez doubtin' ma wurd?'

Plews gobbled. 'Sorry sir, I was looking for a little detail.'

'Ah well, now, Inspector, yez ur an... inter-rusted perty, are ye not? So we shouldnae really tell yez.' Plews was about to protest when he added, 'But if yez just cast yer eyes o'er in the direction o' P C Bryce there, yez might notice that she's hard at work studying the details o' every single Jaguar in the Un-it-ed Kingdom.'

For once, Plews was speechless.

'That's… every… single… wan, Inspector. It's an awfy lot o' Jaguars. Are yez impressed?'

Plews nodded. Then he said, 'Thank you, sir. I'm sorry, sir, I've been under a lot of stress lately.'

'Aye, we a' ken just how hard yer faither's death hit yez.'

Again, Plews looked slightly confused, then said, 'Yes, that too.' Then, after a moment's hesitation, he said, 'Excuse me, sir…'

'Whit?'

'It's actually 'Chief Inspector'.'

O'Malley studied him for a long time, then said, 'So it is now. So it is.'

**

Knox returned home around 7.00 to an empty house. He and Alice had missed each other for almost 36 hours now and he was starting to get worried. The flat had an empty feel about it, as if nothing had moved since the morning, no lights had been on, no cooking had taken place. He made his way into the kitchen and looked all around: she'd taken the post in and set it neatly on a pile on the kitchen table. At first he ignored it, but then his eye was drawn to a handwritten envelope, addressed to him but in Alice's very recognisable hand. A cold chill ran through his body.

He opened all the other mail first – apart from a couple of bills it was all junk mail – then poured himself a decent-sized malt whisky and took Alice's unopened letter across to the sofa. Knowing what was almost certainly inside, he wondered how he had let it get this bad. Was this an occupational hazard for all police officers, he asked himself? Izzy Bryce would never have let work destroy her family, he reminded himself. Then he took a swig of whisky, told himself that Alice was 'just a girlfriend' not a formal partner in any sense, and that perhaps it would be for the best. Or perhaps she was away on holiday. Or on a course. Or was on a round-the-world yacht trip. He ripped open the envelope so quickly that he slightly tore the corner off the sheet of pale blue sheet of writing paper inside.

Dear John

I'm sorry not to be able to tell you this to your face, but you've been very busy at work. To be fair, I have, too. But I feel such a coward doing it like this. You're a lovely, kind considerate man and you deserve better than someone like me.

You'll realise by now that I've left. It's not your fault at all. I wish we could have spent more time together lately but it's not been possible and I'm afraid I just need more than you can give me at present. And I've not been entirely honest with you. You remember my colleague David Lambie? Well, I've been seeing a lot of him, outside school as well inside, and I've decided to move in with him. I used your obvious liking for Mary as an excuse for letting things go further for David and me, but I'm aware I might have done you an injustice there. If I'm honest with myself I need to accept responsibility for my own actions. I've just moved on. And living with another teacher means that our lifestyles fit together much better than yours and mine ever could.

I'll come back tomorrow when you're out and remove my remaining clothes and personal effects, then I'll post the house keys back through your door. And I'll give you something in lieu of the next two or three months rent and housekeeping.

I hope we can always stay friends.

Love, Alice xx

The irony of the little kisses at the end wasn't lost on Knox.

TWENTY-ONE

A S PREDICTED, DAVE LANDER was turning up nothing at all on the CCTV. Knox and O'Malley had given him permission to fast-forward – 'duty o' care', the Superintendent had called it, adding 'we dinnae want tae dae yer head in.'

Knox had arrived that morning looking a little less sharp than usual, something that Lucy had picked up on straight away.

'Everything OK, John?'

'Yes, thanks. What made you ask?'

'Oh, nothing. Just asking.'

Knox turned to Lander.

'Come on then, Dave, there must be something there. Give us a run-down of what's on the CCTV. Anything.'

'There's really nothing. You'd be amazed how boring life is in a typical care home. Nothing happens.'

'Apart frae the odd murder,' said a voice behind. O'Malley had appeared without Knox noticing, and it gave him a start.

'Well, I've checked pretty carefully, sir,' Lander said, now addressing his answers to the Superintendent. 'The only thing that seems to happen is that nurses and doctors come and go.'

'Plus Mary Maxwell-Hume,' Lucy pointed out.

'Right on the stroke of midnight each night,' Lander said. 'Stays for fifteen or twenty minutes then leaves the same way she came in. She never carries anything, unless perhaps she's hiding it under her dress.'

There was a chorus of 'No' from O'Malley and Knox. O'Malley looked at Knox.

'Yez're OK, Inspector?'

'Yes, thanks. Why does everyone keep asking how I am this morning?'

Nobody spoke: they were all waiting for O'Malley.

'On a bender night son, wiz yez?'

'No, sir. Just a couple.'

O'Malley paused for a moment, then said, 'I'd say that wus an Islay, and a peaty wan at that. How about Caol Ila? Wad ah be right?'

Embarrassed, Knox looked down, then said, 'Sorry everyone, I didn't think it was so obvious.' He looked at O'Malley and said, 'Impressive, sir. Caol Ila, got it in one. It won't happen again.'

'I cannae say it's ever happened before so ah presume circumstances demanded a nip or two. Ah think everyone here understands that. Let's go back to you, P. C. Lander. What happens going in the other direction?'

'Towards the fire escape and the builders?'

'Aye.'

'The only other thing in that corridor appears to be a huge linen cupboard. There are regular visits, but they're always by nurses who bring out piles of sheets and so on. I think that cupboard is only for that particular room, though.'

'What about laundry?' Lucy asked. 'How does the stuff get washed?'

'I think that's in the clear – it all comes and goes through the main front entrances, so it would be covered by the metal-detectors and so on. The nurses themselves seem to put the clean stuff in the cupboard.' Lander picked out a sample portion of the CCTV footage to demonstrate what happened in each case. 'They take out the clean bedding from the cupboard each time as they need it. You can even see them open the cupboard at the end of the corridor and lift the stuff out.'

'It's pretty dark in that corridor at night,' Knox said.

'It's so that the patients aren't disturbed. But as the light improves further down you can follow that nurse carrying the linen. That one we're watching is the Polish one, but they all have the same routine.'

'Interesting, though,' Lucy said.

O'Malley sat up. 'Have yez got an idea, Lucy?'

'It's the way that cupboard door opens,' she said. It didn't escape her notice that the Superintendent had referred to her by her first name. 'It's annoying me. Maybe it's nothing, I'll look at it later.'

O'Malley studied her closely but said nothing.

'Anyway, a' o' yez, we need tae remember that the victim wisnae stabbed. It's a red herrin', appropriately enough for a filleting knife. The victim had a heart attack while he wis bein' smothered.' He chuckled. 'While lyin' face-down on top o' another female patient, and we think he'd been dragged there. Then he had his jammies pulled up and doon and then he wis stabbed wi' the knife after he wis deid.' O'Malley shook his head, laughing.

'Everything all right, sir?' Knox asked.

'Whit a palaver, Inspector, eh? Whit a palaver. Why gae tae a' that bother fur a man whae's a'ready deid?'

'To make a point, sir. Would you agree?'

'Oh, ah think ah'd agree a'right. A very sharp point, if ye'll excuse the knifey pun. Ah think whae'ever killed our Mr Plews in yon hospital knew he was a nasty little sex fiend.'

'Doesn't that point to his own children?' said Lander. 'Or even Sister Mary. They'd all experienced him as children.'

O'Malley sat back. 'Aye, son, that narrows the field, doesn't it?'

'Or anyone they happened to tell over the course of their entire lives,' Knox said.

'Aye, Inspector, and that widens it back out again.'

O'Malley took the decision that he and Knox should interview Maximilian Plews together, and that it would look better if they took the same approach with Theodore as well. The Superintendent realised that it would be difficult for Knox to ask even the most innocent of questions of his superior officer, but with such a sensitive subject things were doubly delicate. The Plews brothers were both impossible, and if he could have found a way of arresting them both and deporting them, he'd have done it long ago. Now, however, his patience was being tested to the very limit.

Knox and O'Malley were sitting in an interview room discussing their questioning approach towards the brothers.

'Before yez dae any interviewin', mind, make sure yez have a fair supply o' mints.'

'Yes, sir. And I'm sorry.'

'Naw, son, we've a' been there. Dinnae make a habit o' it, that's all.' Suddenly, he changed subject again. 'Ye ken, John, they Plews brithers fair make me appreciate the social value of hit men.'

At first shocked, Knox wondered if he'd misheard, but quickly realised that he hadn't. Struggling to contain his laughter, Knox said he would ensure that stayed within the four walls.

'Dinnae worry, John, that's kind o' yez, but yez neednae worry. If yez telt anyone, two things wid happen. First, ah'd deny it, and call yez a liar. Naebody wid argue wi' me – ah'm the boss. Second, they'd a' ken ah did say it, but ye'd be kent as someone whae couldnae keep a secret.'

Knox carried on laughing. 'You've got me all tied up, haven't you, sir?'

'Ah hope sae. That's how guid discipline should be. And mind yez can call me 'Jack' inside this office. Only dinnae let that wee nyaff Plews hear yez. He'd want the same, an' ah couldnae bear him tryin' tae be friendly wi' me.'

'I'm sure he has his strengths… Jack.'

'Go on, John, name me wan.'

'He's a good interviewer of some suspects. Terrifying, if that's what's required. I think it's the Hitler moustache – he only grew it to keep up with brother Theodore.'

'You always see the best in folk, John.' Then, for no reason, O'Malley added, 'He spits when he shouts.'

'In a fire, it's cheaper than a sprinkler system.'

O'Malley chuckled. 'Ah kent ah wiz daein' the right thing promotin' you, John.'

'Are you pleased with the new Chief Inspector, Jack?' Plews had been promoted at the same time, but no one knew why.

O'Malley shifted in his seat a little. 'The Chief Inspector caught me in… a compromising position, John.' Then he added, 'Or perhaps ah should say he caught wee Lorna Thompson frae the admin pool in a compromising position.

Dae yez remember her?' He sighed. 'She wis just bein' kind tae me, makin' me feel mair manly, like. But yez ken whit the world's like now, and so does the Chief Inspector. 'Silence is golden,' he said.'

'Ah,' Knox said, nodding slowly. 'Lorna's left now, though.'

'Ma pal in Wishaw got her a nice well-paid job at an architect's office.'

'So she's drawing on the experience, then? That's good.'

O'Malley chuckled. 'Very good, John, I like that. Yes, very good all round. But I had tae… yez ken… gie Plews a guid reference furst.' Then he added quietly, 'Sorry. Makes your job harder.'

'It's not so bad, really. When everyone else thinks the same way, it's a lot easier. And I try to stay out of his way.'

'Staying dry. Very wise.'

Suddenly, O'Malley changed the subject.

'So… did youz dump Alice or did she dump youz?'

'How…?'

'Ah'm a detective, John. Did yez no' ken?' As Knox smiled wryly, O'Malley continued, 'Mind if ah gives yez a bit o' advice, John? Frae wan whae's been there a' too often himself.'

'Please.'

'Get yerself distracted. By yer job, or else find anither wumman – Jeez, even go and watch the fitba', although mind youz, ma Motherwell team wid make yez want tae jump aff the Forth Bridge the now, so mebbe it's no' such a guid idea efter a'.'

Knox acknowledged his superior officer's suggestions but said no more. He really didn't want to discuss his love life with anyone, especially O'Malley. He turned the conversation back to their investigations.

'Exactly what are we going to ask the Chief Inspector?' He wanted to add 'sir' but had been told not to.

'Chief Inspector Plews is only interested in that bloody car o' his. We can soften him up a little through that, though.'

'Are we treating the Chief Inspector as a suspect?'

'We're el-im-in-at-ing him frae our en-qui-ries,' O'Malley said mischievously, stretching out the phrase. 'I'm lookin' forward tae daein' it, tae.'

'But you don't really think…'

'Naw. Why wid he wait until it's almost impossible? He's had a lifetime tae get rid o' his faither. Same wi' the other Plews – whit's his name again?'

'Theodore.'

'Jeez. Maximilian and Theodore. The old man deserved tae be murdered fur that alane. That an' haein' thae two bairns. Caused nothin' but bother.'

There was a knock on the door.

'Aye?'

Chief Inspector Maximilian Plews stuck his head around and asked, and received, permission to enter.

'Excuse me, sir,' Plews said, 'you wished to see me?'

'Aye, Chief Inspector, park yer bum oan a seat.'

Plews screwed his face up at the crude language, but did as he was told.

'We'd like to ask yez a couple of questions, if yez dinnae mind.'

'Is this about the case?'

'Sort of. We need tae clear a few points up.'

Plews drew himself up. 'I hope this is about the cars.' He looked at Knox and added, 'I see the case proved beyond you, Inspector. As I thought, you've a lot to learn.'

'No, Chief Inspector, this isnae about the cars, although we'll come tae that later if yez want. And in my opinion Inspector Knox is daein' an excellent job.'

'He hasn't found the cars, or the culprit. In fact I heard another one disappeared this morning.'

O'Malley ignored him. 'Tell us about yer faither. He hit yez when yez were wee. He was an evil bully – '

'That's my father you're referring to, sir – a murder victim.'

'He was an evil bully, Chief Inspector. He did bad things. He was a sex offender.'

'Sir! I must protest!'

'Really? Dae yez want us tae sort the cars business or not?'

Plews slumped back. 'Yes, of course.'

'Then save us some time by answering our questions about what happened in St Ninian's. The cars are less important. And if yez dinnae agree wi' that, I'll put youz out in front o' the press tae explain.'

Plews sighed, bored. 'Go on.'

O'Malley nodded that Knox should take over.

'Chief Inspector, when you were young, you and your brother Theodore gave evidence in a court case against your uncle.'

'I don't see what that's to do with anything.' Then he added, 'Are you interrogating me, Knox?'

Before Knox could reply, O'Malley butted in. 'Aye, Plews. Answer his questions. Ah'm getting fed up here an' ah want a cup o' tea.'

Taken aback, Plews turned to Knox and said, 'I did. So did Teddy.'

'Why did you lie in court, sir?'

Plews bridled. 'Who says I lied?'

'Contemporary accounts, sir. But you were too young to be prosecuted for perjury.'

O'Malley added, 'But yez're no' now, Chief Inspector. Time tae spill the beans.'

Plews said nothing.

'Help us, please, sir,' Knx said, quietly. 'We're trying to help you, you know. You were a victim, too.'

'I was never sexually abused.'

'Not you, perhaps, but someone else.'

'Who?'

'Yez ken damn well, Chief Inspector,' O'Malley said, impatiently. 'Yer cousin Mary. By yer faither. Now are yez gonnae deny it again? Yez're no' too young tae be prosecuted any mair.'

'I should have a lawyer,' Plews said.

'Why? Dae yez think yer a suspect? Maybe we should be taping this conversation.' He nodded to Knox, who reached over an switched the tape on.

'This is an interview with Chief Inspector Maximilian Plews. Present are Superintendent Jack – '

'Yes, I lied. Don't record it,' Plews said, before quietly adding, 'Please.'

'Very wise, Chief Inspector. We'd just have brought yer brither in an' played aff one o' youz against the other. You know the ropes.'

'So why did you lie?' Knox said, switching off the tape again.

'My father was a very frightening man, Knox. We were terrified of him and his belt. He had a special one made for us, you know. He was a teacher, and teachers could do that in those days. Farmers would make up 'specials'.'

'Doesn't sound very nice.'

'It wasn't.'

'And your cousin Mary got it, too.'

'Yes, we all did.'

'Except she got something else as well, didn't she, sir?'

'If you know the answer, Knox, why are you asking?'

"Cause we want tae hear it frae yer own mouth, Chief Inspector,' O'Malley said firmly.

'Yes, she was… my father… had his way with her.'

'She was only twelve or thirteen,' Knox said.

'My father had lost his wife.'

'Is that an excuse?'

'No. But Teddy and I resented Mary all the same.'

'Why?'

'Because Daddy would feel so guilty that he would take out her for little treats to make up. We boys never got that. Actually, we didn't really understand what was going on then anyway. We just saw her as Daddy's favourite.' Then Plews added, 'I know it doesn't sound very nice, but it's how you see things when you're young. We were just trying to survive. And we all did.' He looked at Knox defiantly.

'In his trial, you gave evidence against Mary Maxwell-Hume's father. You said he was the culprit, not your own father Leonard.'

'Teddy and I were forced to. Daddy said that if we said anything about him, he would take his belt to us harder than we'd ever had it before, then he'd dump us somewhere far away and we'd end up in a home somewhere. Anyway, as he said, lots of fathers beat their children in those days. He was strict, that was all. And I never actually saw him do anything to Mary myself. It happened behind closed doors, if it happened at all.'

'What do you mean, 'If it happened at all?''

'It was only Mary who said that Daddy was to blame. She didn't ever talk about it.'

'But… there were injuries.'

'That's when Daddy said we were to say it was Uncle Philip. Daddy said he'd been trying to protect Mary.'

Knox allowed himself some time to absorb what Plews had just said. He was beginning to see Plews in a new light, as a victim himself as well as a willing accomplice of utter evil. It dawned on him that the story of the Plews brothers was little different from so many others he'd met in his time as a police officer.

'Looking back, what do you think now?' he asked Plews.

Plews looked at him in disgust. 'Inspector, how dare you ask me such a personal question? I am not a suspect, I am not one of your petty villains. How dare you presume to judge me?'

'Sir, we need to look at what might have happened leading up to your father's death. We need to find out how each of the family felt towards your family.'

'You are treating me as a suspect!'

O'Malley had been quiet, but felt a need to offer some support. 'It's OK, Chief Inspector, Inspector Knox is only daein' his job. I'd hae asked the same question masel'.'

'Well I don't like being treated like a common criminal. Especially by a junior officer.'

O'Malley shrugged. 'OK, if yez want it that way… lookin' back on it, whit dae yez think now? O' the business wi' Mary an' yer faither? Are yez proud o' yersel?'

Plews bristled. 'I can enter my own house justified.'

'That's good tae know, Chief Inspector. I suppose yez couldnae help bein' tae weak tae dae the right thing.'

'I really don't like the tone of that, sir. I was a teenager.'

'Yez lied in court. An innocent man went tae jail.'

'Oh, he wasn't innocent.'

'What do you mean, sir?' Knox said.

'Uncle Philip – Mary's own father – was incapable of looking after his teenage daughter. There's no excuse for that.'

'The man was a single parent having a nervous breakdown.'

'Pathetic. Needed to pull himself together. He had a responsibility. But Daddy offered to help out.' Knox, who had been gradually beginning to sympathise a little with Plews, found his sympathies ebbing away again.

'So your cousin Mary ended up in your house,' Knox said. Plews confirmed with an arrogant little nod that made Knox clench his hand into a fist under the table. O'Malley must have spotted it: Knox received a kick under the table that made him wince.

'I still fail to see why you're asking me about all of this, Knox,' Plews said, sharply. 'And I fail to see what all of this has to do with the theft of my Jaguar.'

'We're explorin' a' op-shuns,' O'Malley chipped in. 'We're aware that you' and your brither have been a victim twice over – wi' the loss o' your faither, an' of yer jam jars.'

'Jam jars?'

'Cars – have yez forgotten already, Chief Inspector? I thought ye might have learned that wee bit Cockney rhyming slang by now. Anyway, we wondered if it wisnae a coincidence, like.'

'The cars and my father's death?'

'We have to consider all possibilities, sir,' Knox said. 'I think you'd agree with that. It would be careless to rule anything out.'

If it were possible to strut while sitting, Plews did so now. 'Does this mean you'll be asking my brother the same questions?'

'Of course, sir. And we have to ask your cousin Mary Maxwell-Hume some more, too.'

'I should hope so. I'm sure she's involved in all of this somehow. You're trying to tell me that she had a huge motive, but she doesn't seem to have had the same interrogation.'

'Well, she might have, except that she was nowhere near at the time of death. Nor were you or your brother either, I might add. But we do need to find the answer to a few things.'

'But I'm not a suspect.' It was said as a question with a presumed answer.

'No.'

'So why are you both interviewing me?'

O'Malley stepped in. 'That wis my idea, Chief Inspector. I thought yez mightnae hae taken kindly tae bein' quizzed by a junior officer.'

'Indeed, sir. Knox interviewing me unsupervised by yourself would have been quite inappropriate. It's important that none of us gets above themselves.'

O'Malley smiled. 'Does that include youz yersel', Chief Inspector?'

Plews hesitated, then answered in a low voice, 'I suppose so.'

'I'm sorry, Chief Inspector, ah didnae quite catch that.'

Plews cleared his throat, and said – louder – 'I suppose so.' At no point did he look in Knox's direction. Then he added, 'So, am I eliminated from your enquiries?'

'Chief Inspector, yez ken as well as ah do that we have tae dae everythin' by the book these days. Ye might say we've gone PC daft but that's the way it is. So we have tae ask everyone with a possible motive. Even if we dinnae think yez couldnae hae done the killin' yersel', yez might have helped in some way.'

'And what is your conclusion, sir? I asked you before. Am I eliminated?'

'Naw, we're nae further forward.'

Finally, Plews looked at Knox in contempt.

'And I suppose you're no further forward catching the car thieves?'

'Our enquiries are proceeding, sir.'

'That's all you ever say, Knox. Meanwhile, this 'interview' has just been a waste of time?'

'Well, yez might hae suddenly broken down and confessed. But yez didnae.'

'This *has* been a waste of time!' Plews stood up.

'Ah didnae say that.'

'Are you finished with me, sir?'

'Aye, ah suppose so. Aff yez go.' O'Malley nodded at the door. Plews made to leave, incensed and humiliated in equal measure. Knox could have sworn he clicked his heels before he turned.

After he'd left, O'Malley turned to Knox.

'See that time when he asked about eliminatin' him? I wiz fair tempted to say, 'Only in mah dreams, Chief Inspector."

TWENTY-TWO

I N THE END, O'MALLEY ASKED Knox not to interview Theodore, brother of Chief Inspector Maximilian Plews. O'Malley's thinking was two-fold. First, Theodore – the auction-house manager – knew Mary Maxwell-Hume very well, and there was history between the two of them. Knox had hinted to O'Malley that Mary had been a considerable nuisance in the past. Theodore also knew that Mary and Knox had been very good friends in the past: he didn't know what the relationship was, but was convinced it was an unhealthy one. It meant he was less likely to answer any questions Knox put to him.

Second, O'Malley wanted to annoy Theodore by sending less senior officers to interview him. The brothers would notice such a detail straight away and Theodore would feel insulted. That was fine by O'Malley. In any case, he knew that Lucy Grant would be perfect for the job, and he suggested she take Izzy Bryce with her. The combination of Grant's professionalism and Bryce's refusal to be intimidated was perfect. And, true to form, Izzy dressed perfectly for the occasion in tee-shirt and jeans, with a short leather jacket over the top. (Izzy, meantime, had realised that she probably needed a new pair of jeans, one size bigger for sure. But she'd made it into these ones by lying on the bedroom floor to pull the zip up.)

Lucy had made an appointment to see Theodore, being careful not to say what Izzy and she were going to talk about. Predictably, he greeted them in an offhand, brusque manner, and Lucy was reminded straight away of Knox's description that he was even less pleasant than his police officer brother. Izzy was asked to sit on a wooden chair, and 'not to leave a mess, please.' Izzy had responded by assuring the auction house manager that she had been fully house-trained and knew to go to the toilet if she needed. Plews looked at her with even more contempt.

'My brother's been on the phone,' he said. 'I understand this is likely to be some sort of interrogation.'

'Is it, sir?' Lucy asked, innocently. 'That's not our intention. Is there something you'd like to tell us?'

'Of course not.'

'You'd rather not tell us anything?' Out of the corner of her eye Lucy could see Izzy Bryce tying her shoelaces in an attempt to hide her laughter.

'You know that's not what I mean… Detective Sergeant. Is this modern policing? I'm looking forward to comparing notes with my brother. I understand he's your superior officer, isn't he?'

'One of them, yes, sir,' Lucy replied. Then she added, 'Superintendent O'Malley is in overall charge of the investigation. Please feel free to complain to him if you're not satisfied.'

'O'Malley? Yes, I've heard of him. Rather a coarse fellow. Needs to lose some weight.'

Lucy rather agreed with that, but decided not to comment. She noticed that Izzy had found another shoelace that needed tying.

'Yours was actually the first Jaguar to be stolen, sir. I understand it was quite an upmarket model, too.'

'A 5.0 V8 Petrol 510PS. Silver.'

'Can you suggest why anyone might steal your car, sir?'

'I've been asked all of these inane questions before, Detective Sergeant.' Theodore Plews's default state was 'bristling', but his current mood was a stage beyond that.

'I'm sorry that you find our questions 'inane', sir.'

Plews sniffed. 'I appreciate that you might be a little slow, but please remember that, like my brother, I'm Cambridge University-educated.'

Lucy couldn't contain her surprise. 'Both of you? I didn't know that, sir. Goodness.'

'Ruskin.'

'Well anyway, if you could try to be patient, please, lesser mortals like ourselves need to ask questions in our own time. So – can you think of anyone who might steal your car?'

'The answer is no, of course, apart from the fact that the car is highly desirable.'

'No one has a personal grudge against you?'

Plews hesitated for a minute, then eventually conceded, 'In an art dealer business like Lamberts, you occasionally get disgruntled customers. People who failed to get the price they were hoping for in an auction, or their bid was unsuccessful. And very occasionally someone complains that they've been defrauded by us. It's always nonsense. They're just hoping we'll settle out of court when we've done nothing wrong.'

'How do they take it when you ignore them?'

'Oh we don't ignore them,' Plews said, pomposity emanating from every pore of his body. 'We sue them back. For defamation. We have a standard claim procedure for £100,000.'

'£100,000?' Lucy could hardly believe her ears.

'Lamberts has a reputation, Detective Sergeant Grant. It's worth that sort of money to maintain it. And to dissuade these low-lives from trying to blackmail us.' Then a supercilious smile appeared on his face; it made Grant want to vomit. 'But we're prepared to settle out of court, though. If the blackmailer has children, we'll make sure they have a home.'

'So if Lamberts values something wrongly and someone complains, there's a chance they'll lose their house?'

'As I said, Detective Sergeant, we never make mistakes. And we do try to make sure that children are housed. Not anywhere near this city, though. There's some cheap housing in the north of England that's perfect for the purpose.'

Lucy and Izzy were well trained not to show too much emotion during interviews, but even so, they were struggling not to be shocked by what they were hearing.

'Your car was stolen from outside Lamberts, wasn't it, sir?' Lucy said.

'From my Director's spot in the staff car park, yes.'

'There's no CCTV?'

'There wasn't then. We've had it installed since. Goodness knows why – I almost wish thieves would steal this awful Volvo thing I'm forced to drive by the insurers, and you people don't show any signs of finding my Jag.'

'I can assure you that we're doing our utmost, sir.'

'Nonsense. It's a matter of prioritising, and your priorities aren't the same as the general public's.'

'I understand that they're not the same as yours, sir,' Lucy said. Realising she was getting nowhere, she changed tack.

'When did you last see your father alive, sir?'

'Daddy?' Plews gave the matter some thought, then looked at a diary. '12th April, two years ago. When we finally got Daddy into that home. It took us some time to find somewhere that was free, I should add. Everywhere else seemed to expect the family to pay something. Or sell his house and give them some of the proceeds, which amounts to the same thing, doesn't it?'

'I couldn't comment, sir. Sorry. Just to be clear, are you saying that you haven't seen your father since he went into St Ninian's?'

'I saw him on the day he went in. Not since. Why should I go and see him?'

'You didn't like your father?'

Theodore Plews looked surprised. 'Detective Sergeant, I understand that you never met Daddy.'

'No.'

'That explains your question, then.'

Theodore Plews seemed to regard the question as answered, so Lucy decided to try and irritate him.

'Can I ask what your relationship is with Sister Mary Maxwell-Hume of the Sisters of Mary of the Sacred Cross?'

'That woman! She's a charlatan. A fraud. I mean, that 'order' of hers… have you ever met any other of its members?'

'I admit I haven't personally had that pleasure, sir, no.'

'That's because they don't exist, Detective Sergeant! The woman's a fraud! She's your culprit.'

Privately Lucy had the same thoughts, that Mary's fellow-sisters were imaginary, but she kept her views to herself. 'Mary Maxwell-Hume has as good an alibi for the night of your father's death as your own, sir.'

'I don't mean for Daddy's death, you fool! I mean for my stolen car! I don't care about Daddy at all.'

Lucy sat back, grinning. 'You reckon Sister Mary stole your car?'

'Of course. Who else?'

'We'll take your suggestion into consideration, Mr Plews, I promise.' Izzy seemed to be having yet more problems with her laces. 'You've been very helpful, actually, thank you.'

Just before Lucy brought the interview to a close, she said to Izzy, 'Have you any questions, perhaps, PC Bryce?'

Izzy hesitated. 'Not really, sir. But can I just clear something up?'

'If you must,' said Plews.

'Isn't Ruskin College at Oxford?'

'I was at Ruskin in Cambridge, Constable.'

'There's an Angela Ruskin University in Cambridge, sir.'

'Are you trying to make a point, Constable?'

'No, sir. As you said, as I'm not as well educated as you.'

'Indeed.'

'Were you actually at Cambridge University, sir? We need to get it right for our notes.'

'I think you already know the answer, Constable,' Plews hissed. He turned to Grant. 'Will that be all, Detective Sergeant? I'm a busy man.'

Afterwards, while she was driving them both back to the station, Izzy asked, 'Did we learn anything?'

'Oh yes, Izzy. We learned three things,' Lucy replied. 'First, I learned that you're a bad girl, Isobel Bryce. Well done – I enjoyed that, and I'll look forward to interviewing along with you in the future.'

'Thank you, ma'am. My pleasure.'

'I'll bet.'

'Second, we know that lots of people would have a motive to steal that man's car. He's loathsome. I hope I get the chance to steal his next one.'

Izzy chuckled. 'And the final thing?'

'He didn't kill his father. Had nothing to do with it. He couldn't care if his father was alive or dead, it was obvious. So why kill him?'

***

That same day, Dave Lander had a breakthrough. He discovered that four Sabatier filleting knives had been sold online to UK addresses in the last six months, one of which was to a chef in an Edinburgh city centre restaurant. Not only that, but the buyer in question had asked for the knife to personalised, with his initials engraved on the handle: 'LP'. Lander had immediately taken Andy McFadden to visit the chef in question – a Łukasz Popucewicz – who at the time of their arrival was using the very knife itself. Popucewicz was a recent arrival from Krakow and didn't actually speak English very well, but he'd managed to explain that he'd had to re-order it, as the first knife had gone missing in the post. The package had been left by the delivery driver on the chef's front doormat while he'd been at work – not a good thing to do with a knife, even a knife carefully wrapped – but Popucewicz assured the online seller that it had gone by the time he'd made it home. Precisely to prevent a repeat occurrence, he'd suggested that the second knife be delivered direct to the restaurant; and even Lander had to concede that the chef had little need of two identical knives. All the same, he was certain that the missing knife had probably eventually ended up sticking out of Leonard Plews's back.

News of Lander's discovery buzzed around St Leonard's, but as Lucy pointed out, the Sabatier knife still had to get from outside the chef's flat to inside the ward where Plews had died. Lander still had suspicions of his own.

'The first person to set eyes on the 'lost' knife – apart from the killer – still seems to be Mary Maxwell-Hume. She might not have been the murderer, but she might still know more than she's told us so far. She must know something else.'

Knox said nothing. He was convinced that Mary had nothing to do with Plews's death. But he could sense that others weren't quite so sure, and Dave Lander's success seemed to give extra weight to anything else he suggested.

Sensing Knox's discomfort, O'Malley opted for subterfuge.

'Ah think youz are the best placed tae get stuff out o' yer Sister Mary, John,' he'd said to Knox. 'Use any means yez have tae. Ah dinnae care, although I'll be jealous of course. Ah'm curious about that knife.'

Knox ignored the sly dig about Mary, but pointed out that she was assisting with the car theft investigation. And he was curious about the knife, too.

And so, once again, he found himself parking his car late that afternoon in Mary Maxwell-Hume's little Trinity cul-de-sac. He approached the visit with mixed emotions. He had a job to do, but at the same time O'Malley had given him licence to be genuinely friendly towards her. He was still wondering if she would feel betrayed as he rang her doorbell. As usual, it couldn't be heard from outside so he was slightly startled when Mary opened it.

'My, John! What a pleasant surprise! Please come in – follow me.'

He did as bidden, and as usual she took her time to walk ahead of him, which gave him every opportunity to study her from behind. Never one to hide her figure, Mary was wearing a classic red ankle-length lace dress which appeared to offer occasional faint glimpses of what lay beneath without ever allowing any degree of certainty for the viewer.

When they arrived in the living room, she walked over to her grand piano, which as ever dominated the room, and turned around to face him.

'You approve, John?'

'Of what, Mary?'

She smiled. 'The dress, of course. I know you too well.' As Knox began to blush, she reached towards him and gently brushed his hand. 'It's all right, John, I like when you look at me. It means you're being honest. And you know, of all your fine traits, I like your honesty more than any other?'

'You do?'

'Of course. So, do you like what you see?'

Knox realised that he had lost control of the conversation already. He took a deep breath, and was immediately reminded of Mary's Chanel No. 5.

'Lovely, Mary. I won't lie.'

She smiled broadly. 'No, I know you won't. And speaking of telling the truth, I want you to tell me if you've been practising as we agreed. Please don't let me down.'

'I've been practising, Mary, although I'm sure you'd be disappointed in me.'

Suddenly, she looked serious. 'John, you've never disappointed me.'

'What never?'

Mary knew the reference. 'Well… hardly ever.'

Suddenly she clapped her hands.

'But I must hear you!' Insisting that he remove his jacket, she led him to the piano and sat him on the stool. 'Have you been practising the Bach, John? The *French Suite in B minor*?'

Knox was going to protest when he felt her hands on his shoulders, massaging his neck and back from behind.

'Play for me, John. Play.' She leant her weight on him from behind. He glanced round: her eyes were closed. 'Play,' she whispered in his ear.

And so, as so often before, John Knox found himself playing, like a puppet pianist having all of his strings pulled from behind. Inwardly, he enjoyed the sensuousness, although he spent much of the rest of his time questioning if he was taking advantage of his teacher. At the end, though, she had a surprise for him.

'Thank you, John. I really enjoyed that.'

'Really? Did I play well?'

'Oh no, you're still far too imprecise on the left hand, you missed several notes in the middle section, and your grasp of the dynamics of the piece were really quite poor.

'And there was me thinking you'd enjoyed my playing, too,' Knox said, a little crestfallen.

'Oh, but I did enjoy it. I always enjoy your playing, John. I enjoy sharing your playing.'

Knox was used to being confused by Mary, so he let it go.

'Mary, I came – '

'Oh, John, I'm so sorry.'

Mary sat down on the piano stool beside him, looking concerned.

'What?'

'I can see it in your eyes, John, I'm so sorry, really I am.'

'I don't understand – '

'I can see it. You and Alice have split up, haven't you?'

'How did you – ?'

'I told you, I can see it in your eyes.'

Mary came closer and did something she'd never done before: she hugged him. For the first time since Alice had left, he felt tears in his eyes, and was embarrassed.

'Sorry, Mary.'

'Tell me about it.'

And he did. From the start. He told Mary all about how he and Alice had met, how their relationship had first developed to the point where they'd shared a flat, and how their love had grown cold again.

Eventually, Mary said, 'She was never the woman for you, John.'

'That's a bit unfair. She's a nice person. Attractive.'

'Good in bed?'

'That, too.'

'You can have all that and more, John.'

'What more is there to have?'

'You'll find out one day. One day soon. I guarantee it. But it's not what you need now anyway,' she said.

Knox chuckled. 'I'm not sure what I need at the moment.'

'Well, I do.' She smiled. 'Close your eyes.' He closed them. 'Keep them closed tight or you'll ruin the surprise.' Then eventually, 'John, you may open your eyes.'

What he saw was not what he'd expected. Mary was standing before him, dressed identically to how he'd previously seen her, with one difference: the dress was gone.

'Do you approve?'

Knox was speechless. 'Mary… I don't know what to say.'

'Be honest, John. I can take criticism.'

'You look stunning.'

'So now you know for certain, John. Our order believes we should wear only as much as it is necessary for due modesty. At this moment, modesty is not appropriate for either of us.'

'Are you saying…?'

'Stand up.' She helped him to his feet, then gently removed his clothing. She insisted that she did it herself until eventually they were equally clad.

'You can leave your watch on, John.'

'What now?'

Mary looked at him, a bemused smile on her face. 'What do you think? Come with me.' She took his hand.

'Mary… I'm not sure this is right… I'm taking advantage of you.'

Still holding his hand, she stepped back a little. 'You're taking advantage of me, you think? Tell me, John, is that because I'm a woman and you're a man – '

'Well – '

'Because if it is, I never had you down as sexist. This is my idea, I think. Or is it because I'm twenty years older than you?'

He laughed. 'Twenty-three, to be exact.'

She leaned forward as if to kiss him, then suddenly – very hard – she slapped him across his rear. At first Knox was too shocked to say anything.

'That hurt. I didn't have you down as a violent woman, Mary.'

'I'm not violent, but needs must. If you insist that you're just a little boy, I'll treat you like one.'

'You wouldn't treat a little boy that way, Mary. Be honest.'

'No, that's true. I'd only smack a grown man who deserved it.'

'Am I taking advantage of you?'

'Are we taking advantage of each other, John? Of course we are. It's what each of us needs. You've had your confidence damaged. You need it repaired. This is the best way.'

'And what do you get out of it?'

'Isn't it obvious? What I've missed since my husband Duncan died. I'm not offering you a relationship here, John, we're going to have sex, straightforward sex. While you're enjoying my body, I'll have my eyes closed and be thinking of Duncan. Do you have a problem with that?'

Knox smiled. 'Sounds like I'm getting the better of that deal.'

She led him out of the room. 'Come on, John, enough talking.'

***

'Thank you, John. You made a good Duncan. To be honest, you're a more skilled lover than I'd expected.'

'A better lover than a pianist?'

'Definitely. You're a concert-standard lover.'

Knox chuckled. 'I'm glad I didn't let you down. And thank you, too, by the way.'

'Who were you thinking of? Alice?'

Knox sat up for a moment. 'Mary, I was thinking of you. You should know that.'

'It's nice to hear you say that.'

Knox lay back on the bed beside her.

'Mary, you are the most unusual nun I've ever met.'

'Thank you, John. I'll take that as a compliment.'

'I've never met a nun who rejoiced in sex so much as you.'

'That's because our order has a different attitude to human physical pleasure. For us, physical pleasure is something in which we should rejoice, not to deny ourselves. Physical pleasure is as much part of the human condition as breathing, so long as it's not at anyone else's expense.'

'I like that philosophy.'

'We can go further. We believe that the clitoris is proof of the existence of God.'

'Sorry?'

'You heard. Ask yourself this, John: what function does it perform other than to give pleasure? We believe it's a sin not to glorify the joy it brings. It's our duty to enjoy our bodies, John, not to apologise for them. Innocent, shared pleasure is a gift from God. By the way, the Bible tells us that we are made in God's image, so God must also have…'

'Are you saying God must be a woman?' Knox chuckled, although he suspected Mary was being entirely serious.

'It's the only logical answer, John. The males of most animal species are basically single-use expendable beings, like those carrier bags you used to get in supermarkets before they started charging.' She looked at him intently. 'Look, whoever heard of kings in charge of a beehive?'

'So all this stuff about God being a man, or even both a man and a woman, is rubbish?'

'Utter nonsense. Women have been trying to tell you men that for decades, but you've come to believe your own propaganda. We women are partly to blame, mind you. Throughout history, we've sent men off to fight in wars on our behalf. It was always better that you men got killed rather than us women, but of course men came back full of testosterone and it became hard to control them. And then wars changed, too, so that women weren't safe in their own homes any more. Which is where we are now.'

'Do you feel safe at the moment, Mary?'

She rolled over towards him so that she was lying face down, her head resting on his chest.

'Oh yes, John. I feel safe at the moment. I feel very safe just now, thank you.'

Knox closed his eyes and gently massaged Mary's back. In response, she gently massaged his groin until he started to feel tense again.

'I'm not sure you're quite done, John,' Mary said in a matter-of-fact way. Then she added, 'What was it you wanted to ask me, anyway?'

'Sorry?'

'You came here tonight to ask me some questions, John. About Uncle Lenny or about the cars?'

'It can wait, honestly.'

Mary squeezed him gently. 'No it can't. Ask me your questions and we'll see what we can manage after that.'

'Did you smuggle a filleting knife with the letters 'LP' into St Ninian's?'

Mary looked up at him. Then she kissed the small crucifix that she wore on her neck and said, 'I swear I didn't take any knife into St Ninian's.'

'Can you shed any light on how a knife could have found its way into the ward that night?'

Again she said no, kissing the crucifix. Then she said, 'Can I remind you of something I said before, John?'

'Go on.'

'I said that good detective work is about asking the right questions of the right people. You haven't quite done that yet in Uncle Lenny's case. But you will, I know.'

'You can't give me any more help?'

'No.'

'What about the cars, then?'

'You're staying the night, John.'

'Am I?'

'Yes. And the cars can wait until tomorrow.'

'Are we getting somewhere with the cars, Mary?'

'Getting somewhere? Of course, John. What do you take me for? But it can wait until tomorrow morning, as I said. Tonight, we have other things on our mind. But you have something else on your mind, John. Something else is bothering you. What is it?'

'It's not really about a crime, Mary. Or at least, only a moral crime.'

Mary propped herself up and looked Knox directly in the eye. 'Oh, but they're the worst crimes of all, John. What's happened?'

Knox filled her in about W. Montgomery Bishop's articles about Magda Czeslawska: Mary hadn't seen them.

'His latest one is the worst yet,' Knox told her. 'There's a large photo of Magda, alongside all the patients who have died in the last few months while she's been on duty.'

'But it's a care home, John. People die there, that's what it's for.'

'It's a really wicked article,' Knox said.

'That poor young woman. She deserves justice.'

Knox smiled. 'Justice? There's a nice thought. Bishop is a vile character.'

'I've never heard you say that about anyone, John. He must be truly awful.' She lay back. 'Leave it with me, John, I'll deal with it.'

'You will? Am I allowed to know how you'll deal with it?'

'No. I might need a little help, but remember I can go places that other people can't.' As if to demonstrate the point, she reached down and said, 'Now relax.'

They lay in silence for a while, gently massaging each other. Then Knox said, 'I don't associate you with anything so ritualistic as a crucifix, Mary.'

She stopped for a moment and he wondered if he'd said something wrong. 'It's nothing to do with Christianity, John. It was a present from Duncan.'

'Sorry.'

She started to massage him again. 'Don't be sorry, John. Remember you're Duncan tonight.'

TWENTY-THREE

'**Y**OUZ'RE FEELING BETTER, JOHN. That's a good sight. A bit tired, mebbe?'

'No, sir, I'm fine. I slept very well, thanks,' Knox said. He'd phoned into the office to say that he'd be late in as he'd had to 'pay a return visit to Mary Maxwell-Hume's house in the morning to discuss the car thefts.'

'So… wiz it a satisfactory visit then?'

'I learned a lot, sir, actually. I think we might be making progress on the Jaguars.'

'Really?' O'Malley had been joined by Lander, Grant and Bryce at Knox's 'hot-desk'. 'So yer wumman Mary's deliverin' the goods, is she?'

Knox gave a slight chuckle under his breath. 'I think so, sir. It was a productive visit.'

'Which one?'

Knox looked at O'Malley, slightly bemused.

O'Malley smiled knowingly. 'Yesterday afternoon's, or this morning's?'

Knox looked at him. 'Both.'

O'Malley held his gaze for a moment, then winked. 'Good work, John. What did yez cam up wi' then, between the pair o' yez?'

'Mary reckons she knows what's been going on with the car thefts.'

Lucy Grant looked impressed. 'She does? Well done her. This I must hear.'

Knox took a deep breath. 'Two things are going on. First of all, someone has been able to hack into the DVLA computer in Swansea.'

'I think that's impossible, sir,' Lander said.

Knox looked at him. 'Dave, please don't ask me too much, but I've actually seen a demonstration. Hackers can do what they like, generally. The secret is not to get so greedy that the victim notices. In this case, the culprit is being very clever indeed.'

'Ah cannae wait tae hear this.' O'Malley propped himself on Knox's desk and folded his arms.

'The reason why all the cars have to have personalised number plates is because each stolen car has a history of having its registration changed. The car has its original number plate, then its number plate is changed at the request of the new owner to something like TED 1E or MAX 1.

'Our hacker scans the DVLA site for a car that fits that profile in the local area, then arranges that it gets stolen. It's quickly moved somewhere else, possibly a back street garage, possibly a dealer, where the car is given a third number plate. That's from a car that's been taken off the road, perhaps damaged beyond repair in a car accident. To an outsider, it now looks as though the previous owner has sold the car and taken his personalised number with him, and the car has gone back to having its original number plate. But it hasn't – it's got a new identity altogether. Our hacker simply alters all the details on the database and automatically issues a new registration document. All that remains is to change the plate on the chassis. That should be hard in theory, but there are people out there who can fake almost anything.'

'Why do they bother with the new number?' Izzy asked. 'Why not just use the original number allocated to the car?'

'Because it would be too easy for us to find the cars and check them, Izzy. We'd be watching out for the original registration plates as well as the personalised ones. This way leaves us looking for needles in a haystack.'

O'Malley was impressed. 'And yer Mary found out all o' this fur yez?'

'Off the record?'

'Aff the record.'

'I got a working demonstration.'

O'Malley swore under his breath. 'She's good, John, ah'll gie yez that.'

'She's a private detective.' Knox smiled. 'As she claims, she can go places others fear to tread.'

'Ah'll bet. There's just the wan proablem.'

'Which is?'

'We've nae idea which cars tae start checking for tampered chassis plates. We cannae check every single Jag in the entire country.'

Knox reached into his jacket and produced two sheets of A4 printout.

'Oh ye of little faith in Sister Mary.' He placed one sheet on the desk. 'These are the registration plates of the cars we're looking for.' Then, with a flourish, he placed the other one on top of it. 'And these are the cars that have given up their numbers in the cause of giving each stolen Jaguar a new identity. To be fair, they could be anywhere. Possibly in a crusher somewhere.'

'Well done, sir,' Lucy said.

'Well done, Sister Mary, I think,' Knox said.

'I didn't realise she was so heavily involved in the investigation. That was quite risky, wasn't it?'

'I think wez a' need tae gies yez credit fur stickin' by Sister Mary, John. Ah confess ah had ma doubts. Ah thought ye wuz only interested in her fur her boady last night.'

'And her piano teaching,' Knox added, realising too late that he hadn't denied that he had been tricked into admitting that his stay had been longer than he'd pretended.

'Ah said yez could use whatever methods were necessary, John.' Knox felt his face burning, but O'Malley added. 'It's no' ma business, but yez done well.'

'Thank you. I think we still need Mary, though, sir. She can carry on trawling some of the car showrooms for us.'

'Goin' places no man can go, eh?'

'Going places where no police officer can go, sir.'

Knox and Grant decided that they had to be seen to be giving their attention to the St Ninian's event as well, even if there was never any way that it could ever be proved to be murder. The curiosity of the irrelevant knife stuck into Leonard Plews's back was annoyingly impossible to ignore. Privately, though, Grant was beginning to wonder if she could see a solution to the conundrum of how the knife made its way into the ward.

On arrival, the pair were greeted by a doctor dressed in an expensive suit, whom they hadn't met before. Introducing himself as 'Geoffrey Davis' he explained that he was the medical director of St Ninian's Haven. He spoke with a posh accent: Knox couldn't decide if he was English, was posh Scots, or had simply developed the voice for effect.

'Could you explain what the role of 'medical director' is, sir? Are you full time?'

'Full time?' The doctor guffawed. 'Goodness me, no. What would be the point of that? It would be a terrible waste of valuable funds. No, no – I pop in every two or three weeks to check things are running well. I leave the actual medicine to the young turks, the junior staff, so to speak. I'm sure most of police legwork is done by ordinary constables, isn't it? I mean, why have a dog and bark yourself?'

Knox silently wondered why he'd shown any interest at all. Perhaps reading his thoughts, Davis seemed to see nothing amiss in explaining.

'I'm paid by the St Ninian's Trust, Inspector. My day job, so to speak, is in the city centre. I have a small practice in Ainslie Place in the West End. It's jolly good work, really. Private practice, of course. Mostly medical examinations for BUPA, or for insurance companies. Quite a few large firms send their senior employees to me once a year, too. Almost all nine-to-five stuff, don't you know. Lets me get to the golf course whenever I want, too. Not a bad life, really.'

The mention of golf caused Knox to glance at the medical director's tie.

'I recognise the tie, sir. My Chief Inspector, Maximilian Plews, son of the deceased, is a member there, too, of course.'

Davis wrinkled his nose visibly. 'Yes, I understand both he and his brother, that frightful auctioneer fellow, are members.' It prompted him to change the subject. 'Was it me you wanted to see?'

'Not really, sir, although I'm glad we've met.' Privately he hoped they might not ever have to meet again. 'But I'm afraid I need to check out a few things with your staff. I understand that the night nurse, Magda Czeslawska is on duty again today. I phoned ahead to check.'

'Oh, jolly good. Bad business this, Inspector. Bad business, and bad for business.' He seemed to think his little joke was more amusing than it actually was. 'Are you any nearer to solving what happened? I saw the article in the Mail yesterday. Pretty racist in tone, I'd say. Not that I read the Mail myself, but one of my colleagues pointed it out. This Bishop chappie seems thoroughly unpleasant. Is Magda guilty of anything, by the way?'

'I'd agree about Bishop's article, sir. As far as the case is concerned, we're still pursuing enquiries, sir. We really don't understand what the point of the knife was.'

'Knives generally have a point, inspector, what?'

Knox looked away to try hide his irritation. 'You're a medical man, sir. You know the knife didn't kill Mr Plews.'

'Indeed. It was inserted post mortem. Insufficient bleeding from the wound to be otherwise, so Dr Wolstencroft informed me.'

'Still... someone felt it worthwhile stabbing him. And there's the little matter of how it evaded your security systems here.'

Davis looked a little uncomfortable. 'Yes. Our Trustees are asking the same question. I think they're concerned that we might have to field a compensation claim. Duty of care. All we need is one of those awful ambulance-chasing firms onto the case.'

Knox was sure there would be no claim, but he had no intention of allowing this low-life any peace of mind. 'I understand that the two sons are very litigious, sir.' Davis gulped slightly.

They found Magda coming out of one of the single rooms further down the ward.

'Why am I in the peppers? Am I in trubble?' She looked at Lucy. 'So – vuss those biscuits just a trick?'

'No, Magda, you're not in trouble, not as far as we know. May we call you 'Magda'?' Lucy added. She added, 'I'm sorry, I really am. Look, we can put out a statement if you wish, but I'm almost afraid that Bishop might twist it somehow.'

Magda shrugged her shoulders in resigned agreement.

'Anyway,' Lucy said, 'I'm sorry but we still have a few more things to clear up ourselves.'

Knox had suggested that Lucy lead the questions, as he felt Magda would be more at ease.

'Of curse.'

'Can we go and sit somewhere for a moment?'

Magda led them to a corner of an area designated as a day room. As they sat, Knox watched as Lucy gently coaxed answers from the Polish nurse, now understandably suspicious and far less willing to answer than at their previous meeting. Lucy asked Magda to repeat all of her movements on the night, explaining that it was always possible that some new detail might emerge if she told her story once again. Patiently, Magda explained that she'd looked in on all of the patients about half past ten at night. She'd then returned to her desk which was situated by the doors at the end of the corridor. No one had entered until Sister Mary made her nightly visit at which Lenny Plews's body was discovered.

Lucy asked about access to the room by anyone else from the other end of the corridor. Magda explained that work on the new extension was undertaken during daylight hours, and during that time the old fire escape at the end of the corridor remained completely closed to building workers. Although the old fire escape door had been removed, a mortice lock meant that the temporary replacement door could only be opened from the inside. Only St Ninian's could unlock it, and to prove it she produced a key from a pocket in her uniform. The building was safe, she insisted.

Then Grant asked about something different.

'Magda, I'd like to ask you a little bit about changing the beds. Can I do that?'

Knox was as surprised by the question as Magda herself.

Lucy explained. 'The only cupboard in that corridor is towards the far end, away from your desk and close to the fire exit. Is that correct?'

'Yuss.'

'Can you show us the CCTV console, please?'

Magda led them across to her desk. 'It is all recurded, too.'

'I know, Magda. I just want to try something. Would you please fetch three sheets and two blankets from the cupboard and bring them here?'

'Out here?'

'Please. Just to please me.'

Magda went through the double doors, down the corridor and opened the linen cupboard door. It took her ten or fifteen seconds to fetch out the relevant sheets and blankets.

While she was in the cupboard, Lucy pointed to the CCTV screen, turned to Knox and said, 'Do you see?'

'I can't see very much, Lucy. The door's in the way.'

'That's the point, John. That's the point.'

'But where…?'

'While the linen cupboard door is open, we can't see the door at the end being opened. The knife gets handed in to her, but then we'd see it when the linen cupboard door gets closed. So she has to hide it in the cupboard itself until later.'

'And then she brings it down later into the room where the patients are when…'

'… She has beds to change.'

Knox grinned. 'Detective Sergeant Lucy Grant, you are a genius. A complete genius. Bravo.'

'So Magda's our killer after all?' Lucy said quietly, conscious that the nurse herself might hear.

Knox shook his head.

'No, Lucy, we know from the CCTV that Magda Czeslawska didn't kill anyone that night. And I think that knife's been there for weeks, perhaps even months. Magda didn't mean anyone to be killed at all. I believe she was actually trying to stop someone being killed.'

TWENTY-FOUR

'I DID NUTT STUBB HIM. He vuss a nusty mun but I did nut kill him.'

'The Inspector's not accusing you of that, Magda,' Lucy said, reassuringly. She wasn't quite sure herself what the Inspector was accusing her of, but she knew that wasn't it. 'The Inspector's only asking what you know about the knife.'

'But that journalist made up those things about me. I thought you were being nice to me, buying me chocolate biscuits. Now I am accused of killing a patient. Why should I help you?'

'Because we know that the journalist made up those things, Magda,' Lucy said.

'Tell us about it, Magda,' Knox said gently. 'We know you didn't kill Mr Plews.'

'I didn't mean any harm. But I'd promised, I'd promised...'

'Promised what, Magda?,' Knox pressed. 'You promised something to one of the patients, didn't you? I'm guessing it was one of the women.'

'It was Mrs Gray. She was afraid.'

'Afraid of what, Magda? Was she afraid of Mr Plews?'

Magda nodded. 'He vuss a beast. A beast.' She spat the words. 'He couldn't be trusted at all, we had to sedate him all the time. But Mrs Gray had experienced him, she was afraid he would waken up. And when Łukasz came, it was like a message from God. He had the same initials as Mr Plews.'

'Łukasz?' Lucy asked.

'Łukasz Popucewicz,' Knox said. 'Sous-chef at Benson's in Grindlay Street.'

'The upmarket place? Costs a fortune, two Michelin stars?'

'That's the one, Lucy. Too expensive for mere polis like ourselves.'

'He is a good chef,' Magda said, firmly. 'His work is worth a lot uff money, but he isn't paid vutt he should be.'

'So, explain… how do you know Łukasz? Boyfriend?' Knox asked.

'He is my cousin. He actually stayed with me until he found somewhere of his own.'

'What about the knife, then? Tell us about it.'

'When he moved to his new flat Łukasz ordered it to celebrate his new job as a chef. Ordered it in his name, with his initials. I was always going to steal it but the postman made it easy by leaving the first one outside his flat. I just pretended it had been stolen so he ordered a new one.

'You were corruct, Inspector. Next day, I left the knife outside the old fire escape door then moved it inside into the linen cupboard. Once it was there, it was easy to slip it into Mrs Gray's locker under all of the sheets while I was changing her bed. She was verry grateful.'

'But it was a knife, Magda,' Knox said, still trying to absorb what he was hearing. 'You gave a patient a *knife*?'

'It made her feel safe to know it was there. But I never thought she would use it.'

Knox sat back. 'We're not sure she did.'

'But I do nutt understand.'

'Someone stabbed Mr Plews, but we don't know who it was. They simply used the knife from Mrs Gray's locker.'

'You trucked me. You are like all the other snecks.'

'Listen, Magda, at the moment we just want to find out what happened.'

'Vill you arrest me?'

'Perhaps not. It's not clear that you've broken any laws, to be honest. St Ninian's might not be happy that you brought a knife into the ward on behalf of a patient.'

'So I lose my job?'

'Perhaps they don't have to know, Magda. It depends on how helpful you can be.'

'I've told you everything. It's the truth.' Magda looked terrified.

'When did you smuggle the knife in?' Lucy asked.

'About three months ago.'

'Really? So the knife had been there for a long time?'

'I'd forgotten about it.'

Lucy shook her head and looked at Knox. 'What do you think, sir?'

'I'm not sure we really know any more about what happened in that room that night. All we've solved here is the mystery of how the knife got into the patients' room.'

***

Before they left St Ninian's, they dropped in on Martha Ramsay once again. They didn't expect much, and weren't surprised to hear her back in rambling mode again, this time desperate to tell them that the 'angels would look after her and knew everything.'

As they got into the car to leave, Lucy turned to Knox and asked, 'John, tell me honestly – do you really believe we're going to find out exactly what happened to Mr Plews?'

'You want an honest answer? Given that all but one of those in the room that night is dead, that the remaining one is completely out of it, and that everyone seems more than delighted that old man Plews is dead anyway, I rather doubt it. Add into the mix that we can't even prove he was murdered at all according to Dr Sally, even although we know he was, and I'd say the odds are pretty heavily stacked against solving this. Dr Sally's the one plus that's come out of it, though.'

Lucy smiled at him. 'You like her?'

'I like her commitment to her job, her ability to laugh and yet treat her dead people with reverence. You know she says a little prayer for the deceased before each autopsy?'

'Is that important, John?'

'It seems important to her, and I'm impressed by that. That reminds me, I really ought to pop in to say thanks for all of her careful work on this.'

Lucy smiled. 'You *do* like her, John.'

'She's easy company, that's all.'

Lucy grinned.

'To return to your original question, Lucy, we've known for a long time that we'd never achieve a conviction on the Plews death. But I think we'll need a miracle even to find out what happened at all. Thankfully, things look a little brighter on the Jaguar front.'

***

The next day, a Thursday, brought a bright, clear morning as a woman and her son wandered into Hoggart & Law's with a view to buying a used Jaguar. The woman seemed vaguely familiar, but her son did not. The woman wore a close-fitting green dress, the son was dressed casually, with a jacket and open-necked shirt.

Once again Jason was on duty. It concerned him that he recognised the woman: perhaps he should be able to remember her name. He was aware of her perfume. She took the lead.

'John and I are interested in several of your cars here, young man. Can you provide us with a few details of their previous owners.'

Jason happily explained that each of the cars in question had actually been much-loved, so much so that their owners had personalised their registrations – a common trend amongst owners of prestige Jaguar models like these ones, of course. He complimented the lady's excellent taste. The man asked to see the registration documents, but Jason explained that for security reasons car showrooms didn't keep the cars and the documentation together. The son asked to look under the bonnet of two of them, took a couple of photos on his iPhone and wandered away for a moment. The lady explained that he needed to check financial arrangements with his bank. Jason began to get quite excited at the prospect of anything up to £1000 commission landing in his wage packet.

The lady wandered off to look at a couple of other cars while the man spoke on the phone, then came back and asked Jason for his card.

'Jason Hildersley. Very good, young man. Have you worked here long?'

'About six months, madam.'

'You like it here?'

'Yes, madam.'

'Are you ambitious, Jason?'

'I don't know what you mean, madam.'

'I mean, Jason, are you ambitious? Do you wish to better yourself? Let's see… what does your father do?'

Jason felt he was being interrogated, but the woman was a potential customer for a very expensive Jaguar.

'My father's also in the motor trade, madam. He has a little garage himself. In the old station yard near Portobello. Nothing like this, though.'

'I know the one,' she said. 'But we all have to start somewhere. And I'm sure his business is good.'

'Oh yes, business is very good. He manages lots of holidays. He and Mum are off next week. New York.'

'And do you see much of your father, Jason? Do you ever visit his garage?'

'Oh yes, madam, we see plenty of each other.' Jason seemed keen to steer the conversation back to car sales. 'Can I help you in any other way, madam? By the way, have you been in before?'

The woman in the green dress ignored both questions and simply repeated that she was very interested in several of the cars in the showroom. She left it at that, and wandered away towards the man, whom Jason had clocked as more likely to be her son than her partner, although you could never tell these days. And the woman might have been older – perhaps around fifty, he guessed – but she was very attractive even to Jason. Jason rather fancied her himself.

The woman and 'John' spoke briefly, then John made another phone call while the lady in the green dress approached him again. Jason could feel a little excitement growing inside him as she came very close to him.

'Jason,' the woman whispered softly in his ear, 'I need to ask you something.'

Jason felt his knees tremble slightly. 'Ask anything you like, madam.'

'Servicing a Jaguar can be quite expensive,' she said. 'Do you know anyone who might do it a little cheaper? It would need to be someone I could trust with a Jaguar, of course.'

Jason couldn't quite work out if he should be excited by her close presence or disappointed that her question was about car servicing. He decided to take a chance and whisper a reply in her ear.

'Actually, madam, my dad's a Jaguar specialist. He doesn't advertise the fact but he works on them a lot.'

The woman stood back and said, 'Oh my – but that's wonderful! Will he ever have seen any of these cars here, for instance? I'd really prefer if your father felt a connection with the car we chose to buy.'

Jason walked across and picked out two, a silver 5.0 V8 Petrol 510PS, and an XJ near the window. 'My father worked on both of those before they were traded in,' he confided.

'Oh, but that's wonderful, Jason. I do believe they're two of the cars my son John was keen on, too. He'll be so pleased. Can I go and tell him, please?'

Jason wanted to accompany her, but she held out her palm to indicate that this would be a private conversation.

John greeted her with an enquiring expression.

'What does the lad say, Mary?'

Mary pointed to the cars Jason had told her about. 'That one, and that one.'

'Those two have definitely had their chassis plates changed. Dave Lander's pal down in the police garage could tell from the photos I sent him. In fact I think there are four here. I'm not sure the Chief Inspector's is one of them, though.'

'Oh I think it is, John. So is his brother's.'

'Really?' Knox pointed over to the one in the window. 'The colour's right in that one, but the interior's wrong, Mary.'

'John, our friend Mr Hildersley swaps all the interior parts round. If he can swap it, he does. Look – ' she pointed to another car, '– this car's seats are over there in that car.'

'Jesus.'

'I don't think Our Lord Jesus drives a Jaguar, John.'

'Perhaps not, no. Probably couldn't afford the insurance premiums.'

'I think every part of each car is either here, or at Jason's dad's father's garage. But the pieces of each jigsaw have been deliberately mixed up a little. And they've all been given the number plates of cars that have been declared off-road.'

Just then, two women entered the showroom. Mary put her arm through Knox's like a mother or a lover. 'Time to go?'

'Yes, they're all in place.'

Together, Knox and Mary approached Jason's sales desk. Jason looked up expectantly, but then his face fell when Knox produced his warrant card.

'I wonder…,' Knox said, 'might we have the keys to your showroom, Jason? My colleagues DS Grant and PC Bryce would like to lock up, if you wouldn't mind.'

***

At Hildersley's garage in Portobello, a team led by O'Malley and Dave Lander found most of the other pieces of the 'Jaguar jigsaws' that Mary had suggested would be found there. Mark Hildersley was arrested and charged was a range of offences from 'theft' to 'conspiracy to defraud'. The search team also found a range of ordinary cars that had been involved in serious accidents and which Hildersley was cannibalising for parts, including one part in particular – the registration plate. Hildersley chose to say very little other than that he 'took the blame'.

Jason Hildersley cooperated fully.

To be fair, his father had asked the police to convey his wish that his son should do anything he could to lessen his eventual sentence. That might even have had an effect, except that in no time at all, it became clear that the DVLA computer hacker was none other than Jason himself, skills finely honed during years of playing *Grand Theft Auto*, *Minecraft* and *Football Manager*. Jason created the fictitious documentation online, the false previous owners, and even arranged for the stolen cars to be absorbed into the Hoggart & Law stock and then onto the showroom floor. Jason had persuaded innocent customers to buy new Jaguars cars with a straight cash sale, but then entered each as a trade-in sale, the 'trade-in' car in each case being one of the stolen and altered Jaguars. The fictional 'trade-in value', of course, went straight into the pockets of Mark and Jason Hildersley, over £100,000 for the first three cars alone. The customers, and Hoggart & Law, were completely unaware that anything was going on.

Once it became clear that Knox and his colleagues already knew all of that, Jason's bargaining position began to weaken considerably. From then on, it was 'tell all to save himself,' which meant confessing to everything, including a little bonus: they'd tested the system out before with a Ford dealer. But the police paid no attention to stolen Fords, he explained, whereas it was obvious that the sort of people who owned Jaguars were much more likely to be in a position to make sure something was done about it. But Jaguars brought a much bigger return and it was a risk worth taking. In the end, that was their mistake: the Hildersleys had become greedy.

Naturally, Mary Maxwell-Hume had not been present to hear either of the Hildersleys' confessions. Nevertheless, Knox had a strange sense of déjà vu during the interviews, having already heard Mary's explanation of the father and son's modus operandi. He knew that she'd discovered the little Hildersley back-street garage in Portobello, and had noted the surprising number of Jaguars being serviced or repaired there. And of course she'd already found out about the hacking of the DVLA computer and now, it turned out, the Hoggart & Law system, too. Mary had even managed to find a motive for stealing Theodore Plews's Jaguar first.

Mary, of course, claimed none of the credit for the investigation; all of the plaudits had gone to Knox himself. Even Chief Inspector Maximilian Plews had broken the habit of lifetime and grudgingly congratulated him on 'excellent work'. His closest colleagues knew Mary was heavily involved, but had no idea to what extent and in any case they chose to applaud Knox's willingness to open his mind to alternative methods. As O'Malley put it afterwards, 'There's aye anither way – when yez think yez ken everythin', yez ken nuthin'.'

But, as he listened to first Mark Hildersley, then Jason, tell their respective stories, Knox couldn't but wonder whether he shouldn't be turning himself in for the crime of fraud at the same time.

***

Later that same evening, a journalist sat enjoying a postprandial brandy in the entrance hall in the Caledonian Hotel at Princes' Street's west end. He'd heard unconfirmed rumours that Magda Czeslawska had been arrested, but checking up on that could wait until the following day. In the meantime, he leant back in satisfaction, and looked forward to basking in the glory that he, W. Montgomery Bishop, had broken the story first: a scoop. He was back in top form, another notch for his CV.

His eye was drawn to an older woman who was drifting around aimlessly with a glass and an open bottle of champagne in her hand. Poised and elegant, her calf-length red crêpe dress was simply stunning: it fitted her figure so well that it revealed everything and nothing of her all at once. When the woman sat down at the opposite side of the table from him, Bishop could hardly believe his good fortune.

'There's nothing so lonely as a woman with a bottle of champagne and no one to share it with,' the red-dressed woman said. 'Would you be able to help me?'

Bishop downed the remains of his brandy and pushed his glass forwards on the table that separated them.

'I can't bear to see a damsel in distress,' he said.

'I'm so grateful,' the woman said. 'Perhaps I should sit on your side of the table?'

As she sat down near him, Bishop became aware that the woman was wearing an expensive perfume. She poured a healthy quantity of champagne into his glass and, with a 'cheers', toasted 'to new-found friends.' They chatted for a while, finished the champagne, then suddenly the woman in red suggested that perhaps 'Monty' and she might extend the night a little longer. She had a flat just along in Roseburn, no more than a mile to the west, and if he had a car…

Which was too good an offer for Monty Bishop to refuse. As she said, it was only a short journey and he was perfectly sober. His car was parked just around the corner. She said she needed to powder her nose, he needed to collect a toothbrush, but five minutes later they were in Bishop's car heading west along Shandwick Place.

The car had just passed Haymarket Station when Bishop became aware that a police car was tailing him, lights on, and indicating that he should pull over. Uttering a series of oaths, he stopped the car, whereupon the red-dressed passenger leapt from the passenger side door and ran towards the police car shouting, 'Help, help!'

Ushered into the back seat of the police car, Bishop naturally failed the breathalyser spectacularly, while at the same time the lady in red insisted that she was the victim of an attempted abduction where Bishop had made it clear that he planned on raping her in a country lane somewhere outside the city. No, she didn't have any flat in Roseburn, she'd no idea how Bishop could have made that up; in fact she was actually a virtuous nun and piano teacher who lived quietly in Trinity in the north of the city. She had only managed to escape Bishop's clutches by visiting the hotel toilet and quietly dialling 999 for police assistance. And, of course, by the grace of the Good Lord himself.

Bishop spent the night in the police cells. In the end the police were unsure that they had enough evidence to convict on the abduction and attempted rape count, but the drink-drive charge was a stonewaller. Bishop wasn't to know it yet, but he was about to lose his licence for two years, be fined £3,000, and to lose his job working for Justin Pearce.

A few days later, his car was returned to him, not that he was allowed to drive it. In the glove compartment, Bishop found a little pink Post-It stuck on the inside. It said '*To Monty – don't mess with me. Best wishes, Magda.*'

TWENTY-FIVE

J ACK O'MALLEY INSISTED that every time his team solved a significant crime, it was a cause for celebration. Solving a spate of car crimes might not normally qualify for hanging out the flags, but earning grudging praise from Chief Inspector Maximilian Plews most certainly was. Knox had been concerned that Plews would be in a bad mood: there was no chance that Plews or his brother would get their Jaguars back any time soon as they might be required as evidence in court. But Plews was unconcerned. He didn't want his 'contaminated' car back, and anyway it turned out that the Volvo garage was also a Porsche dealer. Now, two test-drives later, Maximilian and Theodore Plews were each owners of Porsche 911 Carreras, yellow and red respectively – paid for from their hated father's estate. Even the Plews brothers could be made happy, although these things were relative.

The celebration always came in two parts. First, O'Malley arranged that a plentiful supply of fresh warm doughnuts – at his expense – be delivered to the office, to be consumed with plastic cups of coffee from the machine. Second, anyone without family commitments was expected to show up after work in The Auld Hoose just across the road in St Leonard's Street.

Everyone was welcome at the pub, including any support staff, and whether they'd worked on the case or not. Izzy Bryce had excused herself from the Auld Hoose to go home to her family, and to everyone's great relief Plews himself had announced that he'd be giving it a miss, too. A 'drink with lads', he pronounced, wasn't quite his thing. But Chief Superintendent Caroline Richardson, head of the Edinburgh Division, made a point of dropping in for a quick pinot grigio. Knox himself was slightly late, but Sally MacIntosh – still wearing scrubs – arrived at exactly the same time and he was able to slide in fairly quietly. Despite his protestations, Sally insisted on buying Knox a beer.

'What's wrong with me standing a round, John? Does it offend your male chauvinist need to provide for a defenceless woman?' Sally chuckled. 'Anyway, this is your big moment. Well done.'

Knox smiled, said thanks, and bowed in acknowledgement of his defeat. While they were standing at the bar waiting for the drinks to be poured, Sally said, 'I heard about Martha Ramsay. Shame.'

'Yes, died of a stroke this morning. Ironic, really, nothing to do with her dementia at all.'

'And no knives involved,' Sally said. 'So what's happening to the Leonard Plews case?'

'They're closing the file. You're saying he died of a heart attack, there's no way we can prove it was murder, and none of the witnesses are still alive. The witnesses would have been completely unreliable anyway.'

'What about that nurse and the knife – Magda?'

'Well, to be honest, we're not sure she's broken any laws. What she did might have been unprofessional, but she thought she was trying to help. And the knife didn't kill anyone.'

Sally sighed. 'So… dead end?'

'Sounds like it,' Knox nodded, taking a swig from his glass of Peroni. 'Win some, lose some.'

Sally looked past Knox's shoulder towards a corner of the bar. 'I'm intrigued that your friend Sister Mary's here. Is that coincidence?'

Shocked, Knox spun round. Mary was sitting in the corner, all but invisible in a neat-fitting black dress. Beside her sat O'Malley. Making his apologies to Sally, Knox made his way across towards her table.

'Mary – what a lovely surprise! What brings you here to this evil den?'

She smiled warmly. 'The Lord moves in mysterious ways, John.' Then she explained, 'The Superintendent here kindly invited me along. We've been having a very nice quiet chat about your many talents, actually.'

'Yez'd be amazed whit ah've learned about yez, John. Yez're some boy, John, some boy.' O'Malley grinned. 'Ah'd say yez're quite well suited tae each ither, in fact.'

Alarmed, Knox looked at Mary and said, 'What on earth have you been telling the Superintendent, Mary?'

Mary looked towards O'Malley, then back to Knox.

'That's for the Superintendent and me to know, John, and for you to find out.'

'That doesn't sound good,' Knox said.

O'Malley stood up. 'Look, John, ah need tae sir-kyoo-late, and youz need tae be polite tae Sister Mary here. You take ma seat and ah'll head fur the bar again.' He turned back to Mary and said, 'Nice tae talk wi' yez, Sister. Sure yez winnae take ma oaffer up?'

'Thank you… Jack. It's kind of you, but no thanks.'

O'Malley shrugged, and sidled off, leaving Knox to take his place.

'Did O'Malley just suggest to you what I think he just suggested?'

293

'He did, John. And you're right, if you look hard enough he's a very decent, if very lonely, man. The trouble is that he can't whisper sweet nothings in any sort of language I understand. The poor man sounds coarser than he actually is. It's a disability, you know. He should qualify for one of those Blue Badge Permit things that allows you to park your car in special spaces in supermarkets.'

'Don't encourage him. He's takes little enough exercise as it is.'

They sat silent for a moment, then Knox said, 'You didn't tell him… about us, did you?'

'What about us, John? I had a wonderful night with Duncan recently, that's the only thing I remember.' She sipped a little more red wine from her glass. 'Please don't take that away from me.'

'Sorry, I didn't mean – '

Mary gently put her hand on his arm. 'John, don't be sorry. I'm terribly grateful. But I want us to be friends, not lovers. You've said it yourself, it wouldn't be right. You need someone younger than me, and there's a woman out there who's perfect for you, I know that. But I'll always be there for you.'

Knox wasn't quite sure that meant, but he said, 'And I for you, Mary. Thanks for everything. And I believe I've to thank you for dealing with my ex-schoolmate Monty Bishop, too.'

'It was a pleasure, John. Being in the car with him was *not* a pleasure, though. He made my flesh crawl. As you said, he's a vile man.'

'I suspect we've not heard the last of him, though. He has some influential but nasty friends.'

'I'm not afraid of W. Montgomery Bishop, John. I have a higher, more influential friend than anything he can summon. I'm a woman of God, remember.'

Knox chuckled. 'How could anyone forget?'

They sat for a moment, then to break the silence Knox said, 'You'll have heard about the business with your Uncle Lenny.'

'The Superintendent told me, yes.'

'It means we'll never quite find out what happened in there.'

'Why's that, John? Are you giving up?'

'Well, everyone's dead now, aren't they?'

Mary looked away, then looked back towards him.

'I'm slightly disappointed in you, John. I had higher hopes for you than that.'

'I'm sorry if I've let you down, Mary. But what else could I have done?'

'Good detective work is about asking the correct questions, remember? Ask the right questions and the right answers will come.'

'Are you saying I've not been asking the right questions?'

Mary said nothing, so Knox sat for a moment.

'Tell me, Mary, is there anything you know about the Leonard Plews death that I don't know myself?'

'That's a good question, John. Would you like me to answer it?'

Knox laughed. 'It would be nice.'

'Yes.'

'Can you tell me that information?'

'No.'

Slightly taken aback, Knox said, 'This is like twenty questions.'

'I hope it doesn't take you twenty, John. I haven't got that long.'

'Why can't you tell me that information?'

'Because it would be a breach of faith.'

Knox blinked, bemused. A breach of faith? Then he suddenly thought of something.

'Tell me what you do in the middle of the night when you visit those dying patients, Mary.'

'I listen to them.'

'Do you hear their confession?'

'I'm not sure if I'm allowed to hear confessions.'

'If the patients call them confessions, Mary, you'd treat them as such.'

Mary smiled. 'Very good, John. Very good.'

'Did anyone confess to killing Leonard Plews?'

'That would be a breach of confidence, John.'

Knox smiled. 'Mary, I didn't ask you who confessed, I asked if anyone confessed. That's not breaching any confidence.'

'Isn't it?'

'I think you've just told me that someone did confess. I won't ask you who.'

'Thank you.'

They sat in silence for a moment.

'How did Uncle Lenny end up on top of Eileen Lamb, Mary?' Knox asked.

'The usual way.'

'The *usual* way?'

'He got out of his bed and made his way across. He'd done it before.'

'Really?'

'Usually he just stood there then went back to bed.'

'But not this time.'

'No. Not this time,' Mary said. 'He didn't go back to his bed.'

Knox sat quietly for a moment. He didn't want to push her too hard.

'Uncle Lenny did something more, didn't he?'

'Yes. He climbed onto Mrs Lamb's bed. On top of her.'

'But... they still had sheets between them.'

'It didn't matter. He was trying to... he was a horrible man to the core, John.' Mary paused for moment, then continued, 'Anyone who ever met Uncle Lenny knew that.'

'So they decided to stop him? The others managed to do that?'

'I thought you'd said you wouldn't ask me who confessed, John.'

'I haven't asked you who confessed, Mary. I'm trying to ask you what happened. How did they stop Plews? Did someone just hold him down and suffocate him with the pillow?'

'It was the only thing they could do. Or so they thought,' Mary said. 'Perhaps they were right. They just got out of bed and lay on top of him, suffocating the life out of him until he died.'

'And they had the knife.'

'Yes, they had the knife,' Mary said. 'Useful, in the circumstances.'

'Especially a brand-new one with no fingerprints on it.' Mary said nothing, so Knox went on. 'And they just left Uncle Lenny there? Lying on top of Eileen Lamb?'

Mary looked at him, slightly surprised at the question. 'John, those patients were at death's door. Uncle Lenny was the strongest of them by far, and even his lifeless body was a dead weight. Literally. What *could* they do?'

'I suppose so.'

Mary looked out of the window at the street again. 'Satisfied, John? Do you have all the information you need?'

'Nearly. There are one two things I still don't know. Such as who actually did it. Only you know that.'

'Which I'm not going to tell you.'

Knox waited for a moment, then quietly asked, 'How many people confessed, Mary? I know more than one person was involved.'

'You said you wouldn't ask me who confessed.'

'I didn't promise not to ask how many people were involved.'

'Are you expecting me to answer?'

'Was it more than three?'

Mary said nothing, so Knox decided to provoke her.

'I'm guessing six, then. I'll assume six confessed and murdered Uncle Lenny. Everyone did it except the woman who was completely comatose. They're all guilty.'

'None of them are guilty at all, John, and not all six killed him anyway.'

'Ah. So it's a number between four and five.'

Surprisingly, Mary looked flustered. 'John, we're supposed to be celebrating here, and I'm being interrogated.'

'Perhaps I'm just asking the right questions at long last, Mary.'

She didn't reply. Instead she gave a quiet grunt of disgust.

'Go on then,' Knox said, 'tell me how many. What's the harm now?'

'Four.'

'Two of the women suffered from dementia. That means it must have been the three other men and Robina Wallace.' He chuckled. 'So Lucy Grant was right after all – they all did it, just like *Murder on the Orient Express*.'

'I believe that's an Agatha Christie novel, John. Is that a police manual these days? I must say that I do rather approve of Monsieur Poirot. He believes standards should be maintained. But I'm impressed that Ms Grant considered the possibility, however frivolously. You're right, she'll go far.'

She closed her eyes. Knox could tell something was upsetting her.

'What is it, Mary? Tell me,' he said, gently.

'I've let those patients down, John. They spoke to me in confidence and I shouldn't have told you. And they're definitely not murderers in my eyes. If anything, I'm as much to blame for Uncle Lenny's death as them.'

Knox looked at her. 'Why's that, Mary? How are you to blame?'

'When Uncle Lenny wandered over to Eileen Lamb, he was calling out my name. He hadn't a clue what he was doing, but he thought Mrs Lamb was me. The other patients knew what he planned to do. He was the ward bully and the others hated him – were terrified of him, even, hence the knife.'

Knox sat back and took a long slug of Peroni.

'How did they know about you and Uncle Lenny...?'

'Sharing is a two-way thing, John. I thought you'd learned that by now,' she said, looking at Knox intently. 'That applies to secrets, too. So, are you going to arrest me after all?'

He looked away for a moment, took another swig of beer, then turned back towards her.

'Perhaps none of you are killers at all, Mary. Leonard Plews died of a heart attack.'

Mary looked at him, shocked. 'You never told me that.'

Knox described how the heart attack had happened while the patients had been smothering Plews with the pillow.

'You knew all that already? And you never said?'

'It's my job *not* to tell you everything, Mary. You were a star witness. We needed to find out what you knew. But now that I know who did the pillow-smothering, I can work the rest out and make a decent guess about which of them inserted the knife afterwards.'

Mary looked uneasy. 'You're the police officer, John. You're going to tell me anyway, aren't you?'

'It would have taken a bit of strength to drive that knife into old man Plews. I think they did it together. Or tried to, at least. They still couldn't get it all the way in.'

'Uncle Lenny was no loss.'

'I thought you believed that there was good in everyone, Mary.'

'Each and every human being, yes. But Uncle Lenny was a monster.'

'But together those four patients did kill Uncle Lenny, and that's still against the law. Perhaps the law needs to be changed, but in the meantime... we can't prove anything anyway.'

'God watches over us all, John. Might it not be for the best?'

'It might be, but I'd still like to solve one little mystery.'

Mary avoided making eye-contact with him by studying the light as it played on her glass of wine. 'What mystery would that be?' she asked, quietly.

'There were no fingerprints on the knife. But of course it's a hospital, so I reckon they used some disposable gloves.

There were boxes of the things lying around everywhere.' Mary continued to say nothing. 'But those used gloves had to be disposed of. We'd have found anything with traces of blood from Uncle Lenny.'

'Might you have any ideas?' Mary carried on watching her glass as she rocked it to and fro.

'You know, Mary, in all the time I've known you, I've never seen you use a handkerchief before. You had a red silk one in evidence that night.'

'I'd just lost a close relative. I always carry a handkerchief.'

'But I've never seen you use one. And I thought you said Uncle Lenny was no loss.' He paused, then said, 'Those plastic gloves were wrapped inside your red handkerchief, weren't they? Where did you dump them?'

Mary sighed. 'I'd already deposited them into a bin in the staff toilet before you came that night. I was destroying vital evidence, I knew that at the time, but I believed I was doing the right thing. I still believe that.'

'Tell me, Mary, how many disposable gloves did you get rid of?'

She took a deep breath, then shrugged her shoulders. 'Fourteen, I think.'

'Fourteen?'

'They grabbed far too many. They took the knife from Louise Gray's locker, did what they had to do, then dumped the gloves on the floor. They were exhausted – it was an achievement to get back to their own beds. I simply tidied up the mess. They actually rolled up into quite a small ball, you know.'

'So it wasn't hard to hide them in your handkerchief.' Mary didn't comment. Then Knox asked, 'Are you saying that all four did the knife thing together?'

She shrugged her shoulder again, but didn't reply. Then she looked him directly and said, with more than a touch of bitterness, 'Satisfied *this* time?'

'Thank you, Mary. I know it was hard for you. But I needed that last piece of the jigsaw. I think you understand that.'

Mary took a deep breath. 'So, John… will you betray me, just as I betrayed those poor patients? Will you be my Judas Iscariot?'

Knox shook his head.

'I'll not betray you, Mary. I can't prove a thing, anyway. And you've not betrayed those patients either. I won't pass on what you've told me, not even to Lucy. We can each make our own judgements about their 'guilt' or otherwise.'

'God will judge them, John.'

'Her, too.'

It broke the ice: Mary gave a wry smile.

'Can you understand, Mary? I know you have to be true to yourself as a nun, but I have to be true to myself as a police officer.' She didn't reply, so he continued, 'So I hope you can forgive my persistence because I'd rather we didn't fall out.' Then he added, 'My piano playing will never be good enough not to need lessons.'

'No, it won't, John.'

'I'd rather hoped for more encouragement there.'

'Your piano playing shows every promise that it might one day become mediocre. Does that satisfy you? But to answer your other question, yes, I forgive you. To err, as you do on the piano, is human; to forgive is divine.'

When Knox had first met Sister Mary Maxwell-Hume of the Sisters of the Sacred Cross, she could beguile and terrify him in equal measure. In time they'd become close, intimate friends, yet now, in a flash, she'd returned to the woman he first knew. His sense of loss was considerable.

But of course, Mary could read his mind. She squeezed his hand and smiled affectionately.

'I'm not going anywhere, John. I'm still here when you need me. I'll still be around to assist you with your enquiries, and teach you piano.'

'I'll never forget that night, Mary.'

'It was right for both of us then, John. But now you need to move on. I'll never say never, but not now. In the meantime, get up and buy a drink for that woman you came in with. Her glass is empty and it's your turn.' In answer to an unspoken question, she added, 'No more for me, thanks. No, go on, don't be rude. Anyway, I need to go to the loo.'

Knox did as he was asked and tapped Dr Sally, who had found a seat on a stool at the bar, on the shoulder.

'My turn, Sally. What will you have?'

'You don't have to, John, honestly.'

'Is it sexist to want to pay a drink back to a friend?'

'No, it's not. If you insist, I'll have another small glass of red wine, please.' While their drinks were being poured, Sally added, 'I mustn't take you away from Mary, though. You're quite close, aren't you?'

'I suppose we are. She started off as my piano teacher but she's been helpful in a couple of police cases down the years. She's quite a character.'

'Yes, I've come across her a couple of times myself.'

'Really?'

'Here and there.' She raised her glass. 'To you and your team, John, and to many more successes in the future.'

'I didn't do much. I just happened to choose the right people to help me.'

'I think that's called leadership.'

'Now you're definitely flattering me. Good leaders don't normally need to be spoon-fed pasta with green pesto.'

Sally laughed. 'Didn't you like it?' Knox was struck by how easy her company was.

'On the contrary, I liked it a great deal. Being spoon-fed might turn out to be a character weakness.'

'You're always welcome to share my lunch. You could do some gym work at the same time.'

'Lunch sounds the more attractive option.'

'That's because no one's ever shown you how to enjoy being in the gym.'

Knox shrugged. 'I might accept that. Consider it a deal.'

Sally hesitated. 'How will your girlfriend take that? Will you tell her?' Knox sighed. 'Ah, I'm sorry, John. That was clumsy of me. Who broke it up? Or was it mutual?'

'Alice made the decision, but we'd been drifting apart for ages. She's really nice and she deserves better than me.'

'Don't run yourself down, John. You're a lovely man.'

'Thank you, that's a nice thing to say. Perhaps I should say I couldn't offer Alice the lifestyle she needed. In the end she went off with another teacher. I honestly hope she's very happy.' Suddenly becoming more upbeat, he said, 'Listen, can I ask you a question?'

Sally hesitated. 'OK… but can I ask one as well? And will you give me an honest answer?'

'That seems fair.'

Knox was about to speak when he felt a hand brush his rear. He might have taken offence but he recognised the soft touch immediately, to say nothing of the Chanel No. 5.

'John, I really should be going. Please give my thanks to the Superintendent for inviting me here. It's been lovely. Drop in and see me very soon, and keep practising the piano.'

'Mary, please don't leave just yet, come and join us.'

'No, it's time to go.' She reached up towards him and kissed him tenderly on the cheek. As she did so, she whispered very quietly into his ear, 'Enjoy the rest of your evening,' kissed him again, then slipped away out of the door.

Knox looked back at Sally. 'Sorry about that. She's some woman.'

'She is indeed. What were you going to ask me?'

'I never see you except in scrubs. Not always in the same colours, but you seem to like wearing them.'

'They're convenient, John, and I feel good in them. And they let people know what my job is. I like that.'

'Personally, I hate wearing uniform. If I have to wear it for any reason I can't wait to get out of it again.'

Sally laughed. 'That would cause a bit of a stir in my case.'

Knox looked at her quizzically. 'You'll need to explain.'

'Jesus is part of my life, John. I'm a nun. Most people haven't heard of our order, but if you know Sister Mary – '

'Sisters of the Order of Mary on the Sacred Cross.'

'You've heard of us? In which case you might know…'

'That you believe you should only wear whatever is necessary to provide due modesty.'

'Indeed. Sister Mary and I know each other spiritually.'

Knox, who had genuinely come to believe that Sister Mary's order was fictional, was speechless.

'Can I ask my question now?' Sally asked.

'Please go ahead.'

'Are you doing anything tonight? My flat's just down the road.'

'I think I am, actually,' Knox said. Sally looked disappointed, but then he added, 'I think I might be spending the evening with you.'

'That sounds a nice idea.' Then she added, with a mysterious smile that seemed curiously familiar, 'Let's see where the evening takes us, then.'

THE END

ACKNOWLEDGEMENTS

For me, crime fiction is the Everest of writing. The author needs patience, a lot of preparation and endless support. Mary and John were not themselves new characters – they emerged from *The Discreet Charm of Mary Maxwell Hume*, and indeed Mary was originally introduced as the piano teacher of Brian Reid, aka 'Captain', who of course is the central character in *Four Old Geezers and a Valkyrie*. And, yes, it's the same Magda, too.

But *The Midnight Visitor* was a new departure, because it was such a totally different genre from anything I'd attempted previously. Naturally, I needed a lot of help. First of all, I need to thank my good friend and neighbour Katie McGlew for transforming herself from my proofreader into my editor, and a wonderful one at that. We had some amusing moments, though, especially when Katie, who may have lived in Scotland all of her life but is proud of her American heritage, struggled with niceties of Superintendent Jack O'Malley's strong Lanarkshire accent. This book is immeasurably better for Katie's input.

I'm also need to say thank you to my son Al, and to Rosie and Martin Dennis, for each of their perspectives as hospital consultants – particularly Martin, who was at the time a Professor of Geriatric Medicine. I was amazed, and not a little relieved, that none of them felt they had to suspend belief too much, although they pointed out my worst howlers.

On the subject of howlers, though, I need to make it clear that while St Leonard's Police Station in Edinburgh's Pleasance is a very real building indeed, I've never set foot beyond its front reception area. I have no idea at all what the interior looks like, whether it has an open-plan Operations Room, and certainly no idea whether or not the odious Chief Inspector Maximilian Plews would indeed have his own office. This is *my* vision of St Leonard's Police Station, not the real one, not even the St Leonard's of Ian Rankin's Inspector Rebus. I couldn't even find a floor plan of the interior of the building on the internet, which is remarkable in itself. So if there are any police officers who are horrified by my particular representation of their workplace, please accept my apologies. It's a fair cop.

The internet is a wonderful thing, though, bringing help and support from people we'll never meet onto our computer screens. In that regard I need to single out Sue Clayton, who read, commented on, and ultimately pushed out this novel into the public domain: it had been sitting on my hard drive doing absolutely nothing for over two years. (That's a bad habit of mine.)

Finally, I need to thank my endlessly supportive wife Katherine, who seems to spend all of her time forced to stare at the backlit Apple logo on the lid of my laptop. While I've been writing *The Midnight Visitor*, she's been crocheting a massive blanket which she says is for her 'old age in a care home'. If it comes to that, let's hope she fares better than the patients in St Ninian's.

Gordon Lawrie,
December 2021

BY THE SAME AUTHOR

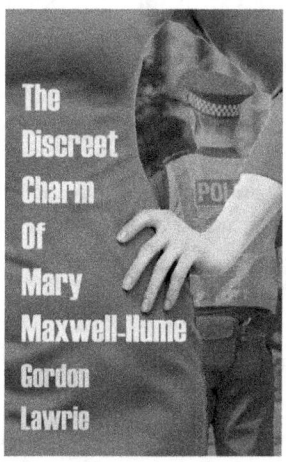

Mary Maxwell-Hume is an enigma. She earns a living as a piano teacher, but also belongs to an obscure order of nuns. Their rules appear curious: although the nuns wear red habits occasionally, the order has a peculiar dress code: nuns wear 'only as much as is necessary to preserve due modesty' – plus liberal doses of Chanel No.5 perfume.

There's the faintest hint that Mary might be a bit of a hustler, but she uses her sensual powers in such a way that nobody really minds – except for the odious Theodore Plews of Lambert's Auction House in Edinburgh. Anyway, who would dare suggest that a woman of God might not all be all that she seems?

Eventually, she engages a young police constable, John Knox, as her faithful 'assistant'...

The Discreet Charm of Mary Maxwell-Hume marks the start of our acquaintance with Mary and John, and is available in paperback, priced £5.99 post free in the UK, or as an ebook, priced £0.99.

ABOUT THE AUTHOR

Gordon Lawrie has lived and worked, mostly as a teacher, all of his life in the Edinburgh area. In 2010, he went part-time in order to turn his attention to writing, and founded the innovative Comely Bank Publishing collective two years later. He has considerable experience as an editor and in micro-publishing, and his book *Self-Publishing, The Total Beginner's Guide*, was published in 2020. Gordon is also the editor of the online flash fiction site Friday Flash Fiction which attracts hundreds of readers and writers each year from throughout the English speaking world.

The Midnight Visitor is his fourth novel.

OTHER NOVELS BY GORDON LAWRIE

Four Old Geezers and a Valkyrie

The Blogger Who Came in from the Cold

OTHER FICTION

100 Not Out

200 Not Out

www.ingramcontent.com/pod-product-compliance
Lightning Source LLC
Chambersburg PA
CBHW070916260626
47162CB00007B/2696